BLACK ICE

BLACK ICE
COLIN DUNNE

St. Martin's Press
New York

For Jim Cheese and the Princess

BLACK ICE. Copyright © 1986 by Colin Dunne. All rights reserved. Printed in the United States of America. No part of this book may be used or reproduced in any manner whatsoever without written permission except in the case of brief quotations embodied in critical articles or reviews. For information, address St. Martin's Press, 175 Fifth Avenue, New York, N.Y. 10010.

Library of Congress Cataloging-in-Publication Data

Dunne, Colin.
  Black ice.

  I. Title.
PR6054.U554B5   1987   823'.914   87-4453
ISBN 0-312-00566-0

First published in Great Britain by Martin Secker & Warburg Limited.

First U.S. Edition

10 9 8 7 6 5 4 3 2 1

1

If you've never come to in the middle of the night to find yourself approximately halfway between New York and Moscow, right up on top of the world, standing outside a block of flats wearing nothing other than a ladies' silk dressing-robe – and that decorated with large scarlet kisses – allow me to describe the sensation.

Confused. That's the word, I think. Confused, and cold around the knees.

I shivered, yawned and did a few push-ups with my eyelids while I applied my brain to some basic questions: like was it night or day? That isn't quite as easy as it sounds. In the summer, about the only way you can tell is by the life in the city. From where I was standing, outside the flats high up on Vesturbrun, the place looked like early-closing day on the *Marie Celeste*.

That made it night. Still.

I looked and listened. Nothing. Only, in the distance, a car chugging and spluttering. An early worker. Or, here in Reykjavik, more likely a late reveller.

I called out her name, then stood there feeling silly. Solrun isn't the sort of name you can go round shouting, not unless you've strayed into one of those operas where all the women look like sixteen-stone milkmaids. In any case, my cry fell into that damp silence like a stone down a well.

Then it struck me. If this was my début in international espionage, I wasn't doing too well. I mean, how would it look on my c.v.? 'On his first operation, Craven actually lost the subject of his surveillance while she was in bed with him.'

Roger Moore never seemed to have these problems.

Once more I called out her name. The wind whipped it away and then frisked me with cold and cheeky fingers. Even with the scarlet kisses, the silk robe wasn't much protection against a breeze that had trained in the Arctic.

Dammit. What the hell was she playing at? Baffled? Oh yes, I was baffled all right. But I wasn't too worried because I knew Solrun. She was a twenty-four carat madcap, that one. Alongside her, other women were prisoners of iron logic. She was governed entirely by inexplicable whim.

Otherwise – let me say it first – what would she be doing in bed with me?

Anyway, at that point I wasn't too serious about my career as a spy. For one thing – as I'd said to Batty – those international organisations who were known by a deadly trio of initials always sounded like television stations to me. 'There's nothing on the KGB tonight, shall we watch the news on CIA?'

Come to that, no one had mentioned spying. 'Give history a bit of a nudge', was the expression Batty had used. From his prissy mouth, it sounded about as strenuous as stamp-collecting.

Right now it was either too early or too late to do anything significant by way of history-nudging. I gave one last shout, one last yawn, one last shiver, and shot back indoors with as much dignity as man can muster when he's dressed like something from a boudoir catalogue. Which wasn't much.

As I waited for the lift, I recalled what she'd said about the two men. Perhaps they'd kill her, she'd said. For a moment, I felt uneasy, until I realised it was a minor attack of those just-before-dawn doubts. She was always saying things like that. That was Solrun, living life downhill without brakes. Death threats, either real or imaginary, probably played the same part in her life as parking tickets in mine. So I shrugged the thought off and hopped into the lift.

That was my first day there. I didn't know what it was all about. Then it was just a good laugh spiced up with a bit of mystery.

Later, the spicing sort of outweighed the laughs.

2

The strongest phrase that William Batty did use, that morning he came sneezing up to my office four floors above Farringdon Road, was 'spot of trouble'. That wasn't much preparation for what was to come, either.

He mumbled on about keeping the old eyes open and a word in the right ear at the right time, and for quite a while I didn't know what the hell he was talking about. I wasn't much wiser when he left, come to think of it.

When I'd moved into that office two years earlier, a pal of mine had said that the sight of all those barrows loaded with second-hand books in the street below would depress anyone attempting to earn a living by arranging words into sentences of interest. It did depress me, but then that was never too difficult. In the film of grease and dust on the window, the same bloke had written 'Sam Craven, Diurnalist and Wordsmith Extraordinaire'. Funny thing about journalists: because their trade obliges them to reduce the English language to a level comprehensible to a four-year-old, they tend to go round talking like Sir Roger de Coverley by way of compensation.

It caught Batty's eye. 'Most amusing,' he said, stooping to read it against the one shaft of sunlight that somehow managed to sneak through the chimneys.

Then he stood up with his hand on his chest, still searching for breath after the stairs. 'My word, young man, you must be very healthy to tackle those every day.'

'You know what they say? You can have all the health in the world but it won't buy you money.'

I took pity on his puzzled face. 'Joke,' I said.

'Joke?' he repeated, then, suddenly smiling: 'Oh yes, I love a joke.'

He sat down gingerly on the rackety bentwood chair I reserved for my most favoured guests. My least favoured guests too, since it was the only one. I had a good look at him.

Late fifties: grey nondescript suit and tie and black shoes, suggesting academic non-striver rather than commercial rat-racer; pale, podgy, with hair that looked like an old tabby that had crawled up there to die, depositing a small kitten on his upper lip on the way.

I was just beginning to wonder about the red rims round his eyes and nose when he suddenly began gasping for air, and tearing a sheet-sized hankie from his pocket he buried his head in it with a volcanic sneeze. 'Hay fever,' his muffled voice explained. 'Dreadful.'

Behind him, the wire coat-hangers on the door-hook tinkled a salute to his effort. He sneezed again, this time a planned and controlled explosion. Afterwards, he gave me a weak smile.

Now it was his turn to have a look. Topless jar of paste with plastic teaspoon replacing lost brush. Chain of paper-clips dangling from large bulldog clip which secured dished shade over desk lamp. Small dented tin teapot wearing smart prophylactic red-rubber spout. Scarred, chipped, scratched and stained desk, with filing cabinet to tone. Two empty lager bottles beside photo of young Sally, clasping kitten. In the loo next door, an echoing baritone's claim that he'd left his heart somewhere was drowned in a noisy gush of water.

'This is what you get for twenty years of honest endeavour,' I said.

Batty nodded uncertainly. If he was impressed by what he'd seen, he managed to restrain himself from showing it.

'Still,' he said, brightly, 'I dare say all a professional like you needs is a typewriter and a bit of paper.'

'And an employer,' I said. I gave him an encouraging smile in case he'd forgotten why he was here. On the telephone an hour earlier, he'd said he was from some international features agency which was interested in commissioning me. I didn't have so many customers that I could afford to let him sneeze himself to death before I'd got the job.

'Ah, yes,' he said, giving me an unexpectedly foxy look. 'Can I ask you something a little . . . well, a little unusual?'

I opened my hands to present an easy target. 'What do you want to know? Shorthand of seventeen words a minute, I can spell Mediterranean some of the time, and my litotes is the talk of Hammersmith – if you'll forgive the hyperbole.'

'Solrun,' he said, ignoring that lot. 'Ring a bell, perhaps, Solrun?'

After a pause, I asked: 'The model?' And he nodded, without taking his eyes off my face.

Whatever I'd been expecting, that wasn't it. While I ran through the implications, I got up and banged the button on the electric kettle on top of the filing cabinet. It began to boil almost immediately. I still hadn't finished my last cup of tea but I needed time to think.

'Yes, I know her,' I said, topping up the tin teapot. 'But you know that already or you wouldn't be here. Tea?'

'Thank you, no,' he said, with a quick glance at the encrusted mug which was the only spare in my catering division. 'You're quite right, of course. Am I right in thinking she is . . . was . . . rather a close friend?'

'You could say that,' I replied. For one heart-stopping moment, it occurred to me he might be collecting divorce evidence. Then I remembered that I was divorced and that Solrun wasn't married, and anyway I hadn't seen her for two years. 'Yes, she's a great lass,' I added.

'Good, good,' he hummed happily. 'You see, she seems to be in a spot of trouble.'

When wasn't she? I nearly asked, then didn't. I sipped my tea and waited for him to explain.

'What it is, Mr Craven, is that she's got mixed up with some rather dangerous types. Undesirables.'

Well, you certainly couldn't call Solrun an undesirable. On the other hand she was very, very dangerous.

These thoughts, together with other warm and pleasant memories, quite distracted me from Batty's explanation – something about a Foreign Office department concerned with British interests abroad – but I returned quickly when he said they understood I was a close (ahem ahem) friend who could possibly use my influence to advise her. That was when he started going on about words in ears and open eyes. At that point I had to intervene.

'I don't really know what the hell you're on about,' I said.

He vanished into his hankie for some more secret H-bomb testing and when he came out his face was as pink as his eyes.

'What we're asking is for you to pop up to Reykjavik as an old friend, see what's going on, and do what you can to steer her away from any foolishness. I'm sure it will all become clear once you're there.'

'It certainly isn't clear now.'

He shrugged and dabbed at his face with the hankie. 'We're offering you rather a splendid opportunity, Mr Craven.'

'Are you?'

'I think so. You could have the chance to give history a bit of a nudge in the right direction. Tempting, don't you think?'

I'd never seen myself as a history-nudger. Personally, I had every confidence that the professionals in charge of our affairs could find the shortest route to Armageddon without any help from me.

'Hang on,' I said, doing a recap to try to straighten it out in my mind. 'You want me to go to Iceland as a sort of temporary diplomat . . .'

'Dear me, no. No, no, no.' He shook his head so quickly that his moustache nearly flew off. 'For us, you see, the whole attraction of employing someone like yourself is that you are not traceable. To us, of course.'

For a moment I had a chilling vision of myself in a mortuary drawer with a question mark on the tag tied to my toe. He must have picked up my reaction because he quickly went on: 'What I mean is that no one will know you're working for us.'

'Ah,' I said, wagging a finger at his beaming face. 'If you're in the line of work I think you're in, Mr Batty, shouldn't you be coming striding out of the sea half-naked with a bloody big knife strapped to your sunburned thigh?'

He straightened in his chair. 'Should I? Why ever do you say that?'

'Ursula Andress did.'

A crafty little smile twisted his lips. 'Really? Was she a civil servant too, Mr Craven?'

'Mr Batty,' I said. 'I do believe you're a bit of a tease.'

3

Just for a minute there, I wasn't sure who was taking the mickey out of who. Or whom, as we diurnalists like to say. By way of celebrating this new rapport, Mr Batty agreed to risk a mug of tea as he told me about his plans for my future.

Not all that surprisingly, I suppose, he had it all worked out. They – his department, presumably – would arrange for one of the Fleet Street newspapers to send me to Iceland on a job. That should give me enough justification to go round asking questions and generally making a nuisance of myself.

'Which one?' I offered him a turn with the sugar-bag containing damp spoon. He declined. Our new rapport wasn't that good.

'One of the pops, we thought,' he replied. 'We have a little pull with them, and they'd be rather fun to work for, wouldn't you say?'

I worked mostly for magazines and the heavies. I'd steered clear of the tabloids ever since they'd taken to printing fiction. Still, this wasn't really work, was it?

'Of course, we'd cover your basic costs and I think we could arrange to put, say, five hundred in your bank account now.'

'That should bring my early retirement forward a couple of seconds.'

'It's all taxpayers' money, Mr Craven,' he said, with some indignation. 'We do have to spend it responsibly. Do you know, I'm convinced that tea tastes much better out of a mug like this, but my secretary won't hear of it.'

I shook my head at him. 'Great mistake, getting physically involved with your secretary.'

'I do assure you . . . let me make it clear immed . . . ah, you're joking again I do believe, Mr Craven.'

'Caught me, Mr Batty. Tell me one thing – how can you be sure I won't nudge history in the wrong direction?'

7

'Excellent point.' He looked at me as, with one stiffened finger, he stroked his sad moustache as though he expected it to bolt for cover down his throat. 'Yes, excellent question. You see, we rather assume that you have the usual sort of loyalty to your country.'

'You could be making a mistake.'

The moustache twitched into a small smile. 'I don't think so.'

'Well.' I looked around my crumbling cabin of an office. 'It's only fair to tell you that I don't feel any sentimental bond to a particular acreage just because that's where my parents succumbed to an attack of lust.'

He went on smiling.

'If they'd had the same attack in the South Seas, we might be having this conversation on the beach over a glass of fresh coconut juice. If you take my point.'

His smile still hadn't shifted.

'Look, let me put it this way. My sole concern is to get this admittedly pathetic little body through from breakfast to bedtime each day with minimum damage. That's my only serious commitment to a philosophical ideal.'

'But you don't have any loyalties which might, shall we say, conflict.' It was more of a statement than a question and I realised, foolishly, that of course he would've had me checked out, even for this errand-boy sort of job.

'Not really.'

He made a brave try at drinking his tea and leaned forward to slide the mug on to my desk. 'Very fair of you to try to explain your position. These days, I think we're inclined to trust someone with your sort of healthy cynicism rather than an old-fashioned patriot. And you do have the incentive of wishing to see that your friend Solrun makes the right decision. Oh, no, Mr Craven. We've made the right choice. You must trust us to do that.'

'In that case . . .'

He was halfway out of the door before I realised what I'd let myself in for.

'One thing,' I said, before he vanished down the stairs. 'This job for the paper – will it be real or is it just . . . window-dressing?'

8

Well, I couldn't say 'cover', could I? Normal people don't go round talking about cover.

'Oh, yes, definitely. We shall see that it's put into their minds to give you a commission up there. You will have to do it, I'm afraid, but no doubt you will be generously paid for it.' He gave my arm a sympathetic pat. 'From what little I've seen of the popular papers, it shouldn't be anything too intellectually demanding. You'll cope, Mr Craven, you'll cope.'

The last I heard of him was a vast sneeze echoing up the stairs. I made another pot of tea and watched the gold dust dance in the one beam of sunlight I was permitted by city by-laws.

That was when it struck me. However they dressed it up in homely jargon, the British Government were employing me – at least, indirectly – to go up to Iceland to see what Solrun was getting up to. And, presumably, to do something about it. That made me a spy. Okay, only Acting, Temporary, and Without Pension Rights, but I was still a spy. I looked around my broken-down office. At least I had one qualification – the ribbon on my typewriter was so worn I could use it as invisible ink.

But exactly what did they expect me to do about it? That was the big puzzle. If Batty had checked me out, which he must've done, then he'd know that I wouldn't be likely to have a deep sense of historic continuity. You don't have a lot of that if you haven't got a mum or dad, like me.

No man is an island? You want to bet? This one is. A private island, and I don't allow picnickers either.

4

Shurring shurring shurring shurring shurring. Shurring shurring. Shurring shurring shurring shurring shurring shurring.

Am I doing this properly? It seems so stupid sitting bolt upright in the office saying one word over and over again to myself. Anyway, here goes. In threes this time.

Shurring shurring shurring. Shurring shurring shurring. Shurring shurring shurring.

Am I meditating yet? I don't feel as though I am. On the other hand, the night I fell down three flights of stairs I didn't feel as though I was drunk. A few more. In pairs this time.

Shurring shurring. Shurring shurring. Shurring shurring.

Just keep saying the mantrap – sorry, mantra – so the teacher said at the class, and my system would sink into the resting state and my mind would be empty of thoughts. Right. Is the mind empty? Whoops, no, there's a sneaky little thought appertaining to an unpaid gas bill. And another about picking up my laundry. I chase those two off and in slips another thought about that bendy-looking blonde in the office downstairs.

Oh, hell, shurring, shurr-bloody-ing, and my mind is wriggling like an ant hill with unauthorised thoughts. The astral plane of selflessness which lies beyond the void didn't seem to have any membership vacancies at the moment.

Shurring shurring . . . I'm not doing all that again. Then I realised. It was the phone.

'Craven?'

'Speaking.'

"Ere. I like this idea you've put up for a feature piece in Iceland.'

Suddenly I knew who it was. Batty hadn't been kidding when he said one of the pop papers. The editor didn't bother to introduce himself because he assumed everyone knew him. He was right. Throughout the newspaper business, he was known as Grimm, on account of the fact that his paper consisted almost entirely of fairy tales. He was a frenzied young northerner who'd found that the streets of London were paved with gold, so long as you didn't mind wading through the sewers first.

'Idea?'

'Yeah, this memo you sent. Secrets of the Sexy Eskies. Brilliant. You're on.'

'Good. I mean, great. Secrets of the what?'

'Sexy Eskies. That's my headline. So you work to that, right?'

I was relieved to hear the headline was his. Even the Foreign Office, with its fathomless resources, couldn't have counterfeited such a classic as that. Even as I was listening to him, I could see the problems of actually putting this into operation.

'So, you get your interview with this Miss Iceland lass – what she does, who with, every pant and wriggle – and we're there. Like I say, Secrets of the Sexy Eskies.'

'Right. Terrific. Just one thing.'

'What?' He sounded irritated. Just one thing sounded one too many for him.

'Strictly speaking, Icelanders aren't Eskimoes. Very, very strictly speaking, of course.'

His sigh burned up a few hundred yards of telephone wire. 'Listen. I shouldn't have to explain this to you,' he said, in the tones of one who bears a heavy burden through life. 'How it works is this. Maybe they are Eskimoes. Maybe they're not Eskimoes. Who can say? But if I think they're Eskimoes then our readers will think they're Eskimoes, and if our readers think they're Eskimoes, then bloody Eskimoes they are. Got it?'

'Got it.'

'Thank God. Tell you what,' he began, in a more generous tone, 'I've seen your stuff around. It's not all crap, you know.'

'I'm glad to hear that.'

'No, fair does, it's not. What I don't understand is why you haven't been on to me before.'

'I was waiting,' I said, marvelling as I heard the unplanned words slip through my lips, 'for a really big one.'

'Love it!' he enthused. 'That's what this business wants – commitment, heart, guts. There's big bucks in this, Craven. Get on your way. Today. Secrets of the Sexy Eskies, eh? Ring in. Ciao.'

I sat there for a couple of minutes looking at the phone and wondering if my attempts at meditation had somehow flung this nightmare figure into my imagination. But no, I knew it wasn't. That was Grimm all right.

It was my only experience of him first-hand, and I must say my immediate reaction was to start a new life in Paraguay under a false name. Still, I wasn't *really* working for him, was I?

I don't know why I bothered dragging my conscience in for an overhaul like that. All I needed to do was to concentrate on the prospect of seeing Solrun again and I could've rationalised the Crucifixion.

One phone call to Icelandair did the lot. They put me on the evening flight, promised to book me a room with Hulda Gudmundsdottir – my, we were back in opera-land, weren't we? – and they also promised to notify the information office where Solrun worked that I was on my way. After that, of course, it was up to her.

Then I rang Sally's convent school near Guildford where eventually I battered my way past the nuns' chorus and got to speak to my daughter. Speak? Did I say speak? Got to listen to her. In no time at all I was apprised of the facts that Natasha had quarrelled with Fiona and she and Henrietta weren't going to bother with them any more, not if they were going to have a pash on that hateful Rowena.

Of course, it all sounded like birdsong to me.

My ex-wife sent her to the convent because they wore boaters in the summer. I think she believed that straw had miracle properties when placed in close proximity to the brain. I made a note to buy myself a straw hat sometime.

I thought of trying the old shurring shurring again, but decided against. It didn't seem to be taking with me. Every time I emptied my mind of the stresses and worries that were poisoning my system (so the book said), someone sneaked up with another lorry-load.

Instead, I sauntered up to the Cheshire Cheese where – gurus please note – I reached astral planes of pure thoughtless serenity on exactly three pints of Marston's best bitter.

5

At first sight you might've thought the flight was a reunion for brother-and-sister twins of a mature age.

People who fly south want to get things: like brown, drunk and laid. People who fly north want to look: they want to look at flowers and birds and scenery, and, as a rule, they stay white, sober and unlaid. They fly north in matching pairs, white-haired, ruddy-faced, retired teachers, husbands and wives who have grown alike over the years.

The flight was full of them. All wearing shirts made from that stuff Scotsmen use for kilts. If you'd asked a question about Jurassic rock formation, every hand in the place would have been raised.

I ate what looked like a bottled brain. It was a herring which, if not actually soused, had certainly stopped off for a couple. Raw and tangy, it tasted delicious. Icelandair haven't yet mastered the art of making all their food taste like wartime soap: how they get a licence beats me.

What with the big twins and the tasty brain, it was all getting a bit unreal and then, when I tried to doze off, I imagined I heard a coach-load of football supporters fly past singing, 'I'm Sitting On Top of the World'.

I opened my eyes. And, would you believe it, the man next to me was apparently trying to steal my shoelaces.

I didn't know what to do. So I just sat there and watched. His face was almost resting on my knee and his hand was scrabbling around by my feet somewhere. When he glanced up and saw me, he mimed, 'Sorry, won't be a sec.' With a wince across his dark impish features, he made a last dive and then surfaced with a plastic carrier bag from which, tinnily, came the music.

Dipping one hand inside, he pulled out a roll of pink lavatory paper on a pink plastic wall mounting which was artistically rendered in the shape of a seated man with his trousers round his ankles. He pushed the man's cartoon-red nose. The singing ceased.

'Clever, isn't it?'

I decided he would definitely repay a little study, so I had a good look at him. Maybe forty or a bit less, thick black thatch of hair, thin features which had been handsome until someone had rearranged the nose with a baseball bat – or similar. It curved across his face banana-style. Yet despite that, all his features added up to an intelligent merry innocence.

'Look, do you see, this chap on the bog is meant to be singing the song . . .'

'Yes, I got that far myself.'

'Splendid, isn't it? Make me a million, this little chap will. By the way, Christopher Bell. Christopher not Chris if you don't mind – I'm not a condensed-name sort of person.'

We managed a hunched handshake, during which he insisted that I drink a brennivin with him. Somehow he dismissed my reluctance – I can't stand the stuff – and whistled up a stewardess and ordered in Icelandic. Before I could express my surprise, a head of silver bristle popped over the seat in front of us.

'An Englishman who speaks another language – and Icelandic of all things. We are seeing miracles.' He gave a dry whisper of a laugh and said something to Christopher Bell in a language that sounded to my ears like sprained Spanish.

Christopher retaliated in the same, then added: 'I'm afraid my Esperanto is pretty shaky.'

'You see,' said Silver Bristle, who had steel-rimmed specs and looked a vital fifty-ish. 'Your friend does not understand.'

'True,' I said.

'Excuse, excuse,' he said, with that dry laugh again. 'I hear this man speaking Icelandic so I ask him if he also speaks Esperanto. And, another miracle, he does. A little, most certainly. Here.'

He gave me his card which made him a German called Bottger who was something big in Esperanto. By this time the brennivin had arrived and Christopher had got a third for

Bottger.

'Do you know,' Christopher said, rotating between the two of us, 'that the recipe for this stuff is still kept secret?'

'Thank God,' I said, as the first sip turned my face into a prune. 'Don't let it out, that's all.'

'I say, don't you like it?' he asked, sounding very concerned.

'Well, if you were an alcoholic it wouldn't stop you drinking, but it would certainly take the pleasure out of it.'

That brought us nicely up to that what-brings-you-here stuff. I told Christopher about my new employer (Grimm, not Batty, of course) and the Sexy Eskies, and he put his hand on my arm and said: 'Look at it this way – someone's got to do it.'

That made me feel like a hangman. Or an undertaker, perhaps. I wasn't sure whether that was an improvement or not.

Bottger, a solo twin, was planning on striding about the scenery in large boots, visiting old Esperanto friends, so they could talk about the rest of us behind our backs. That brought up another volley of the stuff, which Christopher translated.

'He says that if only people would take the trouble to learn Esperanto, we could all speak what is in our hearts.'

'That would mean war.'

'No, no,' Bottger chipped in, in impatient English. 'That is the point. No more wars, no misunderstandings, no troubles. We see into each other's minds.'

'If that stewardess gets to see into my mind,' I said, 'there'll be plenty of troubles, I can tell you. And how about you?' I asked Christopher. 'You're an international lavatory-paper smuggler, I take it?'

He wasn't. But only just. He'd tried a few things. Farming, publishing, salesman. He hadn't hit quite the right thing. He'd heard a tourist boom was coming in Iceland and he'd come north, fallen in love with the country and learned the language. So he was setting up an import-export business, with the musical paper-holder as his first move.

'People absolutely love them. They go like hot cakes at all the seaside places, I'm told.'

'And what are you sending back the other way?' Whatever it was, I thought it had to be better than those. Not necessarily, as

15

it turned out. He planned to ship back shoals of stuffed puffins to an unsuspecting Britain.

I'd seen them in the shops there. Depressed-looking creatures, poised awkwardly on a chunk of lava. I didn't say so, but frankly I wouldn't have wanted to put all my money into stuffed puffins.

'But this,' he said, tapping the plastic bag, 'is my second million. Any chance of a free plug in that paper of yours?'

'Not unless you can persuade a female puffin to take all her feathers off.'

6

That's the time to arrive in Iceland – bang in the middle of a summer night.

Then the sun doesn't set. It just slips off-stage for an hour or two. I gave the other two a lift into town in a Daihatsu jeep I'd hired, and we sat in silence as the narrow strip of tarmac led over the cold grey lava fields, set like forgotten porridge or boiled-over toffee. The first American astronauts practised there: they say they found the moon quite homey after that.

Soon we saw the red and green roofs of Reykjavik and I dropped them in the town and set off for Thingvellir. If she wanted to see me, that's where she'd be.

Out over the lava field I went. A cold blade of a wind fleeced a sheep foraging gamely among the green knobbly rocks and pinned a lone gull to the sky. A herd of ponies truffling for salt in the dust of the road parked reluctantly to let me pass.

Thingvellir was just as I remembered it. Which wasn't all that surprising when you think it's been like that since the world was premiered.

It's a vast plain of lava stretching for miles from the foot of an eighty-foot escarpment of rock. It's the prototype for the House of Commons. The world's first politicians, around the year nine hundred, used to stand with their backs to the cliff to use it as a sound-box while they lied about the budget. Even then they liked the sound of their own voices.

If a country can have a soul, Iceland's is there. And it was there that Solrun and I had together whatever it was we had together. That's why she should be there.

But I wasn't sure. As I drove I remembered what Batty had said about her dangerous friends. The more I thought about it, the more I realised that he wouldn't go to all this trouble to get me out there unless there was *something* going on. What was she up to? And was she okay? Tension tightened me like a banjo as I parked and climbed the steep slope up the back of the cliff-top.

Either the slope had got steeper or I'd got older in the past two years because I had to stoop to climb it, and I found my face only a couple of feet away from the lava, the bare bones of the earth. At the top, I stopped and straightened. The sky was the colour of old jeans. Ten miles away, a line of mountains was a snow-stained smudge on the horizon. Below me, fingers of lava ran out into the wide bright lake.

I'm not a scenery man myself, but if you are given to having your breath took, that's the place for it.

I might've known where she'd be sitting. Right on the edge of the cliff, her legs dangling over the long drop, facing out into the void between earth and sky.

'In that river down there,' she said, pointing, 'they used to tie rocks to unfaithful women and throw them in to drown.'

'That explains it,' I answered.

'What?'

'Why your hair's always wet. How are you, little kiddo?'

What does the name Solrun mean to me, Mr Batty? Well, I'll tell you.

It means a girl who can't see a cliff without wanting to hang her legs over it. It means a girl who's wild and wonderful and wayward.

You know those Scandinavian filmstars like Britt Ekland? They left home because they were sick of being the plainest girls in town, and went to Hollywood where the competition was thinner. And in northern Europe, the Icelandic girls make all the others look sort of dowdy. Even in that aristocratic company, Solrun was something special.

In a race where hair varies from daffodil to snowdrop, hers was about narcissus, cropped short and half-curly in a style that might have looked boyish on anyone else. On her it looked sexy. On her, bald would have looked sexy.

She was slim, the handy, tuck-under-your-arm size, and she was composed entirely of lovely round pieces which were joined up with lovely slim pieces. What she meant to me personally was friendship and sex. It's a much-neglected combination. Without absurd hopes and false promises, like love for instance, you can keep a clear head to enjoy what's going on. It can lead to all sorts of unfashionable abstractions, like trust and respect, and they don't weather too well when love's around.

It happened like this. I was on an official public-relations tour of the country for a magazine. Solrun, who was modelling then but also did some front jobs for things like this, was shepherding us around.

Now anyone who works for a newspaper is by definition a person in whom hope outruns intelligence and this lot – thirty-odd of them – were offering her everything from money to marriage by coffee-break on the first morning. She stood up to it pretty well. But by mid-afternoon, standing here on the cliff-top at Thingvellir, she was almost getting a heat rash from the non-stop battery of leers.

'Make your decision now,' said one smoothie, 'and put the rest of us out of our misery.'

To their surprise, she thought about it for a minute, then she agreed. 'I choose Sam.'

She hit me with a smile that almost knocked me off the cliff, and continued: 'Now, gentlemen, perhaps I can ask you to look at Almannagja, which means All Men's Chasm, which is where the common people used to gather in the days of the ancient assemblies . . .'

I didn't believe her, of course. Not then. I didn't even believe her that night when she came along to my room.

I took a bit of convincing, believe me.

Solrun. Does it ring a bell? One or two, Mr Batty, one or two.

Solrun was Iceland. The wild strangeness of the place burned in her. Fire and ice. Ice and fire. That's what made her what she was – ice-hot.

7

Next time you're young, rich and fashionable and in Iceland, get a flat in Vesturbrun. That's where all the rest of them live. So, naturally enough, that's where Solrun had her flat: six floors up in a tower block which hummed with discreet heat and silent lifts.

In Britain we think light is simply something you switch on. There they play around with it. In her flat, blinds and screens and clever shades sliced up the light and kept it under control. With all that natural wood, bamboo and cane you could've staged *The Mikado* without changing a thing. It was low-level, which is to say that most of the social life was conducted on the floor: the cushions didn't have chairs beneath them, and the two sofas were no higher than a London pavement.

'And have you been faithful to me?' I demanded, not altogether seriously.

When she answered we both burst out laughing. I'd forgotten the way Icelanders say the word for Yes on the in-breath – and the way Solrun liked to string them together.

'Yow yow yow yow yow yow,' she went, like a clockwork cat that needs winding up. It took us over the two-year gap without embarrassment.

We hadn't stayed long up at Thingvellir. Just long enough for me to suck in some of the magic of the place, and to see again how the pearly light swirled around the plain, as real to the eye as the water in the lake. Back home, Solrun had vanished to the sound of splashing taps and re-emerged about five seconds later, damp, pink, fresh and snug inside her silk robe liberally decorated with scarlet lips. From somewhere she'd also produced two small, strong and bitter coffees.

We were both past the pleasure-shock of seeing each other again – and the discovery that all the old feelings were warming up again. It's always nice to know you weren't mistaken. We talked the old nonsense we always did, but I couldn't help but notice the black scimitars of strain beneath her eyes. Her usual playfulness kept failing as a strange unease broke in. Inevitably it reminded me of why Batty had sent me.

'They say at the office that you wish to interview me for one of your wicked London scandal papers?'

'That's right.'

'That is terrible.' She giggled and clasped the front of the robe together to fake respectability. 'Do you think I am scandalous?'

'I was hoping you might remind me.'

She laughed again, a brittle tinkle of sound that died too soon. She slipped down on to one of her squashy cushions and curled up in a way that exposed her legs to potential frostbite.

Or, with any luck, guestbite.

'They tell me you're going to be a star.' I was perched on the edge of the sofa, by her right shoulder.

'Oh, that will not happen,' she said, shaking her head.

That surprised me. She'd gone international since I'd last seen her. She'd been picked up by one of the agencies who fix models for the top glossies. Once or twice I'd been surprised to find her staring up at me from an airport bookstall. She'd done well on the glamour circuit too, and there was talk of her having a go at the Miss World nonsense – and also a few whispers that she'd win it if she did. But she dismissed the whole thing in a way that had nothing to do with modesty.

'That's a shame,' I said. 'I was hoping one day you'd throw me a króna as your Rolls swept past.'

'Only so you could sell your story to that awful newspaper of yours,' she protested.

'You've heard of cheque-book journalism – we do joke-book journalism,' I said.

'Anyway,' she let her head slump back and closed her eyes, 'it will not happen.'

'What?' I said, trying to sustain the jokey tone. 'Not even for the honour of your country?'

I always used to tease her about the way Icelanders almost snapped to attention when you mentioned anything to do with national pride.

'No,' she sighed, not moving. 'Not even for that.'

'Serious?'

'Serious.' After a pause, she added: 'You know that if I could do something – even something as silly as a beauty contest – to help my country, I would do it. But I cannot. Honestly, Sam, it is not possible.'

'I believe you. Why not?'

She scratched her fingers deep into the carpet as though it was a rival's face. I was about to repeat my question when she opened her grey-blue eyes and, in a finish-it voice, said: 'I cannot. That is all.'

Unexpectedly, after another short pause, she asked: 'And how is your little girl? Sally? Am I right?'

Not only did she remember her name, she even knew her age, her birthday, and that she used to have her hair in bunches. At some time, I realised with growing shame, I must've hit her with a walletful of snaps and a bellyful of maudlin-dad rubbish. It was a wonder I ever saw her again.

'Do you love her and are you a good father?'

'Yes and no, in that order.'

'Why?'

'You know why. They shouldn't let people like us have kids. Hell, they shouldn't let us have goldfish. Not without passing exams first, they shouldn't.'

I looked down into her gleaming eyes. 'Don't include me in this,' she said, nipping my leg. 'I think I will be a marvellous mother. Don't you?'

'Well, you won't be short of applicants for daddy, that's for sure.'

'Swine,' she said. She patted the carpet and I slipped down beside her. 'What do you remember best about me?'

'Let me think. I know. You are the only woman I have ever met who doesn't sneak a quick look in a shop window to see how big her bum looks.'

'Do women do that? Really? You understand that all women really believe they are ugly – that's why you are so dangerous.' She nipped me again, so I had to put my palm over my coffee. 'Do you think we would have been good together?'

'We were good together.' I knew what she meant. No matter how adept you are at keeping emotions locked up in the attic, you still wonder what it would be like if you let them out to play.

'You know what I mean,' she replied. 'Properly.'

'I don't think I'm a very proper sort of person.'

'Have you found a wife then?'

'Yes.'

'You have?' Her tone was just too uncaring.

'Yep. But then her husband found me . . .'

She laughed, more naturally this time. Then she snuggled up, the low lamps buttering her legs with yellow light.

'You know I was saying how sorry I was that I cannot win those beauty titles and things for my country?'

'Yes.'

'Well. Tell me, you read books and things . . . who was the famous Englishman who said about choosing between friends and country?'

'I think it was a gent called Forster.'

'Who was he?'

'Not your type for a start.'

'Ah. And is that what he said? If you must choose between friends and country, you must choose friends?'

'About that.'

'Is he right?'

'I don't know. If I had to choose between the two, I think I'd emigrate and find new friends.'

Even as I answered, I thought it was odd. In my entire life I'd had exactly two conversations about patriotism and they'd both been in the last twenty-four hours. Statistically that was a clear concentration.

Gently, I held her to me and breathed in the subtle Solrun scents that were being funnelled out of the top of her robe. 'What's the problem? What's all this serious talk about? You're not going intellectual on me, are you?'

She gave a small sigh. 'No. Not really.'

'A man?' With her, that was always a fair guess. I felt her nod her head.

'Two,' she whispered, sinking deeper into the silk. 'Two men who say they love me. Two men who want to take me away.'

'That's what free enterprise is all about – choice. And your choice not to go if you don't want to.'

Then, in a voice no louder than the soft brush of my fingers on her skin, she said: 'I think perhaps they will kill me.'

Her pretty, sing-song voice faded and left a black chasm of silence. I didn't say a word. Even though I was sure it was Solrun overacting, the moment was still as delicate as porcelain, and I feared my own clumsiness.

Still in a whisper, still half-buried, she said: 'That was why I thought you'd come, Sam. To take me away.'

I coughed. The frightened man's mood-changer. Then I made my speech. 'You can't go away from things, Solrun, you know that. It doesn't work. You can only go towards things. And I haven't got anything to take you towards.'

Even as I said it, I hated myself.

This time the silence didn't last a second, and it was Solrun who smashed the mood. She sprang up, grabbing me by the hand and failing to hold the robe together as modestly as she might.

'You haven't? You have a very bad memory. Before you always took me towards the bedroom.'

There didn't seem much I could say to that. Not with the way that robe was falling open.

Suddenly, it was the old Solrun, outrageous, extrovert, shaking every last ounce of fun out of every day. And if that seems a bit much, you've got to remember that they were road-testing sexual freedom in Iceland when the English were still putting skirts on piano legs. And she was an exquisitely crafted specimen of the non-shaving half of the human race. And it was late. And I didn't need any excuses. That's the truth.

Later, bleary with sleep, I remember her lips touching my forehead and hearing her say 'Bless'. Funny, I thought, through the mists of sleep. 'Bless' doesn't mean goodnight. It means goodbye. Then when I woke all there was beside me was the scented dent she'd left.

The chance had gone. The chance I had to save her. There aren't any excuses to cover that. And that's the hard and bitter truth . . .

8

When I got back upstairs, I tried to search my misty thoughts for any reason why she'd taken off like that. I'm sure I'm lousy in bed but it doesn't usually drive people to move house.

I lifted one of the blinds to let in a little light. The living room had somehow lost its mysterious hot-eyed intimacy of the night before. The coffee cups were still on the table where we'd left them when she took my hand. I looked at my watch. Five minutes past four. In the morning.

Remember, remember, remember. There were the things she'd said about the two men. There was the nonsense about them killing her that I'd taken for wild talk. After all, she was a hell of a drama queen, was Solrun.

So. So let's have a look round.

For some reason I could no longer remember, my clothes were all over the bedroom floor. I opened the wardrobe and immediately regretted it. Anyone who believes that women belong to the same species as men should look inside a woman's wardrobe. You could've taken away six train-loads of clothes without making any impression on it. I was just going to close the door again when I saw the photograph albums. There were a stack of them, and I took them all through to the half-light of the living-room.

I was going to flick through the last one first – the theory being that recent history was more likely to help me – when the book automatically fell open at the last page. It fell open because jammed between the pages was a metal badge. I took it out and looked at it. It was gold-coloured metal, about an inch and a half across; in the centre was a circle bearing the initials AC, with eagle wings on either side. It had been pinned through the page, but had ripped loose.

Immediately above it was a photograph of Solrun playing at proper grown-up ladies. She was wearing an off-the-shoulder number, which, together with the glitter at her throat and ears, made it something of a special night.

The bloke next to her certainly thought so. Cats which had got the cream would've looked suicidal alongside him. If his smile had got any wider, it would've met around the back of his neck.

And why not? He had his right hand, in light but unmistakeably proprietorial fashion, resting on Solrun's bare shoulder. And if he lost her he could always spend the evening looking in the mirror: he was quite something.

He was cowboy-shaped: wide-shouldered and narrow-waisted, in that way that few men ever achieve outside Hollywood. He had a carefully coiffed collection of black curls and an open confident smile that stopped just, but only just, this side of vanity. With the sweet cut of his dinner-jacket, and the general air of a man who'd be handier with a cocktail-shaker than a pick, he looked more Italian than anything else. Only an Italian can carry that much style without going bow-legged.

He was wearing evening dress. An official function maybe? Not necessarily. He looked as though he'd wear a dinner-jacket to bring the coal in.

It was a head-and-shoulders picture so there wasn't much background to go on. All you could see was a display cabinet immediately behind them. As far as I could see, it contained the usual collection of silverware that you find in low-class golf clubs and pretentious suburban homes.

Then I saw the horse-chestnut on top of the cabinet. Only it wasn't a horse-chestnut. It was round, with spikes sticking out, but the spikes were much longer than a chestnut. And it was set up on a small stand – the whole thing looked like plastic – as though it was flying through space.

I knew what it was. I'd seen photographs of it before. I knew exactly what it was . . . but I couldn't remember. Not just then, anyway.

Any chance there was of remembering then vanished when I heard the ping of the lift. I wasn't ready to do any entertaining. I nipped to the window and when I saw what was standing outside I experienced a small but unpleasant heart-leap.

One white Volvo. One Harley Davidson motor-bike. Even when they choose vehicles for their police force, the Icelanders try to show no favouritism between their American and their Scandinavian friends.

I heard footsteps and voices. With the sort of cool reflexes that we spies develop after years of training, I went into a blind panic and jammed the album down the back of the nearest radiator.

9

At Kopavogur I had two hours to sit and contemplate what the descendants of the Vikings might consider a suitable punishment for someone who'd misplaced one of their women. None of the possibilities sounded much fun, so I sat on a plastic scoop in a long empty corridor hoping that Christopher Bell would get my message.

I didn't understand any of it. I didn't understand why I'd been brought to a brown three-storey box of a building in what looked like an industrial estate. The police headquarters I knew was down in the middle of the town.

I'd asked the cops who brought me in, but they treated me as though I was Jack the Ripper after an intensive training course with Black September. Nervous wasn't the word. They may have looked dashingly ornamental in their black-belted uniforms with white-topped caps, but they never took their eyes off me, even when I left the message for Christopher at his hotel reception.

At Kopavogur, they emptied my pockets in plastic sacks, and then an English-speaking officer took a lengthy statement, without all the usual come-off-it-sonny stuff. He took it, and went.

Then a door down the corridor opened and a meaty young face under a thick thatch of white-blond hair beckoned me in.

Cop-shops all over the world retain mementoes of their trade in scarred woodwork or messages of goodwill on the walls. But this place, with its concealed strip lights, pale beige walls, polished wood-block floors, and laundered air, was more like the VIP lounge at an airport. Only I wasn't a VIP.

Looking back on it now, I'm sorry I took the attitude I did to Blondie. But when I'm bullied I get skittish, and this sometimes comes across as impudence.

As if I'd be impudent to a bobby . . .

He nodded me into another scoop by the door and ignored me while I had a good look round.

It was a rectangular room. The far end, to my right, was mostly window. Through it I could see the distant mountains black against the bright sky.

An older man – I could tell that by his thin creamed hair and his seamed neck – faced out of the window. He was making notes. He didn't turn when I came in.

Blondie was opposite me, a couple of yards away, behind a small metal desk. He was frowning as he read through a typescript.

Lots of people make the mistake of thinking that in relatively crime-free countries the police are not much more than an extension of the boy scouts. Don't you believe it. True, Scandinavia isn't like one of those Soviet countries where they chuck you in the loony-bin, step up the largactyl and mark your mail Unknown At This Address, or those equatorial places where they give you a spin in a cement mixer before river-bathing. But up there, they half-expect you to laugh at them, so they have more to prove: they're intelligent, and they can be exactly as tough as you like.

Without glancing up, Blondie began talking.

'Correct any factual errors. Name, Samuel Craven. Age, thirty-eight. Marital status, divorced. Height, five foot ten inches. Weight, twelve stone. Black hair, brown eyes, distinguishing mark, slight scar on left temple, result of car accident.'

He lifted his eyes to check that last item. He needn't have bothered. It only showed against a sun-tan.

'Father unknown, abandoned by mother, childhood in a Dr Barnardo's home in Norfolk, England.'

'Little Orphan Sammy,' I said, as I usually did when that bloodless recitation came up. He didn't acknowledge it. Perhaps he didn't like musicals.

'Next of kin, daughter Sally, aged nine.'

He glanced up again, then added: 'No known security affiliations.'

He put the file down and folded his heavy, tanned hands on it.

'Is that correct? No known security affiliations?'

'I'd say so.'

'What does that mean?'

'Well, if they were known you wouldn't be asking me, and if I have any unknown security affiliations I wouldn't be telling you about them, would I?'

Not traceable, Batty had said. I was beginning to see what he meant.

At the other end of the room, the older man cleared his throat. Blondie leaned forward on beefy forearms and looked at me as though he'd like to see me taken home in a bucket.

'You claim to be a journalist? Can you prove it?'

'I've got a liver and an overdraft, both enlarged.'

I don't think he picked up on all the full humorous implications of that, but he caught the tone. He gave a tough, tired smile and cracked his knuckles. He wasn't impressed with me. He wouldn't have been impressed with three of me.

'You claim in your statement that you met Solrun Jonsdottir at Thingvellir . . . why?'

'Because it's romantic.'

'Romantic?' He gave a laugh that was dangerously overloaded with scorn. 'You meet this . . . girl, you go to bed with her, you say this is romantic?'

'It isn't the way you tell it.'

He gave me the laugh again: three sneers for Craven. 'Well,

well, that is something very new for us. We did not realise that our famous Solrun was romantic.'

'No? Well, I don't suppose you get much time for that sort of thing down at the Hitler Youth.'

The muscles moved in his neck and tightened up his face. That was all. Very softly, he said: 'You are her boyfriend?'

'I would be honoured to be called that.'

'It is not such an honour,' he said, with fastidious malice. 'The lovers of Solrun do not make such an exclusive club. They are men like you. Nobodies. Pick-ups. Drunks. Party scrapings. One night stands.' He added the last word in Icelandic – 'Utlendingar' – with more contempt than all the others. 'Foreigners,' he added, for my benefit.

He switched to a grave, impartial manner. 'It is a shame, of course. Sadly, she represents our country. But I think she will only bring us shame.'

Now, you don't get many puritans in Iceland. That interested me. So I asked him if having a wide and varied social life was illegal these days.

'Not illegal,' he said, in the same tone of controlled menace. 'But it is dangerous. When it is with scum.'

He picked up the documents again, pretended to look at them, and then threw them down with evident disgust. 'Your whole story is a fabrication. It is obvious.'

As he spoke, he pushed himself up on his finger-tips and walked slowly, heavily, around his desk until he was behind me.

'I can see your problem.' I stared at his empty chair, waiting for the blow.

'I don't have a problem. You have a problem. We are not the logga [even I knew the friendly slang word for police] and you should understand this. We are talking about national security. Perhaps you think it is funny that a little island like this should worry about national security? Does that amuse you?'

He didn't wait for an answer. 'It is just as important to us as your Buckingham Palace and Tower of London. Remember that. Remember that before you tell us any more stupid lies. Who are you? Why are you here? Where is Solrun?'

He fired the last three questions into my left ear, so I couldn't help but jump. His face was so close to the side of mine that I had to lean back to get him in focus.

'I've told you. And I don't know where she's gone.'

A pistol shot cracked in my ears and my heart hit the back of my throat. I hung on to the seat of the chair to prevent myself hitting the ceiling. When I opened my screwed-up eyes, he was holding a wide, black plastic ruler he'd slapped on the desk for the sound effect.

'Tell . . . me,' he said, spacing the words a second apart, 'tell . . . me . . . what . . . she . . . said.'

'Nothing.' By now, my nerves were hopping like fleas. 'I mean, she said all sorts of things but nothing you'd want to know.'

'Everything. I want to know everything. Did she say goodbye? Did she mention any friends? Did she say anything about an American? What were her last words? Tell me the last thing she said to you.'

'It wouldn't help.'

'Tell me! Now! Tell me the last words she said.'

'To me?'

'Of course to you. What did she say?'

Well. He had insisted. I did warn him. So I told him. And if they weren't the very last words she said, at least they were the ones I remembered best.

'She said . . . "I don't think I'll ever get my toes uncurled again." I think that was it, more or less word for word.'

His face, open-mouthed, hung in front of me. Slowly, like creeping pain, I watched the understanding rise into his eyes.

'You did ask,' I said, with a winning smile.

Sometimes I do overcook things a bit. Listening to the hot breath whistle through his teeth and seeing the red rage in his face, I thought this could be one of those occasions.

With elaborate care, he raised the black plastic ruler in his bunched fist and brought it down so it tapped me on the shoulder. Once. Twice. He could've been knighting me. I didn't move. Hell, I didn't even breathe. He raised it a third time and held it there above the side of my face. It was only a ruler. In his hand it might as well have been an axe.

The click of a cigarette lighter snapped the tension.

'That will do for now, Magnus. Would you bring some coffee in for myself and Mr Craven. He must be ready for one, and I certainly am. Milk and sugar?'

It was the older man, standing out of sight, just behind me.

'No sugar,' I said. 'Got to watch the old weight. Don't want to die of a fatty heart.'

'I should be very surprised if you live to have the opportunity, Craven,' said the same man, in an even, pleasant voice. 'Two coffees, white, no sugar, please.'

My breath escaped from my body in a flood as the big blond man moved away and placed the ruler carefully on the desk. 'That's better,' I said. 'I don't like talking to the dummy when the ventriloquist is in the room.'

Quite unexpectedly, a neat smile of admiration touched his features and he bowed his head to me in some sort of salute.

10

'Smoke?'

'I gave up.'

'Ah. Iron will. Did you smoke a lot?'

'Sixty a day.'

'That's a lot. Now it doesn't bother you?'

'Only sixty times a day.'

The smoke got mixed up in his rasping laugh and he waved it away from me with his hand. The packet on his desk identified them as small cigars called London Docks: presumably because of the smell.

'Petursson,' he said, extending his hand into the smoke-free zone between us. 'I'm a government fulltrui – an official.' As he spoke he removed his expensive continental tweed jacket and put it on a hanger which he then placed with care in a narrow teak cupboard in the corner. He also flicked at the flawless front of his cream shirt in case a speck of ash had dared to settle there. He was that odd combination of big and neat, the sort of hefty men they say make good dancers.

He must've been sixty and you might have taken him for another of those big men who got into police-type work to get shoes the right size, until you saw the intelligence in the hard slits of his eyes.

'That was very clever.' The chair squealed under his weight as he sat down. 'Magnus was supposed to make you angry. You turned it around.'

He picked up the plastic ruler and wagged it. The crack had split it down the middle. 'It is a delicate subject here.' He gave me a sharp look. 'It is a delicate subject anywhere, wouldn't you say – outsiders who come and take the local girls?'

I knew what he was after, and I wasn't going to let him have it. Father unknown. He'd picked up on that all right. I gave him a smile and let it grow into a yawn to remind him of the time.

Without speaking, Magnus delivered two coffees, and on the tray he placed in front of his boss I recognised the contents of my pockets.

One by one, Petursson picked up the bits of junk, and put them down again. A sleek Waterman pen I never used. A wrist-watch I got duty-free on a plane before finding they were cheaper on the ground. A red plastic rhino, cunningly concealing a pencil-sharpener, that Sally had given me for my birthday. Two chewed pencils. A parking ticket, still creased from where it had been screwed up in rage, then smoothed out again. Ford Escort keys on a Ferrari key-ring. A bill from Rugantino's commemorating dinner with a girl who'd extolled the wonders of celibacy – over the coffee and Sambucca. My passport. My press card. Come to think of it, my life.

He flicked the press card without picking it up.

'Are you really a journalist?' He had a conversational style, not nearly as pugnacious as his apprentice.

'More or less.'

'A scandal rag, I believe.'

'That sort of thing.'

Suddenly he began to pull hard on the cigar, which was threatening to die on him. When he'd kissed it back into life, he grinned up at me.

'You see, Mr Craven, we have people who come here who are not what they seem. Tourists who are not tourists. Businessmen who have no business. You understand?'

'I suppose so.'

'You seem a sensible young man. Why on earth do you work for a newspaper like that?'

'That's what people want to read. Who am I to deny the masses? That's democracy, isn't it? Crap for crap-lovers – I just shovel it.' I'd heard Grimm make that speech once, in El Vino's, but I must admit he did it with more conviction.

Petursson's eyes vanished in a silent smile. 'If that is what you say then I must believe you, Mr Craven. Do you – forgive my asking – do you know a journalist who is also based in London who is called . . .' he made a pretence of looking in a file, 'Ivanov. Oleg Ivanov.'

'Old Ivan? Sure.'

'Well, well. Mr Ivanov is also here in Reykjavik. I believe he works for one of the Moscow agencies.'

'That's what he says.'

'And here you are together. Is this a coincidence?'

I was wondering that myself. 'Unless we're both working on the same story.'

'Of course. Solrun. Don't worry.' He began to chuckle and held out both his hands, palm downwards, in a calm-down gesture. 'I am not so excitable as my young colleague. But she is a little wild. Even for us, Solrun is a little wild. But where has she gone? You cannot help us? You don't want to help us? I wonder.'

At that point, a cough started churning in his chest and then caught in his throat. He glared accusingly at the cigar. A few ambling strides took him to the window and he flicked it out.

'London Docks.' Back behind his desk, he looked regretfully at the packet, then sat back in his chair. 'I lived in London. Over a year.' He stifled a small yawn, then continued with his calculated rambling. 'Yes, a most pleasant time for me. I was attached to one of your government departments. I stayed with a family called Shivas. Charming people. They were very kind to me. I was young, and a little lost. We still write. Originally it was a Huguenot name. I could never understand why it was that they were more proud of that than they were of being British. That is the tragedy of your country, I think. People talk of being Welsh or even Yorkshire but they no longer talk of being British. In Scotland, at your rugby matches, they boo the national anthem. That is what happens when a country loses its identity and its pride – the people retreat into tribalism. Or am I being unfair?'

'I don't know. Does it matter?'

'Perhaps not. But don't make that mistake here. We do care. You saw that in Magnus. We are very close to our history here, and you must remember that.'

'The only bit of history we celebrate is the anniversary of the bloke who tried to blow the whole bloody place up. I've always thought that was a sign of maturity myself. By the way, Mr Petursson, which department were you attached to in London?'

'One of those in Mayfair. I forget the exact title . . .' He let the sentence die.

We both knew what he meant. Those buildings without plaques which you find dotted around Mayfair. Everyone knows what they are. The first principle of espionage is to stay near the good restaurants: they'd rather risk their lives than their lunch.

The phone rang and Petursson listened, then spoke briefly.

'A friend, Christopher Bell, is inquiring for you.'

'That's right. I thought I might need an interpreter.'

'You won't have any problems being understood, Mr Craven, providing that you speak the truth, of course.' His eyes vanished again at his own little joke, and he tipped my belongings in the tray towards me. 'You'd better take these. We do know where to find you, I believe. Ah, one moment. What is this?'

He'd picked up the winged badge I'd found in Solrun's photo album, which was now mixed up among my small change. He held it up and turned it around in the light. 'What is it, Mr Craven? Please enlighten me?'

As he placed it in the palm of his wide hand and held it out to me, I mumbled: 'That? Oh, just a bit of junk I picked up somewhere . . .'

'It looks like a military badge.' I could feel his eyes drilling into me. 'What are these letters? AC. What do they stand for?'

'Afrika Corps,' I said in a blaze of inspiration. 'Military badges, I pick them up for a friend's little boy.'

'Really.' His eyes didn't leave my face. 'Wouldn't AK be more accurate for Afrika Korps? And why would they want wings? Forgive me, but my memory is that they relied rather more on tanks than on aircraft?'

I made a show of inspecting the badge. 'Sorry – you're quite right. That's an air-raid warden's badge from the last war. The initials stand for "All Clear". Quite a collector's item.'

With a leisurely movement, he closed his hand over it and put it in his pocket. 'In that case, perhaps it would be wise if I look after it until you are leaving the country.'

What could I do? Nothing except thank him. So I did. And I was still wondering how he'd managed to outflank me like that when I stepped outside.

'Over here.' I heard a whistle, and then saw a taxi parked down the side of the building. Bell's head was poking out of the window. 'Got your message, but they wouldn't let me in, I'm afraid. Whatever was it all about?'

I told him – or at least an outline of what had happened.

'My word! Stirring times, as they say. They are taking you seriously, aren't they?'

'Why?'

'Petursson's the top chap. Chief spy-catcher.'

'What is that place anyway?'

'Rannsoknarlogrella Rikisins. Literally, Investigative Police of the State.'

'Sort of Special Branch and MI whatsit?'

'Yes. With Miss Marple and Oddjob thrown in. Did they give you a bad time?'

'Not really. Well, they didn't throw their bowler hats at me, anyway.'

11

Maybe it's because I was brought up in dormitories that I don't like sleeping in modern hotels. I always have the feeling that the bedroom walls will fall down and I'll find myself sleeping in a vast five-star dormitory for lost American Express boys.

That's why I always stayed at Hulda's and not at the Saga. I liked a bit of a clutter around me, and there was no shortage of that at Hulda's.

She lived in a barujarns hus – one of the lovely old houses clad in corrugated iron – and the whole place was plastered with evidence of her existence for the last seven decades. There wasn't a surface, horizontal or vertical, that wasn't covered in pictures of human beings on their way from cot to coffin: children, grandchildren, and no doubt great grandchildren, in prams, playing, on bikes, in uniforms, on holidays, and then proudly holding produce of their own. And, since they all had Hulda's clear open forehead, it was like looking down a hall of mirrors.

There were other reasons for staying there, too. Hulda, as frail and perky as a sparrow, knew everything and everyone on the island.

The disadvantage was that she still considered it her duty to introduce me to Viking delicacies – and she wouldn't even let me have a blindfold. She sat there, the light from the half-shuttered windows glinting on the glass of the photographs, watching every mouthful.

'Delicious,' I lied, gagging on the last bite. I don't know what it was. I would've said it had been kicked out of a badly frightened penguin, but I could be wrong.

And Hulda said what she always says at that point in the conversation. She nodded her lovely old head, the grey hair pinned back in a tight bun: 'It is my pleasure and my duty.'

It was coming up for noon. A few hours' sleep and I was

restored, but I had a lot to do. For a start, I wished that Batty had at least given me an emergency number to ring. I'd no idea what to do about a vanishing client. And I wanted to find Ivan and see what he was doing in town. I wouldn't have thought Moscow was interested in Sexy Eskies.

And, now that I'd had more time to think about it, I was comforted by the way Bell had turned out so readily. I couldn't really believe that British intelligence services, inept as they are supposed to be, would send a bumbling amateur like me to do anything more complicated than post a letter. But they might want to use my personal influence – as Batty had said – so long as they had a trade-tested pro keeping an eye on me. As far as I was concerned, they could keep as many eyes on me as they wanted.

'You are seeing Solrun?' Hulda asked, her hawk-eyes searching my plate for signs of leftovers.

'That's the idea.' Even Hulda's information service couldn't have got hold of Solrun's disappearance so quickly.

'She is a most lovely girl.' She sighed as though for her own lost youth. Perhaps it was. Her own beauty was there to see, in the pictures on the walls.

'Is she still single?' I asked, and instantly regretted it. From the look on her face, I knew Hulda had taken it as a reflection on Solrun's desirability, and thus the desirability of all Icelandic women, and by implication the entire nation.

'She could have endless many men,' she said. 'Endless many.'

That was another of her charming idiosyncrasies: endless many.

'Oh, I know, I know.'

'But she has many opportunities for life itself. All the famous magazines wish to take her photograph because she is so beautiful. Yes, that is true. She wishes also to win this title of the most beautiful woman in the world to bring honour on us all. She has men, naturally. Women must have men. But she also has her own life, I think.'

'Quite right too. She's a gorgeous girl.'

'You should know that, Sam.'

'I do, I do. And you're the most gorgeous of them all, Hulda.'

I kissed the top of her head as I passed. 'Don't wait up.'

'And what about you?' she called after me. 'When are you getting married again?'

'The day you say "yow", and not before.'

12

The Vikings fixed on Reykjavik by the traditional, if chancey, method of chucking their furniture over the side of the longboat and setting up house where it landed. If you let your dining-table do your house-hunting, then I suppose you shouldn't complain too much if you end up in an odd sort of place.

And Iceland is an odd sort of place. For over a thousand years after that, they staggered on through blizzards and Black Death, frozen one minute, roasted by volcanoes the next, scratching out a living on a hot cinder still sizzling among the ice at the edge of the Arctic Circle.

Then, after the last war, they suddenly hit the jackpot with their fishing. By the seventies, when I first went there, it was one of the most prosperous countries on earth.

I walked down through the town to see how much it had changed in the past two years. Quite a bit, as it turned out. The pop-fashion explosion had hit them the same as everyone else. Down Laugavegur, blow-ups of Bogart and Monroe smouldered in the shop windows, and on the walkway at Austurstraeti the pavement was knee-deep in Bowie flooding from the shop doorways.

At some secret signal, discernible only to people under the age of twenty, the kids there had changed from skin-tight clothes to floppy, crinkly bags four sizes too big – just like the kids everywhere in the Western world. They lolled in the pale sunshine and tried to feel Mediterranean while they read each other's tee-shirts. Yet they still nibbled the hardfiskur they bought from the pavement stall with one hand, while drinking Coke with the other.

On the hillside opposite, the little toy-town houses in their bright coats of paint looked daintily impermanent. Dress it up how you like, Reykjavik still has the air of the Yukon about it. Only they didn't find gold here. This is a fish-rush town.

I had a coffee in a smart café overlooking the square and wrote a card to Sally. In a doomed attempt to impress the nuns, I'd bought one with a picture of one of the spouting geysers. But I'd spoiled it by writing on the back: 'As you can see, the plumbing here is an absolute disgrace. And guess who's here? – Uncle Ivan.'

Then, in one of those coincidences we deride on the telly but never question in real life, I looked down into the square and saw Ivan. He was sitting on a low wall surrounding a flower garden. Next to him was Christopher Bell.

I was so surprised that when I paid for my coffee I hardly noticed that it cost only slightly less than the down-payment on a five-bedroomed house in Kensington. Icelandic prices rate high on the wince scale.

'Here he is,' Ivan said, as I walked over to them. 'My favourite diurnalist.' He was the pal who'd done the writing on my office window.

'How did you two find each other?'

'Simple really,' Christopher said, a smile breaking out beneath his banana nose. 'I heard this gentleman asking for you at the desk of the hotel.'

It wasn't all that amazing. If you had an expense account and none of my funny twitches about dormitories, the Saga was the place to stay.

'What the hell are you doing here?'

Ivan ignored the question. With an exaggerated roll of his eyes, he replied: 'Never mind that, dear boy. Do you realise I'm missing Sussex at home to Yorkshire?'

'I say,' Christopher intervened with boyish excitement, 'are you keen on cricket?'

'Keen? I adore it.'

'He thinks it's the perfect evocation of man's eternal soul, don't you, Ivan?' I said, just to annoy him.

39

He rewarded me with a petulant blink. 'I still find it impossible to believe that such a bland race as the English could invent a game so rich in yearning. It's a very Russian emotion, yearning.'

'Ah, yearning. Yes.' Christopher didn't look too convinced, but then he'd probably never met anyone quite like Ivan before. He was an original.

In Fleet Street, he was known – affectionately, I hasten to add – as the Gay Red. His parents, one Russian, one English, were academics and he'd split his childhood between the two countries. For years now he'd been based in London for one of the Russian agencies. It was generally assumed, as with all Russian journalists, that his real job was to post bits of information back to the boys at home: this, together with his discreet but clear use of eye-liner, gave him the nickname – and a sort of raffish glamour.

I'd always liked him. When I was married he quite often came back for dinner. He used to entertain us at obscure and grubby East European restaurants which always seemed to be above men's hairdressers in Muswell Hill where the food was invariably a delight. After my divorce, we became good boozing mates.

I knew him as well as anyone, and even I was never sure how much was affectation and how much genuine. The one thing we didn't have in common was cricket. For all it meant to me, it might as well have been Russian. But he used to love to get out to the county games and install himself in a deck-chair among all those elderly couples, tartan rugs around their knees, making faint marks in large scorebooks as they ate damp egg sandwiches.

'And how is the wondrous Sally?' he inquired, with his usual reproving note. He was her godfather. He took his duties – including checking up on me – very seriously.

I showed him the card. 'You'll make the girl into one of those giggly creatures who work in dress shops in South Ken. Tell me it's not true that you are working for the dreaded Grimm – oh my God, it is.'

'What's in it for your Moscow masters, Ivan?'

'Perfectly obvious, surely. The beauty business is the classic example of the exploitation of the innocent by the grasping capitalists. Don't you know anything, dear boy? But I hear you have mislaid, if that's the word, the lady in question.'

He caught my quick glance at Christopher – Ivan didn't miss that sort of thing – and explained: no one had been indiscreet; he'd picked up that information from the Russian Embassy. Not that it would matter, he added.

'I'd no idea you chaps co-operated so much,' Christopher said.

'Believe me,' Ivan replied, 'whether he's in London or Moscow, a boss is a boss is a boss. There is surprisingly little to choose between Sam's ghastly Sexy Eskies and my dreary little pieces of propaganda. Our principal problem, I fear, will be finding exquisite gifts for the wondrous Sally in this desolate dump.'

'I thought we might give her one of Bell's musical loo fittings?'

Ivan's eyes rolled to the skies. 'I declare that out of bounds immediately. Now I must go in search of a vast g and t, and you, Sam, will no doubt wish to have a gallon of that appalling slop you drink.'

'Not here. You can't get beer and there aren't any boozers. We'll have to go to a restaurant.'

'They are a bit restrictive with the old firewater,' Christopher said, apologetically.

'In that case, let us waste no further time.' Ivan rose, a tall stick of a man, his greying hair falling in curtains on either side of his bony face. 'Good Lord!'

At that moment, through a bunch of kids playing around, came a boy with a wad of newspapers under his arm. He looked maybe eleven or twelve. He stopped in front of us and gave a weird funereal wail that was presumably the Icelandic for Three Hurt in Polar Bear Horror. But that wasn't what made us stare. His flat, expressionless face was the one that had become an international symbol for suffering. And you don't expect to stumble upon a Vietnamese at the other end of the world.

'One of the boat people,' Christopher explained. 'About two dozen of them fetched up here.'

41

'Have a care then, Mr Bell,' Ivan said. 'These people are ingenious entrepreneurs, I am told. They may well have plans in the general direction of the stuffed-puffin market.'

We watched the boy with the biscuit-coloured face wander off through the crowds, and then Ivan turned to me, slipping a silver-backed notebook from his pocket.

'Tell me,' he said, flipping it open, 'does the name . . . now where is it . . . does the name Oscar Murphy mean anything to you?'

'Not a thing.'

'Truly?'

'Hell, Ivan, I've only been here one night. Why? Who is he?'

He put the notebook back into his pocket. 'I'm not quite sure. One of our embassy people mentioned him. He wouldn't say any more. You know what those awful Intelligence people are like . . . they won't tell you the time except in code. Come along, my children, Uncle Ivan is ready for drinkiepoohs. Lead the way, Master Bell, you're the nearest we have to a native guide.'

13

In a tight corner, I can eat guillemot without complaint. Pushed, I can listen to a conversation about the art of bowling leg-breaks. What I cannot do – cheerfully, anyway – is both at the same time. So before the coffee came, I left Christopher and Ivan and took a taxi back to Vesturbrun.

My plan was quite simple: get back into the flat and have a good snoop around, particularly at the photo of Solrun's handsome boyfriend. If Petursson had the place staked out, as he almost certainly would, I could always say I'd nipped back to get my razor, and exit smartly.

At first I didn't think I'd get past the foyer. Petursson's man was taking it easy, thumbing through a magazine as he sprawled on a low chair in the small lounge area just inside the door. All that registered on me was his light chamois jacket – they must pay their cops well around here. After that it was eyes ahead and straight towards the lift. I knew he was watching me, and any minute I was expecting to be called to heel.

But not one word. Up I went, and the same god that had installed short-sighted policemen downstairs had arranged for the door to Solrun's flat to be left open.

He'd also arranged for a whirlwind to go through the place. I couldn't believe it. Furniture was tipped over. Clothes were scattered everywhere. Drawers had been ripped open and emptied, books had been swept from their shelves, and even the mattress had been pulled off the bed.

My first thought was indignation that the cop downstairs should sit there reading up gardening tips while an intruder went through the flat. My second was that perhaps I shouldn't put in an official complaint: I was also an intruder. And the third was the photo album. It was still there, down the back of the radiator. The only surprise was that whoever had done the searching hadn't ripped the radiator off the wall.

For the second time, I sat down and opened it. This time, I began – as they say – at the beginning.

Overall, it tended to suggest that Solrun had cancelled her application to the nunnery. It started with boys who didn't look as if they'd ever raised razor to cheek and it ended with the Italian-looking smoothie and the rip-mark where the badge had been. In between were young blokes bulging their biceps beside swimming-pools, students trying to look tubercular and poetic, and sharpies poised with languid cigarettes and bored eyes. Men with moustaches, men with beards, men with shaggy sweaters, men with hand-stitched suits, men with bikes and motor-bikes and cars. And me, out of focus as usual, ringed in red, by a waterfall.

I sat and thought about it for a moment. I wasn't jealous. You couldn't be jealous of Solrun any more than you could hate the sun for shining on other people too. She was a bit on the universal side, was Solrun.

I turned to the last page again. I knew what the long-spiked chestnut was now. It was a few years since I'd seen a picture of it, which probably explained why I hadn't recognised it immediately. It was a model of the first sputnik – you know, the Russians' vintage spacecraft. And the only people who'd be at all likely to give pride-of-place to a junky chunk of patriotic souvenir like that would not be Italian.

Once again I studied the man. Somehow he looked familiar now. He certainly didn't look Russian. I know it's wrong to nominate racial stereotypes but it is remarkable how many Russian men do have faces like overpacked satchels, and Russians don't usually dress like him either.

Or cops. You don't usually see cops dressed in exquisite chamois jackets. That's why he looked familiar. The man in the photograph with Solrun – Russian, Martian or whatever the hell he was – was at this moment sitting downstairs, cool as you like.

I was going to do something about that, right there and then, only this chain saw started at the top of my head and zoomed straight through to my torso and sliced me in two at the pelvis.

Either he was downstairs, cool as you like. Or he was upstairs, in charge of chain saws.

14

It isn't red, it's yellow.

In books, they always say being knocked out gives you a red effect between the eyes. Well this one was a violent shade of mustard, and it swelled and heaved at the back of my eyes until I had to edge them open. Ouch. Close again. The yellow started ebbing and flowing and I realised, like it or not, I was alive.

On the whole, I didn't like it.

This time I opened my eyes and found myself face down on the carpet. A minute later I was face down in the bathroom, over the loo. I felt better for that. So I had a glass of water and did it all over again.

I looked at myself in the mirror. That was a mistake too. I'd gone the colour of candle-fat and I could swear there were sparks coming out of the top of my head where he'd hit me. Chamois jacket. While I was sitting there carefully working it all out, he must have coasted up in the lift and coshed me with a sputnik.

I had another glass of water which, after some difficult negotiations, my stomach decided to accept. Then I turned to go back into the living-room when I saw him.

He was framed in the doorway. Handsome, of course. Elegant, in the fine soft leather. But very very surprised. He should've been running away, I should've been catching him: instead we stood there trying to hypnotise each other.

Then it broke. I shouted something; he turned and fled, and I was so unsteady that I crashed over the sofa as I tried to race after him.

I got to the door in time to see the lift go. I got to the lift in time to see it had reached the ground. And I got back to the flat window in time to see a van tearing down the hill.

That was when I lost my second glass of water.

Luckily, I managed to grab the pan from the floor in time.

A pan? In the middle of the sitting-room floor? Once the urgency had passed, I studied it with some interest. One large pan, orange in colour, wooden of handle, and very heavy. For smacking someone over the head, it was a lot more useful than the scatter cushions or the bits of wicker.

While the latest attack of dizziness passed, I sat on the floor-cushion and had another look at the photo album. The last page had been torn out. Surprise surprise.

I put together the bits of my brain that were still undamaged and pointed them at this chaotic scene. They didn't do too well. Young Chamois wishes to retrieve photo of self so as not to be linked with Solrun. Yes? Well, possibly. So he sneaks in, smashes up the flat, sneaks out, sits reading Harpers until I arrive, sneaks back, wallops me over the head with pan, grabs photo and goes.

On balance, I thought not.

I decided to discard the theory that he carried large pans on

45

his person on the off-chance of meeting a diurnalist in need of treatment. On wobbly legs I went through to the kitchen. Aha. One row of pans, orange with wooden handles. Mummy Pan, Baby Pan, but Big Daddy Pan was missing from the end hook.

So, I tried that one. As I sat admiring his photograph, he tiptoed past me into the kitchen, selected the senior pan, tiptoed back, and panned me. He then threw it down, grabbed the photograph, made his escape . . . and then popped back to see how I was. Little as I understand human behaviour, this didn't sound too convincing either. And if it didn't sound too good to me, how would it sound to Petursson? The flat suddenly looked a very good place not to be. I went.

15

What you do in Britain when you want to play bloodhounds is to start off at the local sub post office. There, when they eventually dig out the electoral roll from under the bacon slicer – invariably covered in potato dirt and still warm from the cat – you can find out who lives where and with whom.

In Iceland, it's the Hagstofa. The official records office is in an old building opposite a green hillock where a statue of Eric the Unsteady, or one of his chums, leans on his axe. With his rat's-tail hair, staring eyes and straggly beard, he looks like a sixties' folk-singer.

I'd nipped back to Hulda's and had a quick shower and change when I realised I could just catch the Hagstofa before it closed. It had struck me that – apart from personal toe-curling information – I knew very little about Solrun's background. I'd been taken there once before by a local journalist and I knew it was definitely the place to start.

The manager – if that's what the three-foot word on his teak door said – wasn't sure. He was a pink hairless man with rimless glasses and a face like a hamster after a three-course meal, and he was torn between their tradition of open government and suspicion of unannounced strangers.

Two things did it. The sight of my Metropolitan Police Press Pass, with my thumb over the last two words as it wafted across his line of vision, and the words Petursson and Kopavogur in the same sentence.

With mumbled apologies, he took me through to a room where the walls, from floor to ceiling, were lined with shelves of metal files.

He reached for one, then froze with his hand up, like a schoolboy wanting to leave the room.

'Allow me,' I said, reaching past him and taking the file down.

'Thank you,' he murmured. 'So difficult. The office girls are always taking away my steps. I think they do it for a joke.'

Naturally, since this was Scandinavia and not Britain, there was no potato dirt and cat warmth. Only sheet upon sheet of computer print-out. Hamster gave a little hop over to the table and began to flick rapidly through the thin skins of paper. Suddenly he stopped. With one small sausage finger, he pushed his specs up his nose and gave me a shifty look.

'For the police?' I don't suppose he'd seen many cops in crumpled old corduroy suits.

I nodded towards the grey telephone. 'Ring Petursson.' He gave me a quick nervous smile and turned the file towards me.

'This is her, I think. Is that her date of birth?'

I looked at his finger. That made her twenty. That would be her.

He slammed that file shut and pushed it away, and brought another one through from the next room.

'In this file there is just the standard information.' He had it open and his finger on her name again. He began to read off her address, occupation, parents' names, father dead . . . 'What exactly are you looking for?'

I was listening but I was watching him too. His lower lip was shaking. His eyes were all over the place. For reasons known only to himself and the computer, my little hamster was telling whoppers.

'Let's have a look.' I turned the file round towards me. When computers first came out I recognised them for what they were, a passing fad, and ignored them. The result is that I still experience deep panic at the sight of those square-shouldered letters. But I made him show me the letter code which followed every name, and what each letter meant. And it was all exactly as he had said: except he'd missed out one letter – a capital C.

'What does it mean?'

The tip of his fat finger whitened on the page. His eyes blinked furiously behind his specs. His lip wobbled again. But he still didn't say anything.

This time I reach over for the telephone. 'Petursson will not be at all pleased . . .'

He leaned forward, his finger still stuck to the page. 'But he knows. He must know. Everyone in Iceland knows.'

I stood there holding the telephone, looking down at his burning face. 'I don't. Tell me.'

With a sigh he sat back, removed his glasses and rubbed the corners of his eyes with finger and thumb. In a quiet, relieved voice, he said: 'She is married.' Then he added: 'You knew, of course.'

I didn't. But he'd led me there by his own fear.

Solrun, married? Well, it wasn't so amazing, was it? What was amazing was that she hadn't told me. Neither had Hulda, come to think of it, when I'd stumbled upon the right question for once. And the little hamster here had nearly chewed his lips off with nerves when I'd asked. Yet it could hardly be a secret: everyone in the country must know.

'Why didn't you want me to know?'

He replaced his specs and looked at me unflinchingly through their smeared lenses. 'I must help you with your official inquiries but I think I must not give my personal opinions.'

Whatever it was he was defending, he was doing his best, and he wasn't a man who had been equipped by nature to stand up to Gestapo interrogation. I decided to leave him with his toenails on.

'In that case, officially, I'd like to see the official record of the official marriage.'

After a moment's thought, he blinked a couple of times and went back to his wall of files.

It was a pink slip of paper, a copy of the marriage certificate. That told me that she had married Pall Olafsson in a civil ceremony. It told me that Pall Olafsson was thirty-four. It told me that he was a welder. And it told me that he lived at Breidholt. That meant it was a love match. If you married someone for money they wouldn't be living at Breidholt – the Rolls-Royces were a bit thin on the ground out there.

All of that was both interesting and surprising. What was a lot more of both was the date. They'd got married exactly nine days earlier.

Which meant she'd spent at least one-ninth of her honeymoon with me. To a little old romantic like me, that didn't seem absolutely right.

'Thank you for all your help,' I said to the hamster, as I left. He didn't even look up.

Across in the park, Eric the Unsteady was looking somewhat wrecked after a day's pillaging, and ready for the next longboat home. I knew how he felt.

16

The Kaffivagninn used to be exactly what it sounds like – a coffee wagon for the fishermen and harbour workers. Now it's grown up into a charming one-room restaurant perched on the edge of the harbour wall.

At first sight you could almost take it for one of those London fish restaurants where they've laid the atmosphere on a shade too thick. Only here the nets outside are still damp from the sea, the fish is practically wriggling when it hits your plate, and no one has ever questioned the authenticity of the scented air. To you it might be the stench of fish, the Icelanders call it the smell of money – and they know what they're talking about.

The Kaffivagninn is the real thing all right, and so's their fish.

I'd planned on digging out Ivan and Christopher Bell. But my head hurt from the pan blow, and I wanted to think about the implications of the revelation at the Hagstofa, so I walked down to the harbour. I had lobster tails fried on a spit, and I sat and looked out of the window. The harbour was packed: everything from little plump plastic tubs to creaking old wooden boats and the big steel jobs, their plates stained with work.

Beyond the forest of masts, you could see clear across Faxafloi Bay to Snaefellsjokull. In the pure northern light, you felt as though you could reach out and touch the cold snows on the side of the mountains. Quite honestly, the lobster wasn't much more than perfect, and I was all set to sit there for a month or two, watching the light and the water making eyes at each other, when the chair opposite squeaked as a wide figure lowered itself upon it.

'The fish is good here,' said Petursson.

'Definitely got the edge on the guillemot.'

'I thought you would be dining with your Russian friend.'

'He's busy taking photographs of all your armed forces.'

'That will not take him long.' He smiled. Iceland doesn't have any forces, armed or otherwise.

'You have had a busy day?'

I wondered how much he'd know about my day. In a place that size, probably everything. Even so, I thought I'd let him tell me.

'So so.'

All he had to do was to raise one big hand to have a girl running out with coffees. I took a good look at him as he sat there. Tonight he was wearing a plain oatmeal-coloured raincoat and an old-fashioned wide-brimmed hat which he placed carefully on his knee, rather than on the table. It surprised me he didn't put all his clothes on hangers before he risked sitting down.

'We were talking about you today.'

'I'm flattered.'

'We are still puzzled, Mr Craven. We still do not quite know where to place you . . . no, no, please do not protest. I know that you are a journalist. The question is: are you something else as well?'

'I thought you did pretty well to turn up all that stuff on me last night.'

He shrugged. 'As I told you, I worked in London. I thought perhaps I would find that you are attached to one of the more informal security sections. Apparently not.'

Brightly, I grinned up at him. 'So there we are then.'

'So there we are. We shall hope so.' He raised his cup with difficulty in his big hand. 'You went back to the flat. I would be grateful if you would tell me about it.'

I was ready for the question, but not for the careful courtesy with which he put it. I had the feeling he was giving me a chance to be straight with him. I had another feeling: if I didn't take it, I'd regret it. So I told him the whole thing: about the way the place had been wrecked, Mr Chamois in the foyer, the crack over the head, even the pan. The only thing I didn't mention was the photograph – well, that had gone anyway.

I ended up: 'Do you think Mr Chamois bopped me, Petursson?'

He rubbed his fingers up the long bones of his jaw. 'No, I do not think he did,' he said, in his roller-coaster accent. 'And now you want to know why. Many reasons. The ones you say, like why would he come back, and how did he get the pan, and so on. But there is another reason. It does not bother you if I smoke?'

He tapped one of his small cigars out of the packet and lit it with a green plastic lighter. He returned both the packet and the lighter to his pocket before continuing.

'He is a diplomat,' he said.

'A diplomat? What sort of diplomat?'

'Not the sort to assault journalists, I can assure you.'

'What nationality is he? What was he doing?'

He rapped the table top twice to silence me. 'Listen, Mr Craven, listen to me. The man who hit you with the pan was hiding in the kitchen.'

He picked a matchstick out of the ashtray and scraped the ash off the end of his cigar before it fell in an unauthorised place.

He wasn't a man for chances, Petursson. That was what made him so good.

'How do you know?'

'Simple. My men were watching the flat. They saw him go in.'

'So why didn't they arrest him?'

'Also simple. They didn't see him leave. He got out by a service door at the side.'

'Was he a diplomat too?'

He chose to ignore the sardonic inflexion. 'No, not this man. I was hoping you might tell us a little about him, Mr Craven?'

I pointed at the top of my head. 'That's all I know about him.'

He sat back in his chair and studied me with an interested, uncritical air. 'That is my difficulty, you see. Am I telling you things? Or am I telling you things you already know? That is my main worry. That, and how much trouble you can make for my country.'

He rose clumsily, heaving the chair back with one hand.

'I'd like you to take a little walk with me, if you would be so kind.'

'Fine,' I said. 'But I didn't know anything about the man in the kitchen, you know. For all I know, he could've been there all night.'

'Oh, no, Mr Craven,' he said, checking the angle of his hat in the window. 'If he had been, you would have been dead. By the way, give me your opinion on the two gentlemen by the harbour as we go, will you?'

He knew how to deliver a line all right, did Petursson, and I hoped I looked appropriately shocked: because he was monitoring every reaction. Before I had time to wonder about the man who might have killed me, Petursson had ushered me outside into the soft light of the late evening. When he took my sleeve to point out the snow on the mountains, I knew he was giving me time to look at the two men dawdling at the water's edge.

They didn't even need to touch each other. The effect that Petursson's appearance had on them was minute but unmistakeable. One, who was throwing stones at a plastic bottle in the water, glimpsed us as he turned. His eyes flicked like knives to his mate, who had his back to us. With a quick movement of his hand, he tossed the remaining half-dozen or so stones into the water and, before the pitter-patter of their landing had died, the two of them were walking off briskly, shoulder to shoulder.

We watched them go before we, at a much more leisurely rate, followed.

'Well? Did anything about them strike you?'

'Obviously they're fishermen.' He didn't look too amazed by that deduction. Men in a semi-uniform of roll-neck sweater, reefer-type jacket, and roll-on woollen hats, all dark blue, seen patrolling a harbour were unlikely to be trapeze artists.

'Yes, that is obvious, I agree. Let us take a look at their vessel.'

By the time we got to the first corner, they were just rounding the next one, two yards ahead. When we reached that corner, they were disappearing up the gangplank of a dirty grey trawler.

'Fishermen – that's all?'

'I'd say so.'

They were men, they were off a fishing-boat, so that was fair enough. What he meant – and what I knew perfectly well he meant – was that they weren't fishermen. From what little I could see of their heads, their hair was too well trimmed. They were too sprucely dressed. They were too clean. They moved with short twelve-inch steps, clipped, quick, purposeful. It's a style that stays long after you've forgotten your drill sergeant's name. Whatever they called themselves now, they were military men.

But just this once I thought it wouldn't do any harm for Petursson to be doing the guessing.

'Very well,' he said. 'Now see what you can tell me about their ship.'

This time, instead of playing stupid, I decided to show him what a bright little fellow I could be.

'Isn't it an AGI?'

Under the brim of his hat, he looked surprised. 'How do you know about such things?'

'Aliens Gathering Intelligence,' I intoned heavily, and I won't say that I wasn't enjoying his surprise. 'Oh, I've written about them.'

I looked over the grey hull with the white superstructure and the name *Pushkin* in Cyrillic lettering on the bows and English on the side of the bridge. The only smartly-painted bit was the hammer and sickle in red on the funnel. That figured. The Russians knock hell out of their trawlers for a few years and then flog them to some poor unsuspecting Third-World country.

'What makes you think it's a spy-ship?' he asked.

Now I really did let myself go. 'Look at all those aerials and DF loops. Christ, you could get the BBC's News at One half-an-hour early with that lot. Even so, I'm surprised it's not got the Hydrographic Service flag flying – you know, blue with a white lighthouse.'

He was just about to give me ten out of ten when a sound above made us both look up.

A fat old man with eyes like holes poked in grey pastry came up to the side to have a look at us. He dragged on a cigarette butt with the urgency you always feel for the last pull, then watched it fall into the oily sea below.

'You are very well informed,' Petursson said admiringly. 'You are correct about the flag though. But don't you think those nets are curious?'

I looked where he was pointing. The deck was covered in a jumble of nylon netting. Why would a spy-ship want nets?

'And this is a stern trawler. So far as I know, the Russians have not yet used a stern trawler as an AGI.'

'So what is it then?'

Again, he ignored my question, as we strolled alongside the scarred grey flanks of the trawler. 'We thought as you did, at first. And of course for the Russians to bring a spy-ship in here – even for repairs, as they insist – would be provocative. As a fulltrui of the government, I sought permission to board her and have a look around.'

'Christ!' From a bit closer, I'd suddenly realised that the fat fisherman who was watching us wasn't a fat fisherman at all. It was a fat fisherwoman. Although how I managed to detect some vestige of femininity in that waddling bundle of rags, I couldn't say.

'A woman, yes. It is not so uncommon. So, as I say, I sought permission to inspect this vessel.'

'And did you?'

'Yes.' He stopped and looked down at me and I saw the twinkle of amusement in his face as he enjoyed telling his story. 'They were most helpful, the captain, the crew, everybody.'

'What did you find?' I asked, which was what he wanted me to do.

'What did I find?' He examined the ship again through narrowed eyes as though he'd only just noticed it. 'I found fish, Mr Craven.'

I was thinking about that when I saw the woman had shuffled along so she was almost above us.

'Good evening, madam,' I called out. 'And how are you?'

No expression touched her pudding features. I heard her hawking in the back of her throat and then she spat solidly and with great relish. It landed an inch away from the gleaming brown toe of Petursson's shoe. He raised his face towards her. She went.

'Yes, lots and lots of fish. Isn't that a surprise? So we gave her the All Clear. Isn't that what it said on that interesting badge of yours. All Clear?'

You don't realise how much you rely on Mother Nature to switch off the lights until she lets you down.

Hulda's thin curtains were useless against the pale steady light of the northern night. I even tried hanging my jacket over the window but it kept slipping down. I wished I'd had some of the tinfoil the American troops use to seal their windows out at the Keflavik base.

It seemed like a good chance to give the old meditation another go. I might've known: the minute I was sitting up all relaxed and shurring-ing away, the pictures started tippling through my mind like a hysterical video. Oddly enough, it wasn't the mystery man in the chamois jacket (a diplomat, had Petursson said?), or the sputnik or the spy-ship that wasn't a spy-ship, or even Solrun, that kept cropping up again in the screen of my mind. It was Magnus, the blondie at the Kopavogur office.

And the way he'd said 'Utlendingar'. Foreigners. Hands-across-the-sea is all very well until the hands start coming in contact with sisters, girlfriends and wives. Before you know it, you've got fists-across-the-bar. Okay, there was a certain historic irony in that the Vikings were supposed to have pioneered take-away women, but it must still be peeving to see visitors coming down the plane steps consulting their phrase-books for 'What are you doing tonight?'

If I didn't understand that feeling, no one would.

Utlendingar. It didn't just mean that you were foreign. It was geographically specific – something like coming from another place. An outsider. And that was a word that had a lot of smoky chemistry for me – outsider. In Barnardo's, that was our name for everyone else in the world. If they weren't Barnardo boys, they were outsiders.

Contrary to what most people supposed, we were the lucky ones and we pitied the outsiders. We had everything, didn't we? Our own village, a cluster of two-storey cottages (as we called them) set around a green, each one named after a famous battle and housing a dozen kids. We counted our gardens in acres, our friends in scores, our toys in hundreds, and our parents were anyone we cared to imagine.

Some days I'd look in the mirror and my hair seemed to be blacker and curlier than ever. Your dad can beat mine? Want to bet? Mine could be Sugar Ray.

17

The next morning at breakfast Hulda got me with some liquidised walrus. By the look of it, I could have used it to repoint the chimney but it didn't taste too bad, so I ate it.

'Hulda,' I said, 'I think you've been leading me up the garden path, you rascal.'

'Garden path?' she repeated, as if she didn't know what it meant.

'Yes. I asked you if Solrun had got married and you said she hadn't.'

Straight-backed, hands folded in her lap, she put her head on one side and asked sweetly: 'And has she?'

'Yes, she has, and you know it very well – like you know everything that happens in this town.'

'I know nothing of this.'

'Hulda,' I began again, in tones of strained patience, 'I have seen the certificate. She married a man called Pall Olafsson from Breidholt.'

She almost bridled at the name. 'I do not think so.'

'I've seen the certificate,' I said. 'With these. Eyes, you know, the things you see with.'

'Ah. You want some more coffee. I go now for more coffee.'

I tried to restrain her, but all I got was, 'It is my pleasure and my duty.'

When she came back with the coffee, she'd worked out a policy line on the marriage. She poured out my cup, moved it nearer so I wouldn't have to exhaust myself stretching, and then adopted her familiarly regal pose in the half-lit room. Her thin, still-supple fingers found one stray hair and slipped it back into place.

'We do not speak of it,' she said.

'Why not?'

She made a fussy gesture with her hand. 'This famous beauty contest . . . is it true she cannot enter if she is married or has a child?'

'I'm not sure.'

'I think that it is so.'

So that was it. They'd all ganged up to keep it quiet so they wouldn't spoil her chances. Off-hand, I wasn't sure about the Miss World restrictions, but I had a feeling she might be right.

'So who's the lucky Palli?' It's one of those names where the affectionate diminutive comes out one syllable longer than the formal name, like John and Johnny.

Her mouth pursed in disapproval. 'He is nothing. He is nobody.'

'Well, he's her husband, Hulda, let's face it.'

She turned towards me, her brows creased as she tried to make me see sense. 'You know Solrun, you know that she has men . . .'

'Endless many men . . .'

'Endless many,' she repeated. 'She would not want this man. It is not a proper marriage. It is not a serious marriage. You must understand that.'

'I did get the impression the vows were a bit elastic.'

'You will not put it in your newspaper? We must not spoil things for her.'

'Don't worry, we won't,' I said. And that reminded me. Sooner or later I had to face up to another conversation with my employer. I had to let him know I was still alive.

'Now then,' he said, going straight into it, 'I'm glad you've rung. We'll want pix of this Sexy Eskie lass. Topless. And is there any chance of getting her next to an igloo?'

'An igloo?' His conception of life outside Britain seemed to be based on the early editions of 'Children of Other Lands'. 'They don't have igloos here.'

'Oh, bloody hell,' he said, in some irritation. 'Not even for show like?'

'No. They never did have igloos.'

'Oh, well, let's have her in the snow then. Topless, making a snowman. That sort of thing.'

Out of the window I could see cool bright sunshine lighting up the coloured houses. 'The only snow here is up the mountains.'

'Thanks for the geography lesson. If our readers wanted educating they wouldn't buy this bloody rubbish would they? So hire a studio, drag the snow down the mountain and let Little Miss Bloody Icicle build an igloo like her granddad used to do. Right? Ciao.'

Compared with that briefing, espionage seemed relatively straightforward – and certainly a lot more honest.

I only had one more job. I stopped off in the town and picked

58

up a postcard of a glacier standing still for the camera. I sat for a while, wondering how best to explain that in Iceland boys take their father's Christian name plus the word 'son' for the surname, and girls do the same with the word 'dottir'. In the end, I simply wrote: 'Do you realise, if you lived here you'd be called Sally Samsdottir? Ask your teacher to explain.'

That was one way of getting my value out of school fees.

Then I called at the Saga and picked up Christopher to do a bit of interpreting. Musical loo gadgets, he'd confided to me on the phone, were proving surprisingly difficult to sell.

18

Alongside the slums of the civilised western world, Breidholt is gracious living.

They don't have the dead dogs and the heaps of wrecked cars and acres of smashed glass that you find in a well-appointed British slum, or the beggars and the pickpockets that you find in southern cities.

You don't find any of these things because in Iceland poverty is practically illegal. There is almost no unemployment, and what little deprivation there is gets mopped up by a social service system that makes Santa Claus look tight-fisted.

So the worst they can show you is Breidholt. It's stuck up on a boulder-strewn hill overlooking the town, high up where the rain and the snow and the wind don't miss a thing, big bare blocks of flats in the glass-and-plastic period of architecture. As I say, in some parts of Naples they'd call it Snob Hill; even so, with shabby washing flapping on the balconies and hardboard up at the broken windows, you could see why the Icelanders weren't too proud of it.

A boy in an outsize tartan jacket stopped chasing a cardboard box, which was being driven by a hard wind, to have a look at us. He tugged the sleeve of his jacket across his trickling nose as Christopher repeated the name and address, then he pointed into a corner of the car park, at an old Ford Escort that had been given a lime-green spray job. By someone, if the paint on the windows and ground was any indication, in the advanced stages of Parkinson's Disease.

As we walked over I heard the international sound of male cursing and spanners clinking. It sounded quite friendly. It didn't look friendly. Behind the Ford, lying alongside an old Triumph motor-bike, was one of the most frightening men I've ever seen. He was on his back, muttering through a cigarette which bobbed on his lip. When he saw me, both the cigarette and the ring spanner in his hand stopped moving.

His head was towards me so that it had that chimpanzee look of all upside-down faces.

When I moved round he looked a lot worse.

He was short in the same way a cement-mixer is short and he looked just as solid. All he was wearing was a soiled red tee-shirt and ragged canvas shorts. His exposed limbs were so bulked up with muscle that they looked foreshortened. Golden hair, sawn off to a ginger bristle on his head, covered his pale hard limbs in a fleece and burst in springy tufts from his exposed belly and over the neck of his shirt. His biceps were blue with tattoos.

Pale blue eyes stared up at us. He didn't move. He didn't speak. He even ignored his cigarette as it flared briefly in the wind.

'I'm looking for Palli Olafsson,' I said, bending down. He gave no reaction.

Christopher said something – presumably the same thing in Icelandic – and although his eyes shifted over to the new speaker, he still didn't reply.

Again Christopher asked, mentioning his name, and then I heard him say the address. The man on the floor grunted and pointed with his spanner at a double-door entrance forty yards away.

As we went he sat up and took a swig from an open bottle of Polar beer. He didn't look like a man with contacts but he must've had some good ones: Polar beer is export only.

'Not the most welcoming of chaps,' Christopher whispered.
'Or places,' I said.

Inside the entrance, the wind, which whirled scraps of litter in a sad dance on the bare concrete, couldn't shift the smell of stale urine and despair. On the metal door of the lift someone had scrawled 'No Nukes'.

The apartment we wanted was on the fourth floor. The door was open. From inside, a gust of wet heat and raw pop music surged out.

That's another old Icelandic trick: when you get your heating cheap – by plugging into all that bubbling just below the earth's crust – all you do is open the door or the window when it gets too hot.

I rapped on the door, rapped again, and then moved slowly down the half-dark corridor. Christopher was a couple of steps behind me. The air was damp and smelt of dead goats. I saw why when the corridor opened out into a large cramped untidy room. The sunset on the carpet had been extinguished by a few hundred spilled dinners and the walls had been used for finger-printing chimney sweeps. Chunks of cheap plastic-covered furniture filled the place. Over the backs and arms of chairs, and from a thin wire stand, hung wet baby clothes. That was what gave the room its own highly individual atmosphere.

In a blue, white-lined cot balanced on a wooden stand, a baby lay with its fat arms above its head like Marciano at the end of a fight.

The mother was asleep too. Not restful angelic sleep but smashed-out exhaustion, sprawled in the sunken seat of a sagging black armchair.

Perhaps a year ago her hair had been in that squared-off blonde shape, only now most of the blonde had gone and it was dull with dirt. The American eagle on the front of her shirt had lost most of its glitter and she wore baggy trousers. She was yesterday's youth suddenly grown old, and on the left side of her face she had the blue-brown bruise that you always find on women like that in flats like that.

'Excuse me,' I said. I had to repeat it twice before she stirred. She opened her eyes and lay there.

A burst of Icelandic behind me reminded me that

Christopher was there. It struck me then that if Batty had sent him to keep an eye on me he was keeping well out of the firing line.

'English?' the girl said, yawning. 'Why come here?' She rooted down the side of the chair and came up with a packet of Camels. She coughed as she lit one.

'Why do you want Palli Olafsson?'

Christopher spoke again, and in bad English she said: 'If it is private you can tell me. I am his girl.'

She rose, smoothing down her clothes and pushing the limp hair back from her bruised face. A soft wail came from the cot. She was there in one movement, changing the cigarette to her left hand so she could stroke the child.

'This is his home?' I asked.

'Oh, yes. His home.' She glanced at a bottle of vodka on top of the television set. 'You like a drink?'

'No, thanks. Is he around?'

Picking her way among the debris of baby clothes and toy ducks and green and red wooden bricks, she went to the window. She made a fuss of opening it, pretending to wipe the sweat off her brow. 'Better,' she said, as the cold wind punched through the rotten warmth of her home.

Again Christopher started talking and she replied to him in rapid Icelandic.

'Sorry, Sam, she's not terribly helpful. Says he's gone out and she doesn't know when he'll be coming back. She wants to know who you are – naturally enough, I'd say.'

As I'd suggested, he told her I was a London journalist who was writing an article about Iceland. That made her laugh.

'Palli can tell you all about Iceland. No problem he can.'

Her sharp laugh halted suddenly. I heard another noise, a cough, a man's cough, coming from the next room. Then it was followed by a deep sleepy groan.

I swopped nervous glances with my friend. Neither of us knew what to do. She resolved it for us then by skipping over to the window and shouting to someone below.

'Damn!' said Christopher. 'That was Palli. With the motorbike. She just told him to run for it.'

We could hear her laughing behind us as we raced for the lift.

When we got down he'd gone. As we went back to the Daihatsu, the little boy in the tartan jacket made his fingers into a gun and shot me. In his other hand he was holding the Polar beer.

19

'What gets me,' I said again, 'is why she'd want to marry someone like that.'

'Oh, I don't know,' Ivan replied, as he shook the dice. 'I think there's quite a lot to be said for a dumb brute. What surprises me is that you haven't tried to claim he's a refugee from the Russian weight-lifting team. Your turn, I think, Christopher.'

Early evening, and the eighth-floor bar of the Saga was still empty. Reykjavik night-life doesn't get into first gear until eleven. By twelve it's a tin-hat job and after that it's every man for himself: or, with a bit of luck, herself.

Right now it was nice and quiet. Sun was streaming through the windows and glancing off the copper top of the horse-shoe bar. Behind it, a young woman in a scarlet waistcoat examined her finger-nails. For a gin and two martinis, she'd just taken the equivalent of a small pools win.

I looked at Ivan and Christopher with the sort of warm glow a mother must feel when she brings home a little playmate for her son and it works. Any minute now they'd be nicking their thumbs with a penknife and becoming blood brothers. I was glad. It wasn't often we had a chance to pick up a new recruit for our rich gallery of English eccentrics, but Christopher Bell was a definite candidate.

He was even winding Ivan up. My old chum had brought out some wretched cricket game that I vaguely remember from schooldays. You each picked a team, and then rolled dice to decide the progress of the game. It went on for hours if you were sufficiently masochistic to let it – rather like the real thing, I suppose. Anyway, Christopher had annoyed him by choosing a side that consisted of luminaries through the ages. At the moment, Meryl Streep was 38 not out, although Honoré de Balzac had been something of a disappointment earlier. He was vulnerable to the rising ball, apparently.

'Another four,' Christopher chortled.

'It reduces the whole thing to a farce,' Ivan protested. 'Meryl Streep can't play cricket.'

'She's batting rather well, I thought.' Christopher fired a sly wink in my direction.

Ivan was also a bit miffed that I'd asked him about the Russian ship in the harbour. 'How do I know what a trawler is doing there? Trawling, I assume.'

He didn't like being appointed champion for his country. At least if he was British, he said with a roll of those expressive brown eyes, he could say Queen and Country. Particularly Queen.

'Wouldn't you ever want to live in Moscow?' Christopher asked. I'd heard his answer before, but I still listened with interest.

He pushed back the wings of grey hair with both hands first of all, so that his face looked even leaner and more aristocratic.

'In Moscow,' he said, with a deliberate shudder, 'I would simply dry up and die. It's an awfully grey place full of awfully grey people. I wouldn't wish to embarrass anyone but Russia simply isn't the place for someone with my somewhat colourful tastes. And of course this is greatly to the convenience of my employers. They know I will do anything – absolutely anything – to stay in the West, and they also know that my own preferences do take me to some rather interesting places. You'd be amazed who one bumps into in some of those rather maley clubs.'

'Gosh, you really are a spy then?' Christopher was wide-eyed at this revelation.

'Oh, I shouldn't think so, dear. What would you say, Sam? No, no, my little pieces of tittle-tattle help to keep the computers busy in Moscow but I don't suppose for a moment they tip the balance in the great conflict between right and wrong – whatever they may be. Isn't that so?'

'I wouldn't know,' I said. I didn't either. You couldn't be sure with Ivan. He always seemed to be telling you too much until you thought about it later and realised he'd told you nothing. I was even less sure since my talk with Batty. Perhaps we were both spies. Perhaps that's all there was to espionage: tittle-tattle and words in ears, games of table-cricket in empty cocktail bars. Perhaps spies were ordinary people with ordinary lives.

'By the way,' he said, fishing out his silver-backed notebook again, 'I have some news for you about your chamois-wearing friend.'

Now that did surprise me. I had to be careful what I told Ivan: even as a friend, I was always aware of the fact that he must have other loyalties. I hadn't told him about the badge with the winged AC and I hadn't told him about the second man in the kitchen. On the other hand, I had mentioned the trawler and the man in the photograph because of the possible Russian connections. Even so, I was surprised when he opened his notebook and began reading.

'His name is Kirillina. Nikolai Kirillina. He's one of the naval people at the embassy, although they don't have proper military attachés because Iceland doesn't have any military.'

Ivan could only be telling me this because someone wanted me to know. Why? 'You traced him through the sputnik?'

He put his fleshless hand to his forehead. 'Ghastly, isn't it? Apparently he has this wonderful flat with a gorgeous display cabinet bursting with silver and porcelain. Bang in the middle of it he puts one of those horrid little plastic sputniks. Not unlike the sort of artifact you might sell, Christopher.'

Christopher grinned up. Then his grin vanished. 'Oh damn, Meryl's out.'

'Thank God. Well bowled.' Ivan kissed the dice. 'Who's in next?'

'Al Jolson.' He slipped me another wink. 'I've heard he's rather useful with the bat. A lot of these coloured chaps are, you know.'

'You see,' Ivan continued. 'What can you do with these people? They have every opportunity, education, money, everything, and they go and put on display a vulgar memento like that.' He reached over and touched my arm. 'I do hope this isn't hurtful in any way, but I am told he was something of a hand with the ladies.'

'Be a waste if he wasn't. He hasn't disappeared then?'

'Apparently not. Drinkiepoohs, anyone?'

As the waitress got the glasses clinking, I walked over to the window and looked out. Poor Solrun. Even by her reckless standards, this was quite a mess. For reasons well beyond my imagination, she'd got married to an Icelandic Hell's Angel who already appeared to be the proud possessor of woman and child. And she was also playing around with a Russian diplomat. It was beginning to sound crazier than the casting for Christopher's cricket team. Who'd she run off with now – King Kong?

The girl came round with the booze and Ivan told her to put it on his bill. I was wondering why Batty thought I could do anything about all this – let alone why I'd want to – when I heard Ivan ask Christopher if he was married.

'Oh, yes, Bella and I have got a lovely little place out at Braintree. I've asked her to think about moving up to Iceland but she isn't terribly keen. At the moment, that is.'

'Would you take out Icelandic citizenship?' I'd been wondering about that.

'Hope to, naturally. Course it's not easy. You have to speak the lingo, of course, and take a local name.'

'After your father?'

'That's right. And since my old man was called Christopher too. I'd have one of these names with a built-in echo. A bit much, I think. How about you, Sam? What was your father's name?'

'Oddly enough, I don't know.'

I'm so used to it that I forget it sometimes makes other people uncomfortable. After a second's silence, Christopher decided not to pursue that one, and started talking about his plans for a sales drive in the morning. I was sorry to hear that. I'd been hoping he might come as interpreter when I went to see Solrun's mother.

'I'll come,' Ivan volunteered. 'It will be just like being a real reporter. I shall wear a Burberry and look terribly louche.'

20

When I come to think about it, I've never actually known a woman who rushed off home to mummy in moments of emotional crisis. My wife used to rush out and spend. To her, the cheque-book was a weapon of retaliation: it gave her a strike-back capability that was awesome.

All the other women I'd known used to go to the hairdressers. Some of them – I'll swear it – used to seek out emotional crises if they'd got word of a classy new crimper.

But I liked the home-to-mummy theory, and I was encouraged by the glint of doubt in Hulda's eyes when I suggested it. Shaking her head like a terrier with a mouse, she said Solrun would never go to her mother's. Since Hulda seemed to be the chairman of the Solrun Defence League, that was good enough for me. I went.

Asta Arnadottir lived in a small flat-fronted terraced house, painted black, in what they call the Stone Village – Grjotathorp – in the old centre of the city. We had to park at the top and walk down. I climbed the three stone steps and gave the heavy brass knocker a bang.

'Hardly Knightsbridge, is it?' Ivan said, in his snobbiest voice.

Actually, it's got a lot of character. Two dozen or so houses, mostly old-style with steep-pitched roofs, dotted around a slope where you could still see some of the boulders that gave the place its name.

Across the road, a skinny woman in a floral pinafore came out and pretended to sweep the pavement so she could have a look at us. There's one of those in every street: self-appointed sentries.

I knocked again. 'It's no use,' Ivan said. 'Empty houses have a definite aura about them. This, I have to tell you, is an empty house.'

67

'So it is,' I said in mock gratitude. As he spoke, there'd been a noise from inside the house.

I called out 'Hello,' and this time used my knuckles on the dark paintwork. In the silence that followed, I put my ear up against it to listen. You couldn't say quite what sort of noise it was – a series of stifled sounds, somewhere between a whimper and a wail.

'Oh, let's go,' Ivan said, moving a step or two up the street. He'd wanted to come in the afternoon. He kept insisting it was too early, meaning, no doubt, too early for him.

'No, there's someone there.' If there was, they weren't opening any doors. I spent fifteen minutes knocking and calling, while the street-sweeper watched in silence, before I gave up and walked back to the jeep.

'You don't think that could've been a child, do you?' I asked.

Ivan was adamant. 'Definitely not. It was a puppy. She won't open the door because she has a dog in there and you know what they're like about that round here. They mow them down in the streets.'

'I'm surprised at you,' I said, as I picked my leisurely way through the morning traffic. 'You mustn't believe what you read in the papers, Ivan. They don't do anything of the sort.'

We were passing the Tjornin and the lake was as calm as a mirror.

I stepped on the brake. Marching alongside the water, in corduroy shorts, baseball cap and boots, was Bottger, the Esperanto-speaker who'd been on the flight out. With his long legs and bony knees, he looked like one of the rarer wading birds.

'Have you found your friends over here?' I asked him.

'No. It is most annoying. They have also gone on holiday.'

'Didn't you write to them to say you were coming?'

'Yes, but I fear there must have been a misunderstanding.'

I couldn't resist it. 'I thought that was what you Esperanto chaps were going to wipe out.'

He gave me a look loaded with reproach. 'And how is your friend with the musical lavatory?'

'He hasn't made his first million yet.'

He pointed a long hard arm out towards the mountains. 'I go

there.' He banged his chest with his fist. 'Fresh air.'

As he loped off, knees high, Ivan patted the lapels of his blazer. 'I go Saga bar. Fresh g and t.'

With a couple of hours to kill, I nipped back down to the harbour to have a look at the Comrades Afloat.

The *Pushkin* was still there, though whether that was a good thing or not, I wasn't sure. And I could see what Petursson meant. The aft-deck was strewn with nets: the Russians don't usually go in for that much window-dressing. Fish too, Petursson had said. That was altogether too much innocence.

I stood for a while watching the harbour move to the rhythms of the sea. A high-prowed steel fishing-boat grunted in its chains. The little play-boats chattered like children. An old wooden warrior's engine drummed as it pushed out to sea, to where the light sky met the dark water.

I turned then and was looking down as I stepped through the sea's cast-offs – the scattering of torn tyres and wooden crates and plastic bottles – when I heard another engine drumming. I looked up. It was Palli Olafsson. He had stopped not six feet away from me.

He was still wearing the tee-shirt and shorts, thin rags on the hard pale slabs and ridges of muscle that looked as though they'd been bolted on to his body. The tattoos showed clearly through the thickets of ginger hair on his arms. You couldn't see his eyelashes and eyebrows, so his light blue eyes seemed to be staring out of a strangely naked face.

'Palli?' I said, wondering how the hell I was going to talk to him without Christopher.

He gave one short, pugnacious nod.

Slowly and deliberately, I mouthed: 'Do you understand English?'

He folded his heavy arms across his chest. 'Bet your ass I do,' he said. And a hard grin bent his lips as he viewed my astonishment.

I took him to a chintzy upstairs café near the lake. Among the blue-and-white gingham tablecloths and spindle-backed chairs, he looked about as likely as a water-buffalo in a dinner-jacket.

He can't have been precisely the sort of customer they were hoping would pop in to encourage mid-morning trade, but they didn't say anything. They didn't even say anything when he spun his chair round and the back creaked under the weight of his arms and shoulders. And they didn't say anything when he flicked the ash off his cigarette on to the floor.

I don't suppose he'd ever had a lot of complaints about his behaviour. Menace hung about him like a low cloud.

I didn't know where to start when I looked at that unnervingly hairless face. 'So . . . you're an American?'

'No. Next question.'

I'd no idea what to make of that. 'You're not an American?'

'That's what I just told you,' he said, in an accent that was pure popcorn and Budweiser. 'Anyway, I don't wanna talk about that.'

'What do you want to talk about?'

'You were looking for me, remember?'

I did, but that seemed a long time ago now. Abandoning all thoughts of subtle interrogation, I swallowed hard and went straight for it.

'You married Solrun, I believe?'

'Who wants to know?'

'Me.' I took his silence as the next question. 'I'm a newspaperman from London. I'm writing some stuff about her.'

He turned his eyes away in disgust. 'Why'd you think I'll buy that shit?'

'You want credentials . . .' I reached inside my jacket, but he was already shaking his head.

'You wouldn't pull that one unless you'd got the paperwork.'

'So how do I convince you? I was a friend of hers. You can ask people. I knew her a couple of years ago when I was on a press visit.'

To my relief he was nodding his head this time. 'I got you. The Brit. The shmuck in the photographs.'

This was no time to be proud. 'That's right,' I said, beaming with bonhomie.

A silence welled up between us as he studied me. If I'd had all day to think about it, I still couldn't have guessed his next question.

'You lay her?' he suddenly snapped out. The silence spread to the other tables. A tall man in a suit who was halfway through the door, glanced around, and went out again.

'Yes,' I said, after a lifetime's pause.

This time he leaned further forward and pushed his crude colourless face towards me. 'You fucked my wife?' he said, in a soft whisper.

'Yes.' My voice bent a bit in the middle but I managed to say it.

He sat back, threw his head back and blew smoke at the ceiling. 'If you'd said you hadn't, I'd have torn your ears off, man,' he said, his eyes, bright with amusement, returning to mine. 'I must be the only goddam guy on this island who hasn't.'

I concentrated on stirring my coffee. There was no sugar in it to stir, but it did seem a fairly neutral activity.

'You wanna write that down for your readers? C'mon, that's a great story – ain't that what you call it, a story?' I had a sudden thought then of Grimm and his ideas about the Sexy Eskies and I wondered what he'd make of reality when it came in this form.

Very gently, I inquired: 'And why was that?'

'Why didn't I get to screw her?' He took delight in spelling it out. Euphemisms weren't needed round here for the moment. 'Maybe she only liked you classy Brits and the way you say "bloke" and "bloody" all the time. Or maybe she was a real patriot and only kicked up her heels for these big dumb fish-stinkin' Icelanders.'

He'd lifted his voice for the last few words and he turned and looked around to see if anyone else wanted to contribute to the debate. They didn't.

He was a puzzle. There was a pride in his bitterness, a violent and defiant pride, and I couldn't see where it came from.

'Course,' he went on, pleased with the discomfort he was causing, 'maybe she didn't like Uncle Sam too much. Some of the folks round here don't. Ain't that right?'

Two stone-faced housewives rose and left. A workman in a donkey jacket followed.

'See what I mean? No, they don't all love the Americanos on this little island. Now I wonder why that can be? I really do wonder about that.'

'But you're not American, are you?'

The smile sank and I was left looking at the hollow emptiness of his eyes. Casually he reached out and took my right hand in his left. He held it softly, without force. Then, with the finger and thumb of his right hand, he took hold of the thin web of flesh between my own finger and thumb. He began to squeeze.

'I know a hundred ways to give you pain.' He watched me with real interest.

At first I felt nothing. I watched his thumb, thick as a truncheon, go into rings of white and red as he increased the pressure. He ground the sliver of tissue until my whole hand felt on fire.

'Well, well, we got a toughie,' he said.

He moved his shoulders forward to get more pressure and he squinted up at me from beneath his bare brows. He was watching me with the detached curiosity of a professional. Inside, everything I had was screwed up into a tight ball in the middle of my chest to stop my face breaking open with the pain, and to stop the shouts from flooding out.

Behind me, I heard one of the waitresses say something which caused a wary look to move across his face. Gently, he released my hand and set it down as though it was a meal he didn't want any more. The pain surged in, white and red lances of it, as the blood moved back.

'I know about pain, friend,' he said, in a quiet, careful voice. 'I was well trained.'

I was nursing my hand, but nothing could stop the feeling that it would detonate with pain.

'You said you weren't American,' I said.

'Did I say that?'

I got up, chucked down some money for the coffee and shook my head at the waitress who was poised to dial for the police.

'Where the hell do you think you're going?'

'A long way from you. I thought you wanted to talk to me, to help me. If you don't, that's fine with me. But what I'm not going to do is to play stupid bloody guessing games with you while you show the world what a big tough boy you are. Now, if you want to go ahead and stamp on my toes and pull my ears off until the cops come and beat some sense into any brain you've got left under that bristle, you'd better do it now – because I'm going.'

I walked out and left him there. I don't know how. Running would've been much easier.

I'd got about two hundred yards up the road by the Tjornin when I heard the big-drum thunder of his bike. The only person near enough for a Mayday call was a small boy in horn-rimmed specs who was shelling the ducks with crusts. He looked nasty enough to handle Palli but not quite big enough. Anyway, without his crusts he was probably nothing.

Palli came up alongside my left shoulder and throttled the engine back to a funereal popping sound.

'Hey,' he shouted over his shoulder. 'You wanna know about the wedding?'

I walked on. He wobbled, swung the front wheel for a balance he failed to find, and then tore down the street with a mighty grunt of the engine, braked hard, spun round, and came back. He turned again behind me and came up once more on my shoulder.

'Guess I was out of line back there,' he said, shouting over the engine.

I stopped. He put his foot down.

'You were.'

He put his head on one side and ran his nails through his stubble of hair. 'Guy comes along, says he's a fucking writer or something, starts asking all sorts of questions . . .'

'Forget it,' I said, and I'd begun to move off when he called me back – politely.

'Let's talk. Don't be so goddam nervy.'

'Where?'

'Not now. Tonight. Seven. You good for a coupla drinks – Icelandic prices?'

We arranged to meet that evening at one of the few hotel bars – all the bars are hotel bars. As he roared off, I nursed my throbbing hand and hoped it was going to be worth it.

21

When I walked into Ivan's room, he was holding the bedside phone out towards me.

'Excellent timing. Your guru, I believe.'

It was Grimm. Hulda had put him on to the hotel. ''Ere, was that that bloody Russian who's always hanging round the industrial boys?'

'Mr Ivanov, that's right.'

'You want to watch him, he's a spy.'

'So he says.'

That one flew straight past him.

'I've just been looking at today's paper and you know what's wrong with it?'

'No.'

'Adjectives.'

'Adjectives?'

'Sodding bloody adjectives, stupid useless bloody adjectives. I've told 'em all here. Anyone else uses adjectives and they're up for the chop. So remember it when you write your stuff. No bloody adjectives.'

'I will.'

'Oh, aye, and that pic of the bird and the igloo. You can always bung her five hundred if it'll help.'

'Five hundred pounds?'

'Well, I don't mean five hundred snowballs, do I? Ciao.'

Ivan was silent and withdrawn on the way up to the Stone Village. We'd arranged to have another go at Solrun's mother. Even my account of Grimm's phone-call didn't raise more than a thin smile.

'Tell me,' I asked, because I'd had time to think about it, 'why did you tell me about Solrun's Russian boyfriend?'

He kept looking straight ahead, his face drawn. 'Because you asked,' he said, with a funny little shrug.

We could hear the noise from Asta's house as we walked down the street.

'Yes, folks, those super singers from Oklahoma City will be at the Top Four Club tonight at twenny-hundred hours . . . the menu for the enlisted men's dining facility is corn chowder soup, shish kebab or southern fried chicken . . . make a note, our calligraphy class is due to start again soon at the Hobby Shop and anyone who's interested . . .'

It was the radio from the NATO base out at Keflavik and it poured out from the now half-open door of her house. The woman with the broom came to the door of her house and called out to us, but Ivan and I just exchanged glances. I knocked on the door. By the third time, with no answer still, I pushed the door gently open and stepped inside.

It was the home of a house-proud woman. You could see it in the gleaming paintwork, the shining windows, polished tan furniture, the kitchen in which every appliance nestled cosily on its hook and every substance had a labelled tin. Judging by the condition of the carpets, the occupants had mastered the mystery of flight. If a germ had got through the door, it would've died of loneliness. Everything was in its place. There was no sign that the perfect order of this dusted haven had been disturbed.

But there was no sign of Solrun's mother either. And fear hung in the air as unmistakeable as the smell of stale gunsmoke.

I'd switched off the parroting American voice, and we stood looking at each other in the perfect silence of her home. Then a soft gust of wind blew over the carpet and I saw something move.

At first sight you'd have taken it for thistledown. It was only when I bent down and held it between my hands that I could see it was a ball of hair. Silver hair, curled up, so that it rolled like a puffball on the lightest breath of wind.

Kneeling by the living-room door, I looked out into the hall and saw two more, then another one, another three or four drifting over the green carpet. I chased them and picked them up.

The specks of blood on the end were still wet.

I must've ripped open every door in the house before I saw the cupboard in the hall. It was set into the wall and painted white so you'd hardly notice it.

When I opened the door, she didn't fall out like they do in films. It took me a few seconds to see why. They'd used a snapped-off broom handle, three-foot of it, wedged wall-to-wall across her chest to hold her jammed against the back of the shallow cupboard.

They must have got her out of bed because she was wearing a pretty cream-and-white nightie with white lace trim and a matching housecoat over the top. It wasn't the sort of thing a middle-aged woman would buy herself: perhaps Solrun had got it as a present, and her mother would have said it was too young – and been delighted.

The blood had soaked through both garments on her shoulders and all down the front where her head hung forward. There were splashes all over her bare feet and on the floor where it had gone on dripping. I'd never seen anything like her head. Jesus. Nothing, ever, not like that. At first glance it didn't even look like a head. It looked more like an Easter egg that some kid had inexpertly daubed with paint and decorated with fur and fluff. It was only when you saw the face beneath that you realised it was a head, and the decorations were blood and the few sad sprouts that were all that was left of her hair. Those, and some gummy strands glued to her head by the congealing blood.

I had to say the words to myself to make myself believe them. 'Dear God,' I said, 'she's been scalped.'

I kept saying that to myself, over and over again, when I heard a faint bubbling sound. With my left hand under her chin, I lifted that dreadful head, and I felt like Salome with John the Baptist. I heard the scrape of air in her throat. Incredibly, she was alive.

'Get the doctor. The police, anyone – she's alive!'

Then I heard Ivan in the kitchen and I knew he was being sick. I made the call myself and when I'd finished Ivan was leaning in the kitchen doorway. He looked as though he was dying himself.

'Your shoe.' He put his hand up to his mouth again.

When I looked down, a tendril of silver hair had attached itself to my shoe. I bent down and brushed it off. It was the blood at the roots that made it stick.

'I've never seen anything so terrible.' For the first time he sounded like a foreigner. He patted his mouth with a hankie and muttered to himself in Russian.

I soaked a towel in the kitchen and tried to clean up her nose and mouth to help her breathe. I didn't try to unfasten her. I was scared of what would happen if I did. She was still hanging there when the police arrived, and in the disturbance I saw those balls of white hair rolling like tumbleweed across the shining blue tiles of the kitchen. I hadn't the heart to go over and pick them up.

'She was young to have white hair,' Ivan said. It was one of those fatuous things you do say when you're in shock.

22

As afternoons go, that one didn't. It lasted about a month.

Back at the hotel, Ivan lay on his bed with his arms folded across his chest like a crusader on his tomb. I hardly liked to speak to him in case his brimming brown eyes overflowed and embarrassed both of us. He was an old softie.

I tried to raise Christopher but he was still out on his rounds, and even a couple of hefty drinks did nothing to shift the lead weight in my gut. At first it had all seemed a bit of a lark. not any more, it didn't.

When Magnus marched in with three uniformed officers, we were both glad to see him. Separately we gave our statements, and that helped to eat up more of the dragging time. I had a stroll outside the hotel – conscious all the time of the uniformed cop eyeing me from his car – and watched the flags of all nations stand out as stiff as boards in the streaming wind.

When Petursson arrived, I waited in a downstairs side-room in the hotel while he read the statements and then interviewed Ivan.

'Well, Mr Craven,' he said, as he came through to me, 'a pretty pan of fish we have here, have we not?'

'Kettle – not that it matters.'

'Of course, kettle. I am out of practice. A pretty kettle of fish, to be sure.'

Together we went over my statement in detail. I was watching him with interest. If the scalping – that was how I'd started to think of it – had affected him, it was only to make him more steady and painstaking than before.

When we'd finished that, I left him sitting at a green card table with copies of the statements in front of him, and wandered over to the window.

That was when his assistant Magnus jumped me.

'Now!' Petursson suddenly snapped. To my amazement, Magnus spun me by the shoulder and – with a merry smile on his face – swung a useful left hook at my jaw. As I went reeling back, he did his level best to stick his right arm up to the elbow in my stomach.

Luckily for me, he'd telegraphed them fairly well; at least I was able to lean back so that the first punch only glanced my jaw, but the second one went in deep, and hurt.

'I hope you are all right,' the senior man said, as he reached down with one hand to help me up from the carpet.

'Is this what they mean by helping the police with their inquiries?' I gasped.

'You see,' he said, talking straight past me. 'You were wrong. He is untrained.'

'Untrained?' I looked from one to the other but they weren't very interested.

'Yes, Sir,' said the blond. 'No self-defence, and I gave him every chance.'

'Look pal, next time you give me notice and we'll soon see...'

Well, I was annoyed. I've been in my share of saloon-bar bust-ups and I've still got all my own teeth. They're not all in my mouth, but at least I've got them.

Patting me on the shoulder as you might a fretful child, Petursson led me to a chair and sat me down. 'Do not take it personally. After our last conversation, Magnus was of the opinion that you were a ... professional gentleman in these matters. I was not so sure. So we devised this little test for you.'

'Great. Have I passed?'

I held my head between my hands. By now the pain from my jaw had linked up neatly with the pain from the top of my head.

'What do you think?' Petursson looked at Magnus, who shrugged and moved over to the door. Then he turned to me again: 'You are a puzzle for us, you see.'

'Well, I'm sorry about that.'

He turned his impassive face towards me. His eyes – like a lot of Icelanders' – were so deep they must've been riveted into place.

'You went to see Solrun – what happened to her? You went to see her mother – what happened to her?'

He had a point there. Even I could see that. He didn't much care for the rest of my activities either, and he didn't seem to have missed much. He didn't like the way I'd bandied his name about the Hagstofa.

'And you have been keeping bad company,' he went on. 'Palli.'

'I thought he was a fine example of your country's youth.'

That brought some warmth into his voice. 'He's no Icelander. He is the dregs of the American military and even they don't want him any more.' Sitting back, he lit another of his small cigars. This time he held it between his middle fingers to cut down nicotine stain. 'Magnus knows all about Palli.'

Magnus stayed on guard at the door and spoke in an official-report voice. 'Palli Olafsson? His parents were both Icelanders. They divorced when he was three years of age and his mother married an American from the base. They moved to Chicago, her new husband's home, in the northern part of the United States. He grew up as an American ...'

His boss cut in: 'See, his environment and his upbringing were all American. Carry on.'

'He served with the American marines. Later he was many times in police troubles and had to receive psychiatric treatment.'

He stopped. Petursson said: 'He's a bum.' He looked round the room for an ashtray and then crossed and tapped his cigar ash into a potted plant on the window-sill.

'How did he end up here?'

'What was that television programme they had in America? Roots. It was that sort of thing. He wanted to come here to try to be an Icelander. Crazy idea. He is a crazy man. Sometimes he can be very dangerous. His head is full of wild things. He should be in the kleppur.'

An alarming thought suddenly came to me. 'You don't think he had anything to do with Solrun's mother?'

He sat there, shaking his head. 'No, not Palli. We blame him for many things but not this.'

'So, who do you blame?'

Magnus coughed and spread his feet. Petursson began to straighten up the papers in front of him. The cigar smoke was a blue mist in the beams of sunlight from the window.

'Did you see a lady who was sweeping her pavement when you called? She tells us that she saw a man in a corduroy suit with a swarthy complexion call at the house. She says he was with a tall skinny man who walked like a woman.'

Neither Ivan nor I could quarrel with those descriptions. 'Go on.'

'Very well. Before you two went in, she saw three men go to the house. She believes two of them were wearing dark uniforms. They were inside the house when you called the first time, but left, apparently in a hurry, before you returned.'

'They were inside with . . . with Solrun's mother?'

'Yes. Torturing her.'

I remembered the whimpering noise we'd heard that Ivan insisted was a puppy. That must've been her. I swallowed hard on the thought.

'Were they looking for Solrun too?'

He nodded. 'That is my belief.' He beat me to the next question. 'She had been there. She arrived and left at night but the woman across the road saw her. You know what those women are like.'

'What exactly did they do to her, Petursson?'

In a matter-of-fact voice, he recited it, as he packed his papers into a soft leather briefcase. They had been professionals. The torture was graded so that she would be systematically weakened. Each time they gripped one lock of hair – he demonstrated how they wrapped it round a finger – and ripped it out. She must have been very brave. They had torn out almost all her hair, but she had told them nothing. The ordeal brought on a heart attack, and then I had disturbed them.

There wasn't much I could say to that. I followed the two of them out to the door and just as they were going I remembered about the man in the photograph. It made a handy banana skin to slip under his foot as he was going.

'Perhaps,' I said, 'that nice Mr Kirillina will be able to help you find Solrun.'

He stopped, and slowly his big shoulders turned so that he faced me again. He was clearly surprised that I'd picked up his name.

'Why do you think that?' he asked.

'Well, he was a leading member of her fan-club.'

He weighed that for a moment, and then, with considerable caution, he added: 'I think Mr Kirillina would be very pleased to find her himself.'

That didn't seem to advance the sum of human knowledge very far, or not the section of it that I was supervising. I had one last try as he waited for the lift.

'If it's not top secret, I'd like to hear the detailed description of her attackers from Solrun's mother. Will she be able to talk by tomorrow, do you think?'

The doors opened and he and Magnus stepped inside. 'Didn't I say? There won't be any descriptions, I'm afraid. She died at sixteen-twenty.'

He balanced his wide hat on top of his creamed head, and the doors met.

23

I found Palli on a stool in the hotel bar he'd named. He hadn't got any smaller, any lovelier, or any sunnier in his disposition.

'I was drinking a brenni-and-coke but for you I'll have a vodka – that big.' He opened his fingers to the barman to indicate about half a pint of vodka. Then he gave a silent jeering laugh.

As the glass landed on the bar, I grabbed it and held it at arm's length.

'Now, before we start, there's one thing we get straight. No pain. No hand-squeezing, no tooth-pulling, no eye-poking and no neck-breaking. Got me? You're going to sit up there like a nice big boy and smile and say thank you to the kind gentleman.'

He came slowly up off the stool. No one had spoken to him like that since he was seven, and they'd probably regretted it then.

'I'll say what the fuck . . .'

'Or,' I said, silencing him with one raised finger, 'you don't get to know about today's murder.'

'What murder?' He sank back. I was quite relieved. Although Petursson had said it was nothing to do with him, he would've been my number-one suspect for any crime north of Glasgow.

'Solrun's mother,' I said, handing him his drink.

'Shit. The old lady. Why'd anyone want to do that?'

I told him what little I knew about it, and news of a juicy killing seemed to calm him down. He'd certainly found a drinking place to match his personality. It was a bleak dark barn, and the only other customers were two men: one singing softly to the fruit-machine as he tried to waltz with it, and a man on the next stool who was trying to guess his own name.

Brain-damage boozing used to be quite a problem in

Iceland. He'd managed to find the one place where traditional values still prevailed.

'Your turn,' I said, without any ceremony.

'How's that?' he said, squinting up at me over his second drink.

'You said you'd tell me about you and Solrun. The marriage – remember?'

To my surprise, in a quiet and reasonable tone he began to tell me.

'Have you heard of Frimerkjapeninga? Sure you haven't. Why the hell would you? It's just another of them crazy words that's three blocks long – they got plenty of those here, believe me. Frimer-crap, whatever the word is, is what they call the stamp money the government here pays all the school-kids for their vacation work. Like picking up leaves in the parks and picking the weeds out, all crummy jobs like that. They stick the money away in the bank for them and when they're twenty-two or so they can pick it up. Worth having too. It can be a couple of thousand bucks.'

'As much as that?'

'That's right.' He drained his drink. 'You okay for another of these? Thanks. It's a long time between drinks when I'm paying. So that's what they call their stamp money. There's only two ways of getting your hands on it. Either you wait till pay-out day, or you get married.'

He pointed his thick blunt finger at me. 'You got it. They call them stamp weddings – I think that's frimekjagifting, or something like that. Some of the kids get married just so's they can pick up the cash. Then they get divorced. Who cares – they got the money.'

'She only married you for the money?'

'You got it.'

I remembered what Hulda had said. 'And it wasn't a real marriage. There wasn't anything between you?'

'You mean true love?' He gave his sour laugh again, took a slot out of his new drink and wiped his mouth with the back of his hand. When the jeering, ugly look drained from his face, something a good deal more pleasant moved in. On anyone else you might've taken it for general human decency. 'Truth is, he added, 'I was standing in for my best buddy.'

'How'd you mean?'

'Well,' he clamped a hand over his flat stomach as a belch erupted from his mouth, 'I said I'd tell you so I will. She was my best buddy's girl. He wanted me to marry her so's she could get the money and that's what I did.'

'And you're not going to tell me who your best buddy is?'

'No sir, I am not. He asked me to look after his desert-bike and I did, and he asked me to look after his baby and I did. No problem.'

'That's the Triumph Trophy, is it?'

The glass stopped halfway to his mouth and his face burst into one big grin.

'The six-fifty?' I went on.

'Hell, how about that, we gotta guy who knows about desert-bikes.'

The truth is that I don't know much about them at all. I'd recognised it: but then, with those old-fashioned sit-up handlebars and high ground clearance, it wasn't all that clever. I knew that they were the great classic bikes of the sixties. You had to be able to handle them too – not like these modern rockets that the kids strap themselves inside before they close their eyes and pray. What might've been a little bit clever was that I'd noticed the chain, clean enough to wear as a slightly oily necklace – the sign of a man who loved bikes.

What had happened was that somewhere along the way, among the thousands of people I'd chatted to and thousands I'd interviewed, or among the thousands of bits and pieces I'd written and thousands I'd read, someone had told me about desert-bikes, and a bit of it had stuck. But for the next thirty minutes he told me how much he knew about them – which actually was a lot – and he still thought I was an expert.

And as he talked, I saw the way he changed. He'd begun by wanting to demonstrate his fury and his cruelty. But when he talked about something he loved, you could almost see the bunched muscles soften and pleasure drive the tension out of his gripped face.

'Pinky's?' My eyes were on the girls – romantic rather than pornographic – who writhed in smudged blue and red beneath the hair of his arms. It was a fair guess. A lot of Americans in their thirties had picked up tattoos at Pinky's on R and R in Hong Kong.

By way of reply, he pushed up the short sleeve of his tee-shirt where it stretched over his football of a bicep. There were the two tattooed words I knew would be there.

'Some of the boat people ended up here, I believe,' I said.

Slowly, he nodded his cropped and colourless head.

Casually, I went on: 'I saw the little kid selling newspapers in the town.'

'I seen him too. First time I was so scared I started shaking. I was thinking about the kids who used to come up to us carrying grenades.'

He slapped the bar with his hand. The crack was so loud that the man who was now proposing to the fruit-machine turned and glared at us, then carried on.

'Now I see him and I know he's just a kid, like any other kid, nothing special. You know something? This place is too damned dull. You know what the guys out at the base call this island? Icehole. I know what they mean. Sometimes when it's been raining for about a year and the wind takes the goddam coat off your back every time you step out, it can be rough. But you go to the right place, it's Fun City, coupla laughs, coupla drinks, coupla girls – each. Fun City, man.'

By two in the morning we'd had those coupla drinks a coupla dozen times, and he'd had all four girls – his and mine – crawling all over him. Now he was down to one.

We were watching a strange tribe engaged in a frenetic fertility ritual which involved self-dislocation of all the major joints while being tortured by the most advanced sound-and-light techniques. It was a disco, half-a-dozen floors of it from what I could see. To me it looked like a high-rise hell, but then these days I find whist over-stimulating. Palli – even though he was my age – and the rest of the young savages thought it was wonderful.

'Kids fly in from London to this place,' he told me.

'Can't they shoot their planes out of the sky before they land?'

We'd reached an agreement over the booze. Palli had

stopped being so punitive about it and reverted to his brenni-and-Coke. He was the only non-native I knew who actually liked the stuff. It's known locally as Black Death, some say because of the colour of the bottle and some say because they have to carry you home in a hand-cart afterwards. I'd settled for martinis, which they served in the same measures as beer and at the same price as gold.

'Shall I tell you about my daddy?' There was a lot of self-mockery in his question, but something else too.

'Tell me about your daddy.'

We were spread all over the table, facing each other. The last of the girls was sitting on the floor, looped disconsolately around his thigh.

'My daddy was an Icelander.' I tried to make the right sort of surprised reactions. 'So was my old lady. They bust up. She married a guy from the base, and I ended up back in Chicago.'

He stopped. To spur him on, I said: 'You enlisted?'

'Yeah. Afterwards I had problems. Shrinks, all that garbage. Shit, man, I didn't know who the hell I was.' He shuffled the girl around so he could lean over the table to get nearer to me. She didn't mind. She didn't even notice.

With one scarlet talon she was tracing the blue, blurred letters at the top of his arm. She did the V, then the I, but gave up halfway through the E, and yawned instead. Someone ought to do a study of the incidence of boredom in beautiful girls: it's phenomenal.

'I didn't get this off the shrinks, I swear it, and maybe I don't explain too good, but I'll try. Look. You gotta know what you are. You think, here I am, I'm a goddam peasant from Chile and my pa's a fisherman, and that's what I am. I started thinking like that, and naturally I started seeing what I really was. I'm an Icelander. My daddy's an Icelander. So let's get the hell to Iceland.'

'Did you find your father?'

He had turned his face towards the band. They were doing their best to wake up Greenland. Even so I still heard him give that sour, edgy laugh again.

'I found him, okay. That was something. That was really something.' He went quiet for a moment while he thought about that and I thought then that he wasn't going to tell me. He raised his glass to me. In a much better English accent than he could've managed sober, he said: 'Sam, you're a bloody good bloke.' He slapped the girl on the rump and said: 'He's a bloody good bloke, this Brit. He's one of the good guys.'

He put his drink down and rearranged the girl and then started again. 'Yeah, I found him. We stood staring at each other. Just staring. He was crying, for Christ's sake. Tears pumping down his cheeks. So was I.'

'I can understand that.'

He shook his head. 'No, you can't. You see, we couldn't speak to each other. He didn't speak any English. I didn't speak any Icelandic. So what else could we do? We stood and cried like two fucking big babies. That's something.'

'Do you like living here?'

'Do I like it? Look at these girls, for chrissakes! They don't look like this in Chicago, I'm telling you. Have you seen the country? All those mountains and rivers. It's a helluva country.'

I knew why he hadn't answered my question. I also knew he would, in his own time. It only took another half-minute's silence.

'I hate it, man.' He patted the girl again as she whispered into his ear: 'Sure, sugar, sure.' Then he carried on. 'Sure, it is a great big wonderful place, I know that. But do you know what lonely is? I look at those mountains and I feel so lonely I could cry. Spend most of my time round at the Marine House – the guys on embassy security duty give me a game of pool and a few Buds. Hell, at least I can tell what they're talking about.'

For all his toughness, he was just a little boy who'd turned one corner too many and lost sight of home. Now he was just very lucky that he happened to tell me. At two in the morning, with enough of the right stuff down my throat, there are few problems I can't solve. And this was one I knew something about.

'Go home,' I said.

'This is my home.' He stabbed a finger against his bicep. 'I got Icelandic blood in these veins. Pure one hundred per cent Icelandic blood.'

I shut him up with a wave of my hands. 'Blood doesn't have a nationality. It's just the red stuff that fills up your tubes. You're an American. You look like one, you talk like one, you think like one, you are one. Go back and be one.'

'Yeah, but my daddy . . .'

'He's got nothing to do with it. Look, I'll tell you my theory. Shall I?'

He hitched the girl up a bit higher and gave me a big grin. 'He's going to tell us a theory. My bloody good bloke. Let's hear it, Sam.'

He was so drunk that if I'd told him the story of Goldilocks he would've hailed it as the solution to the human predicament. The story of Goldilocks probably makes more sense than my theory, but I told it anyway.

'You are alone. I mean, so am I and so's everyone else too, but for the purposes of this drunken explanation, you are alone. Right?'

'Right.' He tipped his drink up and somehow managed to keep his eyes on me at the same time.

'People are frightened of being alone, and they use anything to try to disguise the fact. They use sex, they use love, they use marriage, they use friendship, they use all these things to try to kid themselves that they are not by themselves. Most of all they use family. They give them special names like uncle and sister and grandma to try to bind them closer. Sometimes it works. Sometimes – say at a family party at Christmas – you really feel as though you belong to a sort of club. Or if you're with one of these girls, or the two of us having a drink.'

He raised his glass. 'You're a bloody good bloke,' he said again. 'And you're right, I just know you're right.'

'These,' I said, jabbing him in the chest, and that's not a tactic I'd risk sober, 'are fairy-stories we tell ourselves so we won't be afraid of the dark. But they don't mean a thing. In the end, there's just you, Palli Olafsson, that's all.'

The girl on the floor yawned. 'Too much talking.' Then she curled round his leg again.

Palli was leaning forward again, frowning in concentration. 'It's like a new deal when you're born?'

'That's it.'

'It doesn't matter who your father is?'

'No. Not a bit.'

He clapped his hands on his legs to applaud himself as he triumphantly yelled at me: 'Okay, so if your father – your own father – was, say, Adolf Hitler, would you still say all that?'

'As a matter of fact, my father was an American.'

At first he took it for a joke whose meaning had got misted over by the booze.

'Well, don't you go near any of those Klansmen down in Alabama, not with your hair, buster . . .' He stopped as he saw my face. 'Hey. You ain't joking?'

I shook my head. 'All I know about my father is that he was an American GI stationed in Britain.'

'Wow.' He took a gulp at his drink. 'Wow,' he said again.

I was nine when the letter came. As soon as I opened it, I felt my nerves sizzle. I don't know why, but I remember that quite clearly.

'Dear Samuel,' it began, and no one, not even the superintendent, called me that. 'I thought I would drop you a line to say that we hope you are getting on all right. You'll be ten next month, won't you? Quite the young man, I expect. I want you to know that your mum had to put you in the home because of the problems it would have caused in the family. I expect she thinks about you a lot and I know I do. I was thinking the other night that you don't want to grow up thinking you weren't loved, so I decided to write this letter. All the best. Your grandma.'

Looking back now, I suppose I was devastated. I was excited, but it was excitement with a touch of terror in it, I think.

Although she had written her name and address quite clearly, I never made any attempt to reply to it or to get in touch with her. Now I'm not quite sure why. Perhaps I never thought of it. Perhaps I did, and rejected it. I don't know.

And I never told anyone about it either. I kept it, folded in its envelope, as a secret. Often when I was alone I took it out and reread it, testing each word for different meanings and interpretations. Eventually, it disintegrated.

It wasn't until three years later, when I was thirteen, that I went to the superintendent and said I wanted to know who my parents were. He told me my mother had been a local factory girl and my father was a US serviceman. 'As far as we can establish,' he said, 'they only met on the one occasion.' He warned me against digging too deep. People who did were almost always disappointed, he said. His advice was to let well alone. When I said that was what I'd do, he looked relieved.

After that I never asked again.

Not that I told one word of that to Palli.

'Wow,' he said, for a third time. 'Don't you know who he was?'

'No. I don't know who my mother was either.'

'Can't you find out some way?'

'I could – I don't want to.'

'That is very, very cool.' He shook his scrubbing-brush head, grinning and giggling. 'You don't want to know and you carry on as though nothing's happened?'

'Nothing did happen to me, did it?'

'I guess not. That's it! Christ, you are right!' He reached over and grabbed my hand and started shaking it. I thought mine was coming off at the wrist. 'So what the hell does it matter about your old man, you're here and you're having a good time. It's a new deal. Every time, every life, it's a new deal.'

As he was calling up some more drinks, he suddenly remembered something. He leaned over the table and put his hand on my arm. 'You know what I said . . . you know, about the Alabama Klansmen, shit, I was only joking.'

'That's okay, Palli.'

'I mean, fuck, you don't look anything . . .'

'Forget it, Palli.' Somehow, through the seas of booze, I managed to recognise that as the key moment. 'You know that Solrun's done a runner, don't you?'

'She has?' He tried to look surprised but failed. He knew. Without a doubt he knew.

'Look, I know you've got to be loyal to your pal but do you think she could've gone to him?'

'No chance.' I could see the effort it took for him to face me with steady eyes. 'He's back in the States, working in a muffler shop in Jamaica. You know, near Kennedy.'

'Where you should be? Back in the States?'

'Oh, yeah.' Again the slow smile softened his face. 'I'm going fishing tomorrow. Why don't you come along, Sam? Few beers – real American beers – see what we can haul in?'

'Why not?' I replied, in that easy-going carefree way that means you haven't the faintest intention of doing it.

But then what a dull old world it would be if we all told the truth all the time. Like that business over the AC badge. I wasn't in any rush to tell Petursson but I'd recognised the badge the minute I saw it. It was a miniature of the US Marines breast insignia for Air Crew. The real one is about four inches across but this smaller version was the one they gave to girlfriends to 'pin' them. In the same way that little boys at parties stick their fingers in the tastiest cakes to reserve them.

That was the badge. Somehow that slotted in neatly with a spare name I'd got rolling around in my mind unclaimed. I'd been fed two names. Solrun had talked about two men. One of the names, Kirillina, fitted the young Russian diplomat. Logically then ... Oscar Murphy ... or was I jumping to conclusions?

There was only one thing to do. Try it.

'What I don't understand is this, Palli,' I said. I didn't have to act drunk. This was Method School where you have to live the part.

'Whassat?' He had one eye closed to focus on me. The girl had gone.

'This.' I wanted to bring the badge and the man together in one sentence for maximum impact and with the state my brain was in it wasn't easy work. But eventually I got there. I took a deep breath. 'If your buddy Oscar Murphy had got his helicopter wings and was doing so well, why the hell did he want to quit the marines like that?'

His face registered a bull's eye.

Show me a conclusion and I'll jump to it. If I had a family, that'd be the motto.

24

As soon as he picked up the phone, I went straight into my nasal-yankee voice. 'You gotta Mr Vale there?'

'Jack Vale speaking,' he said, in that mellifluous Edinburgh accent that made the rest of the English-speaking world sound like woad-smeared savages. 'Can I help you?'

'Sure you can, Vale, unless you wanna wind up at the bottom of the river with a nickelodeon around your neck. You can keep your stinkin' hands off my wife.'

A long pause followed. After all, it was five in the morning in New York.

'Behind that atrocious imitation of the great Mr James Cagney, I do believe I detect the unmistakeable voice of an old friend. How are you, Sam? And what do you mean by attempting such clumsy deceptions at this hour of the night?'

Since he went to freelance in New York ten years ago, I'd rung Jack about once a year, in a variety of causes and accents. I'd never survived the first minute without being spotted.

'Just testing, Jack. I was wondering if you could check something out for me.'

'Do you have to tell me now? Oh, it doesn't matter, I'm awake. Who's it for?'

'Grimm's sunny stories.'

'Surely you're not reduced to that, are you? Tell me the worst then. But I warn you, under no circumstances will I even contemplate doing Sexy Secrets of the Stars again.'

I told him. He didn't sound too hopeful.

'Jamaica's out by the airport. He works in a muffler shop, you say?'

'Yes. I assume that's a place where Americans buy colourful woollen scarves to keep the cold out, isn't it Jack?'

He gave a sigh of elaborate weariness. 'You don't assume anything of the sort. But I must tell you that there are hundreds of those back-street exhaust centres – as you would put it, in your quaint British way. However, leave it with me.'

We were finishing off all that whatever-happened-to-old-thingy when I saw Christopher coming in through Hulda's door. Five minutes later he was having breakfast with me and rabbiting away with Hulda in Icelandic.

'Absolutely delicious,' he enthused, smearing what looked like jellied seal on to his toast. He made his finger and thumb into that Gallic ring of approval. 'Superb, Hulda, superb. Try some, Sam. It's a sort of potted lamb.'

I'd been tucking mine away behind the geraniums but now I didn't have any choice. He was right. It was delicious.

'If it wants to get eaten, why does it go round looking like that?'

'Don't be so squeamish,' he said. Then he rhapsodised some more at Hulda. She was presiding – no lesser word would cover it – at the head of the table, delighted at last to have an appreciative audience for her efforts.

When she spoke back to him, in Icelandic of course, I knew what she'd be saying by the formal way she tilted her head.

'You really ought to learn some of the language,' Christopher said to me. 'You miss so much.'

'Oh, I wouldn't say that. She just told you that it was her duty and her pleasure.'

His head spun towards me. 'Gosh, you do after all.'

'Sam knows me too well,' Hulda said, and they both laughed. I might've fooled him but I couldn't kid Hulda for long.

When she went through to the kitchen, Christopher began to talk seriously. He'd heard about Solrun's mother when he got back from the north the previous night. Even at second-hand, he was horrified by what had happened, which set me wondering if he could be Batty's man sent along to throw me a lifeline. There was his nose: surely that would pass as credentials for one of the shadier trades.

What he wanted, when he got around to it, was to express his doubts about Ivan. Knowing we were friends didn't make it any easier for him, but in the end he did manage to say it.

'He's up at the Russian Embassy again now.' He was whispering, his eyes on the door for Hulda's return.

I wasn't going to join in the whispering. 'Why not? He works for the Russian government.'

'Yes, but doing what? I know he's an old friend of yours and all that, but I must say it – I think he's a spy. A proper spy.'

'Like all of us, he operates as best he can in a world of limited possibilities.'

'An awful lot more limited in Russia,' he grumbled.

He'd come round to offer his services as interpreter again. He'd had a disappointing trip to Akureyri. No one was interested in his lavatory gimmick. It was hard to believe that he was genuinely surprised by this, but he was clearly quite crestfallen. Now he was having problems getting authority to move stuffed puffins out of the country.

His gypsy face looked quite pale. 'I'm beginning to think I may not be cut out for business after all,' he said. I had to hide my smile. 'Anyway, not to worry. At least it gives me the opportunity to offer a small present to your daughter.'

He swung over a plastic bag. Without looking, I knew what would be inside. It was. A stuffed puffin. I assumed it was stuffed but, to be honest, it looked alive to me. Alive, and very still. I'm sure you can't get that quality of malevolence into glass eyes. The look on its face was the sort of expression you'd expect to see on your worst enemy as you fell down a manhole. Malicious satisfaction. With its webbed feet clinging to a chunk of lava, it stood with its head cocked, gloating.

'I'm sure she'll love it.' He was almost prompting me.

'Oh, yes, I'm sure she will. Although I'm not sure Uncle Ivan will approve.'

'Any use for a passing polyglot today?'

For a second, I couldn't think what he meant. Then I realised. I was tempted to include him. I might well need an interpreter. But since the old lady's death, it had struck me I was involved with some deeply serious people.

'I can manage,' I said. 'But thanks, anyway.'

25

The coughing man was bothering me. I don't know why. There was no reason why Palli's girlfriend – if that's what she was – shouldn't have a male guest in the spare bedroom. She didn't altogether look like a girl who was saving herself for Mr Right. On the other hand, maybe it was her poor old granddad, or maybe an out-of-town hack like me who was staying with her.

When I'd heard him cough, she'd shouted out of the window at Palli and that was when he'd taken off. In the rush, I'd forgotten the coughing man.

I'd intended asking Palli about it last night. I'd also meant to ask him about the girl and the baby, although I'd somehow picked up the impression that they didn't belong to him in any permanent sense. All that had gone the moment I'd mentioned Oscar Murphy. That sobered him up all right. It sobered me up, too – for a second, there was a fair chance he was going to redesign my face. Then, without another word, he'd got up and thundered out. He crashed through the party crowds with as much ceremony as a Sherman tank.

I remembered he'd said he was going fishing. Maybe that would give me a chance to try to talk my way into the flat again. At the worst I could keep watch.

It was raining. Heavy sheets ceaselessly poured down, swinging and swirling in a gusty wind. In Iceland you don't let that keep you indoors. If you did, you could be there for a month.

As I drove up the long hill towards the Breidholt flats, I saw Palli's female flatmate rushing down behind an encased pram. If I'd thought about it, perhaps I would've turned back. But I was still suffering from brain damage from the night before and I wasn't up to flexible forward planning. So I carried on. In the car park I couldn't see any sign of Palli's Triumph.

Which meant, if the coughing man wasn't there, that the flat was empty. Me, I'm like nature, I abhor a vacuum.

Since my last visit, the only improvement to the environment was a fresh vomit stain in the lift. The corridor was empty. From the flat next door came the sound of American voices from the base radio and a small child's monotonous pleading. Happy-family time.

On the door of Palli's flat, swinging from a central drawing-pin, was a note. It was scrawled in thick blurred pencil lines on the back of a computerised bill. I read it, and read it again – 'Lykillinn er a sinum stad.'

It didn't mean a lot to me. In fact, it didn't mean a thing to me. Not many Icelandic words do.

I took a closer look at the door. It wasn't much more than a thin board on a frame with a key-turn opening, which meant it only had one fastening. Under pressure from my hand, it gave a little before springing back. One bash would do it. One heel kick would rip out the screws that held it to the jamb.

It would also rip all the neighbours out of their flats to see what was going on. And what would I find inside? Maybe Palli lying on his bed reading comics and smoking while a friend borrowed his bike. No: whatever real spies may do, kicking doors down wasn't the answer.

I examined the note again in the hope that my Icelandic had improved. It hadn't. Next door the woman was singing and the child was crying – which was cause and which was effect was anyone's guess. Two doors down, I heard a man's voice getting louder as he got nearer to the corridor. His door opened and his voice, echoing in the tiled corridor, stopped when he saw me. He was a weathered-looking man, heavily built, in an old leather jerkin. He stood there, scratching his belly, then went back inside.

Then I remembered the credit card trick beloved of private eyes. The latch didn't take Amex, but thought seriously about Diners before rejecting that too.

I stared at the door again, hoping it would talk to me. In a way it did. Woman, child and Palli resident, plus one more man who may be resident or guest. Keys. How did they all come and go? Did people like that have a selection of keys ready cut for house guests? No, they did not. So what did they do?

Bruce Willmott, who was at school with me, had five brothers and two sisters. They didn't all have keys that was for sure. So what . . . I remembered.

I reached up and ran my fingers along the shelf above the door. The key was there. They did what most people did who weren't too worried about burglars because they'd nothing worth nicking. They stuck the key in the nearest hiding place and left a note saying, 'Key in Usual Place'.

The door opened easily. I stepped inside and closed it behind me.

The coughing man suddenly became an eight-foot Viking in my imagination. Every creak became a footfall, every shadow an ambush. Even my breathing was deafening. I leaned back against the door and calmed down my fears. I was inside. I couldn't go back.

'Hello,' I called out in a breezy voice. 'Anyone at home? Palli? You there, Palli?'

With thumping, confident steps, I strode into the living-room. Some of the steamy smell had lifted, otherwise it was the same. If I abhorred a vacuum then she abhorred a vacuum cleaner.

The first bedroom was hers and the baby's. His too, lucky feller. Her clothes were heaped in a jumble on a chair, spilling down to the floor. She'd propped a chipped mirror against the window. That, with a few flattened tubes and topless pots, took care of her glamour requirements. Over the duvet cover, Snow White and the dwarfs scampered, presumably looking for somewhere to have a wash. Both pillows were badly bruised.

The second bedroom was unfurnished: no bed, no chairs, no carpet, nothing. But someone was camping out there just the same.

It was the tidiest corner of the whole flat. One olive-green sleeping-bag had been rolled up and stacked against the wall. Beside that stood a nylon tote-bag. A few items of clothing had been folded and put into a neat pile: roll-neck sweater, patch-pocket canvas trousers, a camo-shirt. A green woollen stocking hat held the pocket debris: a handful of American coins, an airline boarding pass, a pair of nail clippers, a book of matches from a bar in New Jersey inscribed 'No Faggots Allowed', two ballpoint pens. Next to that lay a duty-free carton of tipped Camels, ripped open with several packs missing, and a bottle of Jack Daniels Black Label, either half-empty or half-full, depending on whether you're a pessimist or an optimist.

Whoever he was, he liked things neat and tidy. The map of Iceland might have unfolded itself if he hadn't been careful to pin it down with a good solid weight.

But that's the thing about a Colt .45 automatic – they do weigh a lot. Now I don't know a lot about guns – when I first read James Bond I wondered why he shot people with the Pope's hat – but I do know that this one was very big, very wicked, and very dangerous.

If you could manage to lift it, that is. I could, with an effort. I held it in my handkerchief while I inspected it. Full magazine, one up the spout, safety on, which is how a working pistol should be if you're thinking of putting it to some use. And if you're not, why not carry a willing smile instead?

It wasn't new, but it was well cared-for. Which was more than you could say for me.

Then I thought of the ID tag which marines have on their shirts, inside and just below the collar where they have their name, rank and number. Someone else had thought of it too. Name rank and number had been snipped off. All that remained was the assurance that this shirt met USMC specifications. It was when I was trying to fold the shirt as neatly as I'd found it that I felt the photograph in the pocket. I say photograph, but it was only one of those instant snaps, so the focusing wasn't too good and there was a lot of glare from the snow.

Even so, it couldn't have been anyone but Solrun. She was standing on a wooden verandah outside what looked like a sumarhus – the country cabins the Icelanders race to for their summer weekends. You could see the snow in the background and Solrun was wrapped in hood and gloves. So was the baby she was holding up for the camera.

If that's what it was. It was baby-shaped. It wore baby clothes. But that was all you could see. It looked like one of the in-arms models – much the same as the one I'd seen here earlier – rather than the running-around ones. That was about as far as my infant recognition took me.

I wasn't expecting to find that. I wasn't expecting the knock on the door either.

The first knock was hesitant. The second was more forceful. The third rattled the door on its hinges, and there were raised voices behind it too.

By then I'd shoved the photo back in the shirt and put it back on the pile. As I raced through to the bathroom I was taking off my jacket and tie, and I prayed that the shaky-looking shower-fitting worked as I stuck my head under and turned it on. It did. Then all I needed was a towel – I found one that had apparently been used for mucking out elephants – before I answered the door.

What I saw was the man in the leather jerkin I'd encountered earlier, and a watery-eyed woman he'd pulled in as a witness. What they saw was a half-dressed man who was in the middle of washing his hair.

'Ja?' I asked, giving my head another scrub.

The man, who'd been poised for action but had now dropped back a step in puzzlement, aimed some hesitant Icelandic at me. I retaliated with a minute and a half of rapid German along the lines of my being Palli's best friend from Hamburg. I mentioned Palli's name four times just to make sure.

'Ah, Palli?' he said, eventually.

'Ja,' I said, congratulating him as though he'd just won the pools. 'Friend,' I said in English, tapping myself on the chest.

'Friend,' the woman said, treating me to a brown-toothed smile. Still trying to smile at me, she shot a volley out of the side of her mouth at her husband. What it said, at a guess, was what the hell was he playing at, dragging her out of her flat with a lot of nutty talk about burglars and then disturbing innocent tourists in the middle of their toilet preparations. After all, whoever heard of a burglar hanging about to wash his hair?

'Guten morgen,' she said to me, in a moment of inspiration. She led him off by the arm and the moment their door closed she was at him like an angry monkey.

Five minutes later I left. It may not have been a very profitable morning, but at least I'd got my hair washed. I wanted to look my best for the US Navy top brass, didn't I?

26

Forget East meets West. Forget about those places like Berlin and Korea where they've scratched a line in the dust across the road so they can stand eyeball to eyeball. These are quaint rituals, as formalised and lifeless as the quadrille.

Instead, turn the globe on its side. Up on top of the world, that's the place. Without walls or barbed wire, without salutes or ceremony, no check-points, no stiff courtesies, no furtive soldiers' button-swapping, the two sides are already engaged. Battle is joined. Warfare has commenced. Only so far this is an exhibition fight: like karate killers demonstrating their skills, they stop always a fraction short of death.

Between Canada and Scotland there is a 1600-mile stretch of water that has been called the most strategic highway in the world. From their naval base at Kola, the Russian submarines slip unseen down this highway and out into the Atlantic. There, if they felt like it, they could stand between America and Europe, or simply sit on America's front doorstep slotting rockets in at short range.

Anyone who enjoys a symbol might like to think about this: the name which the Russians give to the base from which all this wickedness is unleashed, in America – phonetically at any rate – is the name of a fizzy drink. Kola. Cola. The sinister, the frivolous.

It's not quite so charmingly simple, of course. The Americans don't just sit around with their Cokes. Slap-bang in the middle of this route south is Iceland. As long ago as 1920, a man who later earned something of a reputation as a tactician was talking about the strategic importance of the country; his name was Lenin. Early in World War II, the Brits and the Americans grabbed it before Hitler could, and after the war the Americans left, then moved back in.

The Russian submarines – some twice the size of jumbo jets –

may be unseen but they are not undetected. Like cuddly black-nosed pandas, Orion P-3C's and AWACS with the giant mushrooms on their backs, trudge backwards and forwards, to and fro, over the cold sea. Beneath it electronic eavesdroppers called sonar buoys pass back details of all the passing traffic. So finely, so accurately can they do this, that the Americans can recognise individual vessels. 'I see old Igor still hasn't got that bearing fixed,' they say. They sit there counting the ships as easily as little boys collecting train numbers.

It is a game of blind man's bluff. Both are blind. Both, we hope, are bluffing.

That would be an acceptable way of preserving the status quo if it wasn't for one thing – the chance Russians have of changing it. They can't invade, of course. This isn't Afghanistan: it is a part of Europe. They can't nurture revolution: it's one of the few countries in the world that is prosperous and classless.

No, they have one chance. And that is to make the Americans so hated that they have to pack up and go home.

27

'That's what I'd do,' said Andy Dempsie, sawing off a chunk of steak no bigger than a standard house brick. He held it in mid-air as he finished his statement. 'Make 'em hate us. That's what I'd do if I was sitting down in Gardastraeti. You bet.'

The steak brick vanished.

He wasn't in Gardastraeti where the Russians had their embassy. He was facing me across a bare-topped table in the Navy Exchange snack bar on the NATO base at Keflavik. It was one of those places you couldn't hope to describe without a hatful of hyphens – it was a no-frills, fast-food, stand-in-line, serve-yourself place. All the phrases that in Britain guaranteed you a hamburger you could heel your shoes with, but here it meant a pizza as deep as his steak and just as delicious. And the Milwaukee beer was sweeping up the remains of the hangover from my long night with Palli.

'So,' he went on, 'when you phoned so early this morning – a London newspaperman, would you believe – and said you wanted to talk about one of our guys, I thought, here we go, it's happened. What's he done, this Murphy? Murdered a coupla dozen Iceland kids and every damn one of them as cute as hell? It's got to happen. One of these days. But it's not like that, you say?'

I told him again that it wasn't like that. I'd told him before when I arrived at the Public Affairs office, and he'd left one of his clerks to pull out the records on Oscar Murphy while we ate.

It wasn't hard to see why he was their Public Affairs man. With his wide-open face and non-stop chatter, plus a hair-trigger laugh, he was one of those blessed men who made you smile the minute you saw him. I've met a few with that gift, but not many. It's the sort of talent that opens doors and minds and mouths and if I could choose any talent, that's the one I'd go for.

He was a big-framed man and, although time and good times had added another chin and stomach, he still looked fit. He was wearing loose, colourful golf-course clothes.

'Another beer? Sure you want another beer. Now, where was I . . .' He'd kept up three lines of conversation since we met, and still managed to keep eating. 'Oh yeah, the doc. So I says to him, sure I smoke, forty-a-day, sometimes fifty. Do you drink? he asks, and I says, you bet I do, a few beers, a jugful of martinis before dinner, wine, a few big brandies later. I thought, dammit, I'm not going to lie to these medics, they rule our lives. He writes it all down then he looks up and says, "Mr Dempsie, you're in great shape. Whatever you're doing don't stop." Not bad, huh?'

Rich laughter rolled from him at the thought of how he'd cheated the medical profession. He finished off the steak, and speared the last dozen chips before pushing the plate away.

As he sat back, rocking the chair up on its rear legs, he lit a menthol cigarette and said: 'Nothing personal, Sam, but I truly am sorry to see you here.'

'Me? Why?'

'Because you're the guys who win and lose wars. Most of the time you win 'em for someone else and lose 'em for us.'

'But you're the country that invented advertising and public relations.'

'I know. And we keep getting whipped at it. Stay there.' He got up and came back a minute later with two more beers. 'One of the political boys was up from Washington doing a report and he said,' Dempsie puffed out his chest and lowered his voice, ' "The greatest threat to the American presence in the North Atlantic is the interface between the American male and the Icelandic female." That's what he said and it's true. But you wouldn't believe what we do to stay out of trouble.'

He recited it. They vetted servicemen to make sure they were suitable. They brought as many married couples as possible. Single men only stayed a year. They gave them everything they could to keep them on base: food at a quarter of Reykjavik prices, shops, clubs, sport, country lodges for fishing and skiing and night-classes in everything short of nuclear physics.

They were so low-profile, he said, they were almost underground. No men were permitted off base in uniform. Even out of uniform they had to be back on base before the Reykjavik night-life had begun to move. They even piped their three television channels around the camp so that it wouldn't get into the Iceland homes and corrupt them.

'You ever seen a US serviceman walking around in uniform in this country?'

I thought about that. 'I've not seen a US serviceman at all, as far as I know.'

He slapped the table with his non-smoking hand. 'There you are. Five thousand here, including dependents, and you wouldn't even know it. We are so careful, Sam, I'm telling you – so very very careful.'

'You're winning, then.'

With a sigh and a shake of the head, he murmured: 'We don't stand a chance.' He waved his cigarette hand at a man in aviator glasses who was feeding the juke-box. 'That's the man who's getting the computer to cough up on Oscar Murphy.'

'Why don't you stand a chance?' I didn't want that to get lost.

He assumed an expression of candid philosophical despair.

'Have you seen these Icelandic women?' He ground his cigarette out in an ashtray. 'And we have to persuade our fellers to stay in and study basic home economics? That's the interface he meant. Oh boy. Now you're going to tell me that Murphy's mixed up in some girl trouble?'

'Well . . .'

That was enough. He came bolt upright and rested his arms on the table and stared at me, waiting for the rest. I couldn't have lied to him. He seemed to have half-guessed anyway.

'Not necessarily trouble, but I'm writing a piece about an Icelandic girl and he's been . . .'

I pulled an apologetic face. He nodded and chewed his top lip.

'To be absolutely honest,' I added, 'I don't think he's here any more. But I thought you might have something on your records. Now I suppose I don't get any help?'

He scrubbed that out of the air with his hand. 'We can help, we will. That's where we're so stupid. Free press, open society. Christ! No wonder we don't have any control.' Somehow he dredged that big laugh up from somewhere. 'Don't look so grim, Sam, we'll sort it out.'

He lit another cigarette and the hospital smell of menthol drifted over.

'What I was saying before, I have a lot of sympathy for the Icelanders who don't want us here. They'd only just got their full independence from Denmark when we moved in during the war.'

I thought it was time I showed that I'd done some homework too. 'But don't all the polls show that two-thirds want you here?'

'They do, sure they do. Politically, rationally they know that. But I think that emotionally they'd like to be neutral. All those hundreds of years when they had the shit knocked out of them day after day by good old Mother Nature – I mean, if you weren't suffocated in a ten-foot snow drift then you had your ass burned off by a volcano – no one was interested then. Now it's strategically important, and they're pulling in the bucks too as it happens, and suddenly everyone wants to be their best friend. I can see they wouldn't like that. I can see they'd feel mightily inclined to tell us all to get the hell out. I'd feel like that too. It wouldn't take too much to turn that two-thirds one-third round.'

'What would it take?'

'Like I said, we pick our guys very carefully and we look after them too. But one day one of our fellers will sniff something or drink something or just go off the wall like people do sometimes, in the best ordered societies, and he'll run round burning Reykjavik down and we'll be in big, big trouble.' He drank some beer from the can. 'I hope to God I'm not on duty when it happens. Come on back to my office for some coffee.'

It had stopped raining, but spiteful clouds still tumbled around the sky. Two young blacks in track-suits jogged past.

'That's something you wouldn't have seen at one time,' Dempsie said.

'Jogging?'

'No, blacks.'

'How's that?' I'd heard the story but I still wanted to hear his official version.

'When we first came here we had to make a deal that only "first-class" troops would be stationed here. You know what "first-class" meant then?'

'White?'

'White.' He stopped and looked out over the lava plains. With some care, he went on: 'These people had what I call an excess of national pride. They were pure bred. Literally, I mean. No newcomers had landed here for a thousand years. That doesn't seem important to mongrels like us but to them it was.'

'You mean they were racists.' I put that in to see what he'd say. He handled it well.

'I don't know. I don't think so. Certainly not in the sense of a racist in Birmingham, Alabama. Or Birmingham, England, for that matter. They didn't look down on other races because they didn't have any other races to look down on. A lot of the older people still feel the same. When they were discussing admitting two dozen boat people you would've thought they were landing battalions of Martian rapists.'

'Know what you mean. All those years, locked in here battling with the elements. I suppose after a few centuries you begin to think you belong to the most exclusive club on earth.'

'That's it,' he said, moving off again. 'The most exclusive club on earth, and membership's closed.' He gave me a grin over his shoulder. 'And if I was in a club with lady members like that, I'd close the membership too.'

Back at his office, we drank some coffee and talked some more until his assistant, the one who'd been playing the jukebox, walked in.

'We hit a snarl-up over this Murphy,' he said.

I can't say I was all that surprised.

'Sam was saying that he thinks maybe he's no longer with us,' Dempsie explained, but the man cut him off short.

'Oh no, Sir, he's still stationed here but he's not on the base today and I can't get in touch with him.'

He turned to me, looking even more apologetic. 'I'm sorry about this, Sir, I really am. What I was going to suggest was that maybe Mr Dempsie or myself could bring Corporal Murphy down to your hotel tomorrow.'

Now that did surprise me. And on Dempsie's large and genial features I thought I caught a glimpse of satisfied amusement.

28

I drove back into town alongside the Tjornin. I stopped and stared at it. You know how it is when you're sure something's wrong but you can't see what it is.

Then I realised. It was deserted. A bold band of ducks was leading a raiding party on the land and ransacking a paper-bag

106

of slices of bread, squabbling in their glee at putting one over on their patrons. Further along I saw a toy yacht beached on the side, and a coat and picnic bag beyond that. But no people. Then I saw where they'd all gone.

A crowd of thirty or so people were taking the road that led up the hillside among the smart villas. From somewhere up at the front, out of my sight, I could hear the sweet burble of a motor-bike. Only one machine on the island sounded like that.

There was no way of pushing through the crowd, so I did a few nifty turns around the town centre and pulled round the corner into Gardastraeti when I saw the mob advancing down the road.

In front of them was Palli with a roped prisoner.

Sitting back on his machine, his bare blue-stained arms were alive with muscles as he bent his wrists down, juggling throttle and clutch to hold it down to walking speed.

Beyond him, thirty yards or so distant, was the shuffling muttering crowd. They daren't come nearer; they couldn't go away.

And between them, secured to the bike by twelve-foot of orange nylon cord around his neck, was a young dark-haired man.

At first I didn't recognise him, but then, neither would his mother. His face was blood and bruises and not much else, and he was holding his head back in a queer sort of way. He stumbled and staggered along and it took me a minute to realise it was the Russian. The one in the photograph with Solrun. The one in the chamois jacket. Only now he looked about as elegant as a scarecrow. His jacket was ripped open and as he walked his knee poked through a tear in his trousers.

When he saw me, Palli gunned the bike and eased the clutch a fraction. It was beautifully judged. The bike jumped forward a yard, the rope tightened and Kirillina was jerked forward on his knees. I saw then that his hands were tied behind his back.

'Said I'd run you home – here y'are,' Palli called out. He didn't even bother to look round. He smiled at me all the time. 'Know who this lulu is?'

'I know.'

By this time I was out of the car and unfastening the cord

around his neck. At least it wasn't a noose. And the fastening on his hands fell away when I touched it. 'What the hell are you doing, Palli? The cops'll lynch you for this.'

He pulled an innocent face. 'Me? I was only giving the guy a lift home. I didn't touch him. Ask the bum.'

I knew I had to. Kirillina was mauling at his face and generally trying to bring himself round.

'No,' he said, when I put the question. 'Not him.'

'Who? Who did it? I'll get the police.'

'Police?' His eyes opened in alarm. 'No police.'

Close to, I could see the damage. His right eye had gone completely under a blue-black mound. The blood from his nose had soaked up the grime and grit of the road where he must've fallen, so that his face looked like a dropped lollipop.

He didn't seem to know he was outside the Soviet Embassy. It's a cream and grey building, which somehow manages to look thickset and heavy-shouldered, as though anxious to conform to its national stereotype. It was the sort of building where a Victorian might have kept his second-best mistress. Now it was bursting with life. Faces appeared at the basement windows behind the security bars, and higher up the building.

'He was playing around with Oscar's chick,' Palli said. He'd obviously decided to try to justify it. 'You gotta hand out a warning now and again.'

I didn't reply. Then I heard him say 'Hey, this could be fun,' and I looked up and saw the door to the embassy, on the side of the building, had opened. Three men were coming down the steps, two of them trying to restrain a third who was shouting and waving his one free arm. Down the road the crowd watched this loud incomprehensible drama.

As he burst free and rushed to the gate, I led Kirillina to him. He put his arm round him lovingly, and coaxed him up the stone steps and into the embassy.

One of the two remaining men pointed at Palli and bellowed a fierce threat. Then they all withdrew and closed the heavy green door behind them.

'Some show, huh?'

'You must be mad. Are you trying to start a war or something?'

He pushed two fingers down into the pocket of his sleeveless denim jacket and pulled out his cigarettes. As he lit one, he said: 'I told you, it wasn't me. But if it was I've got the perfect defence.' He drew on the cigarette and then leaned back on his bike to blow the smoke skywards. 'Yes, sir, that bastard was screwing my wife.'

'Your wife?'

'That's right. Solrun.'

Then I saw what he meant.

'Now leaving out what I know and what you know, on paper she is my wife and that guy – who is reckoned to be a smart-ass diplomat or something – has been taking advantage of her loving disposition. Now she's gone missing and he's got the nerve to come to my apartment looking for her. Shit, man, no one would convict me on that. They'll say I shoulda killed him.'

He pretended to get off his bike to go and find the Russian again, then sat back. He was fire-proof and he knew it.

'Did he really come to your apartment?' Somehow I had to try to salvage some truth from all this.

'That's right. A real foolish thing to do.'

'Why?'

He began to paddle the bike along with his feet. I walked with him. The crowd had almost all gone now, back to their boats and empty bags of bread.

'He said he was looking for Solrun. Friends of Oscar he ran into thought he might know that himself.'

'And did he?'

'Well, he didn't say, matter of fact.' He scrubbed his fingers in the ginger matting of his chest.

He stopped the bike and motioned me nearer with a movement of his head. The jeering triumph left his face.

'Look. After last night, some things I wanna say, okay?'

To him, a beating-up was all in a day's work. He obviously thought I was getting far too excited about it.

'All right. What?'

'I'm sorry I walked out on you. I don't know where you got the name, but yes, sure, Oscar Murphy was my buddy.'

'And he isn't here?'

He kept his hairless face directed towards me and his pale

109

blue eyes were steady enough. 'I told you that. He's working in a muffler shop in Jamaica – New-York Jamaica that is, not the one down in the West Indies.'

He saw me glancing back anxiously at the embassy.

'Don't worry about it. They just roughed him up a little. He'll be okay. Sam,' he said, 'I wanted to tell you I was hearing you last night. You talked good sense to me. Better than I've heard for years. I'm going back. I'm going back to Chicago.'

'Great,' I said, and he managed to look quite hurt by the sardonic way I said it. For some reason he wanted my good opinion.

He halted the bike with his feet on the road again and held out his broad hands with their tufty golden hair. Then he turned them over, palms and padded muscles uppermost.

Whoever had beaten up the Russian would've had hands like a slaughterman. Palli's wouldn't have got a second glance at a needlework class. Not only were they unscratched, they were surprisingly clean.

29

From the top bar of the Saga we watched the bulging black clouds chug across the sky and tip their endless drenching loads on the city. It wasn't a scene to lift the human spirit, but right then you couldn't have budged Ivan's spirit with heavy-lifting gear.

His face, one of those long and mournful models at the best of times, hung in grey folds and his soft brown eyes were veined and rimmed with red.

'I know, I look ghastly,' he said, when he saw the expression on my face.

'What's the trouble?' I asked, waving up a martini for me and another gin for him.

'The usual.' He shrugged and turned his face towards the windows which were draped from the outside with nets of rain.

I don't know why I bothered asking. That was all he ever said: the usual. It was frustrating really, because he was disbarred from the one activity that all us diurnalists have in common – group grizzling. Somehow we manage to combine a mawkish affection for our worthless trade with a deep contempt for those who employ us. Grimm, admittedly, was an extreme case, but in general we were right.

And poor old Ivan couldn't join in.

'They're giving you a bad time?' I said. He didn't even nod. They probably had nod-detectors in every room in the place.

'I wish I were like you – independent,' he said, unexpectedly. There were only three businessmen at the bar, and we were tucked quietly away in a corner.

'You are independent.'

'Not really. Not like you. Not emotionally independent. I'm terribly vulnerable, as I'm sure you know. It's inevitable if one is . . . gayish.'

He always qualified gay by adding the last three letters, as though the process was somehow incomplete and a little bit of him was still heterosexual. If so, it was a little bit I'd never seen.

'I suppose they can always haul you back to Mother Russia.'

He lifted his hangdog face. 'Don't.'

'Are you filing anything so far?'

He shook his head. I was glad about that. What can happen on those sort of jobs is that some agency bloke files to Moscow, one of the Moscow-based western reporters picks it up and does it up for London and New York, and before you know where you are you have an editor ratting at you.

'Apparently,' he added, 'I'm on ice for a policy piece.'

'That shouldn't affect me too much. Unless it's a topless policy piece.'

'You?'

That was my chance to tell him about offering Grimm a story on Solrun's mother. I'd caught a call from him – and just missed one from Jack Vale in New York – when I got back to Hulda's. At least the story about Grimm might cheer him up.

'He said it was too fish-and-chippy and they'd got a dozen

like that down the Old Kent Road every week. So I suggested that there might be a security angle to it and my esteemed editor squealed with laughter. "What are they after up there," he said, "the secret recipe for fish fingers?" He told me to stay on the trail of the Sexy Eskies and he also authorised me to go up to a thousand quid to get the right pictures.'

Ivan did manage a tired smile. He wasn't being drawn by that reference to a security angle. All he said was: 'But you haven't got your model available for the pictures, have you?'

'We're working on it, Ivan. By the way, you know about your embassy chap being beaten up, do you?'

'It was nothing much,' he said hurriedly.

'Nothing much? I saw it. He'd had a damn good kicking and he was hand-delivered, in public and daylight, to the embassy door. Well, gate.'

Ivan looked agitated. 'I gather there's no official protest anyway.'

'Odd. Very odd.' That covered the two questions I'd wanted to put to him. Which left me with one small item of information which I wished to slip into his drink – or wherever else he might best swallow it. And I wanted to watch his face while he did it.

'Hey,' I said, breaking off mid-swallow as I suddenly 'remembered' something. 'One of your tips came up nicely, Ivan.'

'Did it?' he replied, listlessly.

'Yes. Oscar Murphy.'

'Oscar Murphy.' He ran his thin fingers around his mouth and began to pull himself up from his slouched position.

'You remember. Our first day here, I think. You said you'd picked his name up at the embassy.'

'Oh, yes, I remember.' He looked relieved. He didn't know what was coming next. For all he knew he was in for a nasty shock. He was.

'I've got an appointment with him tomorrow.'

Then he did drag himself up and he couldn't keep the amazement out of his face. 'Oscar Murphy? You're meeting him? That can't . . . I mean, are you sure, is it the same man? I'm sure there's some kind of mix-up.'

'Why?' I almost hated myself for doing that. He was in

enough trouble as it was. But it was Ivan who'd fed me the two names in the first place, both the Russian and the American, and it was only fair I should bounce one of them back at him.

He cast about for an answer. 'I had the impression that he was . . . abroad somewhere.'

'Not at all,' I went on, breezily. 'Chap up at the base has fixed it all for me. I'm seeing him at ten tomorrow.'

'Where?' he asked, too quickly. Then he added lamely: 'You don't want to have to bother going all the way out to Keflavik again, do you?'

'No, they're bringing him down here. That's one thing about the Yanks, their PR is terrific. So I see him here and let's hope he can give us a lead on Solrun.'

What he should've done was to ask if the mysterious Oscar Murphy knew Solrun, because as far as Ivan was concerned, he didn't. But he was tired and he was missing a few, and he let that one go.

He sat back again and rested his head on the cushion. Wearily he closed his eyes. I felt sorry for him.

'This wretched business,' he murmured. 'Do your bosses ever make you do things you find distasteful?'

'Only every day.'

'Like what?' Above his closed and hooded eyes, his brows furrowed into a frown.

'Like getting out of bed. Picking up the telephone. Talking to their readers. All pretty grisly, I can tell you.'

After a short silence, still with his eyes closed, he asked: 'Have you found anything for the wondrous Sally yet?'

'I thought maybe something in sealskin.' I didn't dare tell him about Bell's gift of the stuffed puffin.

'How ghastly.' His eyes half-opened. 'I won't have that, I'm afraid. Not the skins of those dear little creatures. Why don't we look at some of the knitwear here? It's gorgeous.'

'Then we'll run into the save-the-sheep mob.'

As I walked through the door at Hulda's the phone was ringing. It was Jack Vale.

'What a busy little bee you are to be sure,' he said. 'This is the third time I've tried you.'

'How'd it go?'

'I managed to run him down all right. He's your man, no doubt about that, Sam. Hang on while I check my notes. Here we are . . . ready? It's Corporal Oscar Murphy and he was with the jar-heads.'

'Jaw-heads?'

'Jar-heads. Marines. They are known by this fine example of muscular American English because their caps fit so tightly on to their cropped heads that they look as though they've been screwed on.'

'Can we have the rest in English English please?'

'And who better than a Scot to answer that plea . . . yes, of course. On his first tour of three-to-four years he was a crewman on helicopters out of MCAS Cherry Point, North Carolina. Okay?'

It was a clear line. I could even hear his notebook rustle as he turned the page.

'That's right, Cherry Point. He was a gunner on CH-46s. Is this what you want to know?'

'Couldn't be better.'

'He made E4, that's corporal, on his first tour, and – this is interesting – to do that you have to be what they call squared away.'

'English, please?'

'It's a reference to the way they have to do their beds at boot camp, like hospital corners for nurses. A squared-away marine is one who is well trained, highly-disciplined, a good soldier in other words. He was doing well, your man.'

'Was doing?'

'I'll come to that. On his second tour he came up to Iceland and they put him on security duty at the embassy there. Again, they don't give jobs like that to the ground-pounders.'

He was enjoying this. Oh, he really was. I didn't even have to ask.

'A ground-pounder, as I'm sure you're wondering, is also known as a meatball or a shithead. This refers to the more basic type of marine. Oscar Murphy was an altogether more superior type. At first, anyway.'

'What happened?'

'I don't quite know. The story is that there was some trouble over a girl out there and he was transferred back to the States. He hit the booze – also hit a sergeant apparently – and when he tried to re-enlist they wouldn't have him. So from being blue-eyed he sank to bum status in no time flat. Lives with a girl called Vicky.'

'He is there, isn't he, Jack?'

'Here?'

'Yes. In America.'

'Oh yes, he's here all right.'

That was what I wanted to know. More than anything else.

'So what's his explanation?'

'Ah. I thought you might ask that. You see I picked this up on the old white man's whispering wires.'

'You didn't go down there? You haven't seen him?'

'No, I managed to raise his brother at the muff... the exhaust centre, and he filled in all the background. Murphy's off work with 'flu, in common with about a million other people this week, so I didn't see a lot of point in driving all the way out to Jamaica to see him.'

He didn't want to drive out to Jamaica like people in Kensington don't want to drive out to Hackney. Even so, I wanted to know what he had to say about the girl, and Jack couldn't get that from his boss. I asked him to go out there.

'It'll cost.' Jack Vale charged a hundred quid for picking up the telephone. If you wanted him to speak into it that was another fifty.

'Charge it to Grimm,' I said.

'I will, I will.'

'I can only leave you with the advice Grimm himself gave me this afternoon, Jack. His final instruction, in fact.'

'What was that?'

I quoted it exactly as Grimm had said it to me before he rang off: 'Walk tall.' Then Jack actually replied what I'd only thought.

Anyway you looked at it, that was interesting. Jack was going out to see Oscar Murphy in New York. I was going to meet him in Reykjavik. Oscar Murphy, the model soldier who fell from grace. Either he was unusually adept at international trans-

115

port, or there were two Oscar Murphys. At least. If ever they all got together in the same country they could have a reunion. As it was, I'd be quite happy just to meet one of them.

I started hanging my cord suit and spare shirts over the window, to keep the northern night at bay in the hope of a good night's kip, when Hulda tapped on the door. There was someone to see me downstairs.

'I hope you have not been a bad boy,' she said, archly.

'I believe I have, but it's so long ago now I'm no longer sure. Why?'

I got the answer when I went downstairs into the sitting-room. Petursson was standing there. He was sighing impatiently and dabbing at his hat with a hankie.

'Raindrops,' he explained, in some irritation. 'Do you think they will mark it?'

30

After a blow like that – raindrops on your hat – it wasn't easy to settle him down. But, with Hulda's ministrations, he made a fairly good recovery.

She obviously knew him well, and there was a good deal of affection mingled with her respect. She bore off his precious hat and coat to a place, presumably, beyond the reach of acts of God. She then placed him in her own rug-wrapped rocking-chair, with a table and ashtray at hand.

While she was making coffee, I told him what had happened in Gardastraeti earlier that day. That was why he'd come. Or so he said. At the end of it, to my surprise, he was happy with my conclusion that Palli hadn't handed out the beating himself.

'He's going back, by the way.'

'Who – Palli?'

'Yes. Back to the US. He's decided he's not an Icelander

after all.'

'For this we should be very grateful. I am a policeman and to me he only means trouble. Even so, I look at him and at those Vietnamese children down in the town and I think it is strange that the human wreckage of a war on the other side of the world years ago should be washed up here. Strange, and sad. What do you think about Palli Olafsson, Hulda?'

She'd just come in with a tray of coffee and some volcanic biscuits. She placed it on the table and began to pour the coffee. As she did, she recited with great emphasis a couple of short bursts of Icelandic.

To me she said: 'That is an old saying which means that we cannot save those who are doomed to die and we cannot send to hell those who must live.'

It sounded sinister, delivered by this spry little woman in her darkened room cluttered with the past. The twentieth century seemed a long long way away. With a small bow of her head, she left the room. Petursson eased the atmosphere with a gentle laugh.

'You must not make the mistake of thinking we are like you central Europeans,' he explained. 'For centuries life up here has been ruled by storm and fire. People – the older ones especially – do have some strange beliefs.'

'Too many books and long dark nights,' I said.

He looked at the stacked shelves and the heavy drapes which she'd drawn against the light and laughed again. Then, to my surprise, he asked me to call him Pete. That was what his friends in London had called him.

I was happy enough to go along with that. Quite instinctively, I liked him. He had none of the cop bully-boy about him. With small twinkling eyes in his solid face, and his fastidious patience, there was something elephantine about him. He didn't get going too easily, but I bet he took a lot of stopping.

'Of course,' he said, sipping from an elfin-sized cup with some difficulty, 'you are a man with no past yourself, aren't you? Wasn't it Barnardo's?'

To my own surprise, I went and told him about it. And that is unusual. There aren't three people who've heard that story.

'Does this mean you love the Americans or you hate them,

then?' It was a shrewd question. I'd spent quite a few hours with that myself.

'Neither. It doesn't matter. Parents don't matter. Where you come from doesn't matter.'

'What? None of it?'

'No. You go from birth to seventy or whatever, you try to avoid pushing old ladies under buses, you try not to slip under too many yourself, and that's it.'

I wasn't quite sure whether he was appalled or fascinated. He sounded about half and half.

'That is a most unusual view. But what about collective responsibility? As a member of a family, or your country, or the human race?'

'Baloney. They're just so many clubs people join to light fires against the dark and the cold, but they don't mean anything. You're still alone.'

'So when the nuclear holocaust . . .'

'And the whole of mankind is wiped? That proves what I'm saying. If you die with a million people in a nuclear war, for the individual it's exactly the same as stepping off Beachy Head. Your own individual death's the only one that matters. To you.'

'You're not serious, surely. It was an Englishman who wrote that no man is an island.'

'Just because someone wrote it and everyone keeps saying it doesn't make it true.' He really had hit on one of my favourites this time. So I presented him with my slightly more pragmatic version: 'Send not to inquire for whom the bell tolls, because it's only someone else.'

He gave a shocked laugh, and they're quite hard to extract from policemen.

'You teach all this to your little girl?'

'Do you have children?'

'A son. He is grown up now, of course.'

'Seriously, did you teach him anything at all? Did your advice and example really influence him in the long term?'

He sat staring into his coffee cup. Then he raised his head. 'I'm not sure, maybe not, how can you say . . .'

'There you are. No. I don't try to teach my daughter

anything. I love her. I try to help her. I try to make her laugh. But in the end what happens to her life is down to her.'

I sat back smugly and looked at him. I was pleased with my plough-a-lonely-furrow philosophy. What I liked about it was that it didn't accept any religion or political philosophy or social system so far devised by man. Really, it was incompatible with almost anything right down to joining a book club, but I was prepared to cheat over things like that. One thing, it had certainly silenced old Pete Petursson.

'Do you still remember the address?' he asked, after a while.

'What address?'

'The address of the grandmother who wrote to you.'

'Oh, that. Since you ask, I can actually remember it. It was in Chelmsford.'

He rose ponderously and brought the coffee-pot over to me. 'A refill? Yes, of course, that explains it. But it is still unusual.'

'Explains what?' I was getting a bit annoyed about this sudden change of tack he'd pulled on me.

'Why you should go to such lengths to erect an explanation for the fact that you were afraid to go to that address. You were afraid to face your past. That is why you and Palli understand each other. Isn't that so?'

No, it was not bloody so, I told him, and I said so several times and at some length. It didn't do any good of course. If what I was saying had about the same philosophical value as a dustbin full of old fishheads (which was what I sometimes privately believed) then he'd just emptied the lot over my head.

On the other hand, if it was all true (which was also what I privately believed, and sometimes at the same time), then he'd got me.

I was glad to steer the conversation back to Solrun. I was glad, too, to see that Pete – after the first two or three times, the name came easily – wasn't too worried about her. At first, he said, they thought she might have been abducted. Now they were almost certain she was in hiding and he thought that was no bad thing.

After what had happened to her mother and to her boyfriend, I was inclined to agree. It was why she'd gone to ground that was bothering me more than where.

'You know who this Kirillina is?' Pete was giving me one of his searching looks as he lit up another of those small cigars.

'A Russian. One of her boyfriends?'

'You do not know, I see. That was also why I came tonight. I will tell you.'

And he did. He once again did that trick of moving the cigar on a notch to avoid nicotine stains and he began to talk about the Russian as though he knew and loved him. In a way, I suppose he did.

'He was a bright boy, Nikolai. He was spotted at seventeen and selected for officer training. He went to the Frunze Higher Naval School in Leningrad – do you know of it? I'm sorry. No, I'm not trying to catch you out. Sometimes I forget what you know and what you don't know. He went to the Frunze which many people would say is the best of them. All the rest of it is quite normal. First he went to a ship as a lieutenant. He did the four jobs that a Soviet naval officer usually does – a group head, a department head, first lieutenant and then CO, all on the same ship. I forget which one. All I remember is that it was a Krivak class frigate. And here he is as a captain, third rank, and in effect an assistant naval attaché at the Russian Embassy here. You understand they do not have military attachés, because Iceland does not have any military. But that would be his speciality.'

'He's a talented boy, isn't he?'

Petursson concentrated as he held the cigar over the heavy brown glass ashtray and knocked the ash off with his finger. Then he sat back again and resumed the story of Captain Kirillina.

'He is, Sam. Because he has a talent that is worth much more than his brains to the Soviet Union. Much much more.'

'What's that?'

'In a woman you would call it allure. I don't know what you would say for a man.'

'Charm, maybe?'

'Charm, certainly. But charm combined with looks and with personal magnetism – social graces, too. These qualities are unusual anywhere but in the Soviet Union they are like gold.'

He let that sink in. It did. I remembered the photograph and my first reaction to it. He was a hell of a good-looking man and if I'd noticed, it was a reasonable bet that one or two women had. You could see, even in that picture, the composure of the man.

'He turns up here in the Russian Embassy. You know the building, you were there today. The Russians attach so much importance to their Iceland embassy that they have eighty people here – three times as many as the Americans. And no non-Soviet ever gets inside. They even have their own plumbers and joiners.'

'What's that got to do with our dashing buccaneer?' I asked. I tasted my coffee. I'd been listening so keenly it had gone cold. I put it back on the table.

'I tell you that to show you how reclusive these Soviet diplomats are. They live in their own ghetto. They are secretive. Not only do they not mix, they positively shun any offers of friendship.'

'So how does Nikolai administer his fatal charm at that distance? By satellite?' I must admit I was being a bit waspish. Male A does not usually wish to hear about the irresistible charms of Male B, particularly when Male B has been known to knock off Male A's girl.

Pete reached over and touched my arm with his hand. 'It isn't personal. That is what I am showing you. We are talking about a highly professional man.'

'He was in the diplomatic ghetto . . .'

'No. That's the point. He never was. He rented a beautiful flat over in the west of the city, facing the sea. It was beautiful – I went there a few times myself. We have some rich people here, but there are very few apartments here that were so lavishly furnished. For the most, in excellent taste. He had been well taught.'

'Apart from the plastic sputnik.'

First his face registered astonishment, then amusement and he sat laughing at the thought of it. 'You know about that? Sometimes I do wonder about you, Sam. You are quite right. There, in a cabinet filled with beautiful silver and porcelain, is a model of the first sputnik. The Russians never get it quite right.'

'Now you're going to tell me that he gave parties like Gatsby and the women fell at his feet.'

The Icelander flapped a big hand at the cloud of cigar smoke which was building up around him. A single beam of light through the curtains laid a gold bar across his silver hair.

'Of course. It is so obvious. Wonderful food, wonderful drink, wonderful company, too. He was immensely popular. With men as much as women.'

'You don't mean. . . ?'

He held his hands up in horror at the idea. 'Certainly not. He was a professional, I tell you. You are right, women did go for him. And he was – what shall we say – associated with three or four.'

'Associated?' He'd picked that word very carefully.

'Yes. He took them out. Oh, I forgot to tell you, he had a beautiful car too. An English sports car, a Morgan I believe. Can you imagine – a Soviet diplomat driving around in a Morgan? Sorry, where was I? Yes, these other women. Girls is perhaps more accurate. He took them out, went to parties, went skiing and skating, and bought them lovely presents. But he did not go to bed with any of them.'

'Perhaps they said no.'

He pulled a face at that. 'Sam, our girls do not suffer from fake modesty. He didn't ask them, that is the truth. If he had, the answer would have been yes.'

'If they were like the Icelandic girls I know, they must have asked him.'

'They did, naturally. He declined.'

'Ungrateful Commie rat,' I said just to show where my sympathies lay.

'Politely, he declined. Can you imagine the effect this had on our girls? We are only a little country, gossip travels very fast. Here was this man who looked and lived like a film star and who insisted on sleeping alone. They were like bees around a honeypot, I can tell you.'

'Perhaps,' I said, because of course I could see very well where his narrative was leading, 'perhaps you're wrong. Perhaps he was an impotent Russian naval diplomat of private means?'

He allowed himself a small smile, and began to push himself to and fro in the rocker. He was enjoying this.

'Obviously – I need not say this I am sure – the extrovert Soviet diplomats are invariably attempting to penetrate the skin of the society in which they are living. There are also two other tests that invariably apply.'

He grabbed the index finger of his left hand with his right hand. 'One: at some point in their careers they must have received training. After his command of the frigate, and before he surfaced in diplomatic life, Kirillina disappeared for two years. He was not in any naval institution. He was not in any diplomatic institution.'

'I warn you, Pete,' I said. 'I have a very high resistance to overworked initials like KGB.'

In a soft voice he replied: 'Then perhaps it is as well it was the GRU.'

'GRU? Who the hell are they?'

'Much the same sort of thing. And two,' he grabbed the second finger, 'they are the only Soviet diplomats who criticise the regime. Kirillina did so several times. With people he had got to know a little. He would say that the Eastern Bloc countries were too backward, and they could learn a lot from the West. "Communism has never learned to live with fun," he used to say. And his impotence very rapidly disappeared when he encountered Solrun.'

'Gosh, I am glad to hear that,' I said.

There are times when I astonish myself with my generosity, I truly do.

He looked at his watch. 'Good heavens, it is so late. I apologise. I had so many things to tell you I forgot the time.' As he got to his feet with the nimbleness I'd noted before, Hulda came zipping into the room with his coat folded in her arms so that his hat rested on it, like the Crown Jewels on their cushion. If he was worried about her listening, he didn't show it. For some reason I liked him better for that.

And because of that I was flattered when he asked me to have dinner at his flat the following evening. I had this feeling he didn't throw a lot of invitations around. 'It will be pleasant to talk about London again,' was his explanation.

We were on the door-step before I asked the question that had been niggling at me all night.

'Why?'

'Why what?' He put his hand out to make sure it wasn't raining: then he put his hat on.

'I'm glad you have told me so much. I'm grateful you've taken me into your confidence, but why me? Why tell me anything?'

'We must all follow instincts, I think. My instinct is that you are here for a purpose, and that purpose has yet to be disclosed. In the meantime I would like you to understand how I see these things in case one day you can help me.' He turned his face towards me. 'Are there things you could tell me that would help?'

The Oscar Murphy story – both of them – was on the tip of my tongue. Just as I was going to tell him, I had this alarming vision of the elusive Oscar turning up to find the place ringed with police.

'I'll think about it,' I said, feebly.

'I would be most grateful. We have some very powerful people playing games in my country and I would welcome any help. I am, as I'm sure the Americans will tell you, very Mickey Mouse.'

I watched him walk down the street and almost called him back to tell him about Oscar. Never mind, I thought, it'll keep until tomorrow.

It didn't keep, of course. And if I had told him I could have saved at least one life.

31

'Sam Craven,' said Andy Dempsie, 'meet Oscar Murphy.'

'Hi,' he said, like he would. Powerful handshake, square tough face, reddish-brown hair and a scattering of freckles. He was wearing standard inoffensive clothes: well-pressed grey trousers, dark blue blazer-style jacket, light blue shirt, mid-blue knitted tie, and black slip-on shoes. Late twenties, short thick-torso type that usually make good boxers, and an open intelligent face.

He gave a little whistle as he looked around. 'We don't get in here much on corporal's pay,' he said.

'So here's your boy, Sam,' Dempsie said, as though Murphy was a freshly-landed trout. He'd booked a private room and he was examining the full range of breakfast food that was laid out on a table at the side. 'Coffee, boys?'

'Yes, Sir,' said Oscar, and I nodded.

'You're still in the corps?' I was keen to get started.

'Yeah,' he said, almost as though his honour had been queried. Then his face lightened. 'Oh, I get you – we don't wear uniform off base. That's so, isn't it, Sir?'

'Certainly is.' Dempsie grabbed my arm in a muscular hand and spoke quietly to me as he headed towards the door. 'Leave you with him, okay? He's a good guy. He'll tell you about the girl, too – no problem.'

As he left, Murphy got up and grabbed some toast and a croissant. I did the same. A bit of togetherness never did any harm.

'This is just for my information and doesn't go into any official report or newspaper report for that matter.'

'Fine, Sir.'

'So you were Solrun's feller?'

'You too,' he said, then he added quickly: 'Hope you don't mind me saying it like that.' When he saw I didn't, his face set in a smile of sheepish pride, but at least it was better than the barnyard bristling I'd been expecting. In fact, Oscar wasn't what I'd been expecting, but I didn't quite know why.

'You knew about me, then, Oscar?'

'Uhuh. She told me. Hell, you know Solrun – crazy as a monkey, but totally, totally honest.'

'You were seeing her at that time, then?'

He pulled an apologetic face and gave a long sigh. "Fraid so. I knew she had to spend a lot of time with these foreign newspapermen. Later she told me she'd taken a shine to one of them . . . kapow, that's Solrun.'

He unbuttoned his jacket and loosened his tie. 'Don't get me wrong. If I'd caught you then I would've broken your goddam neck. I cooled down a lot since then.'

'Thank God,' I said, to take any competitive sting out of the air. 'Tell me about you and her. How you met. Everything.'

'Well . . .' He glanced at the door as if he was afraid Dempsie might be listening. 'They don't encourage US servicemen to take up with the local girls. I'm not complaining about that. They tell you about the place before you come out here, and you can find every damned thing you want on that base.'

'How did you meet?'

'Skiing.' He pointed out of the window towards the ever-present mountains. You could see them clearly today. The mists and rain had gone. Now you'd think it was another country.

'That was one of the things I promised myself,' he went on. 'I was going to do some studying, get some exams, save some money, take a trip round Europe, and do some skiing. First trip into the mountains, I meet Solrun. End of studying and saving.'

Listening to this, I couldn't see how serious he was about her. He sounded almost too casual. 'I thought you two had a big thing going?'

His smile died. He looked down at his polished shoes. Then he glanced up. 'That's right. I try not to get too heavy about it now – what's the point? – but at the time I worshipped that girl.'

He rose so he faced me. 'I wasn't some guy on a business trip looking for a piece of ass.' You couldn't miss the cool venom in his voice.

'I didn't think you were,' I said, as gently as I could, and I was relieved to see his shoulders sink down a fraction. It was too early in the day for all that say-that-again stuff.

He flapped his hand. 'Sorry about that,' he said, rubbing the back of his neck as though easing tension. 'Sometimes it still hurts.' He lowered his voice and asked: 'Is she okay, Craven?'

'I think so. Yes, I'm sure she is.'

'She's got into some trouble?' He didn't wait for an answer. 'No surprise, huh? Like I was saying, she knocked my socks off. I wanted to marry her and the whole bit, and the personnel people out at the base, they really tried to warn me off, you know. They say they don't do that, but believe me they do their best to build a wall a mile high between us and these Icelandic chicks.'

'Why?'

'Why? Come on now. Why? Because all the local guys will go bananas if we take all the best girls. Because no one nowhere likes to have foreign military around. And because a few hundred half-American kids running around is the quickest way to screw up international relations.'

'All of which you forgot the minute you saw Solrun?'

He held out his open hands in a gesture of guilt. 'Almost forgot my own name. I wanted to take her back to the States. I was very, very serious.'

'So where did it go wrong?'

He examined his immaculate finger-nails. 'Guess I found out what I knew all the time really. About the others. The guys like you. She told me. I suppose I couldn't take it, that's the truth of it.' Once again he was raiding the breakfast table, loading his plate. 'Can I get you some more coffee, Sir? No? Okay. Look, Dempsie said I wasn't to hold anything back. She was screwing a Russian. It's true. A diplomat from the embassy. I loved her because she was wild and dangerous but, believe me, that was a bit too wild and dangerous for me. That's why I wanted out.'

Squared-away. That was the expression. And I could see it applied. He was clean and bright and all the things officers like to see when they open a barracks door.

'You used to work for your brother. In a muffler shop I think you call it?'

He spun round so that he had to hold the croissants on his plate. 'How the hell do you know that?' Then he began to laugh. 'You reporters really do your homework, don't you? Yes, that's right. Joe's got a back-street place, down in Jamaica. He does okay.'

'And Vicky?'

His eyes narrowed down and he stood there without moving for several seconds. 'Jesus H Christ, you don't miss a lot. Vicky was my girl.'

'Still is?'

He shrugged. 'Who knows?' Untroubled again, he went on

127

eating and waved to me to do the same.

I felt as though I'd strayed into a dream: reality was out of focus. This was Oscar Murphy. He had the same job and the same girlfriend as the one Jack Vale had checked out. He knew all about Solrun, he even knew about Kirillina. But Jack said he'd left the marines and was living in New York – and I was watching him tear a croissant to pieces. Somewhere, time and place had got seriously out of tune.

Then I remembered. There was something else that didn't match up, too.

'That about does it then, Oscar.'

'That it?' he spluttered through the crumbs. 'Okay if I finish this? I mean we eat well out there but this is . . .' He pushed another piece in as evidence of his sincerity.

'And it's been all over between you and Solrun for weeks?'

'Months. Finito. Forget it.'

That was my cue. 'So you don't really mind about her getting married the week before last?'

For one nasty moment I was sure he was going to take a swing at me.

One minute he was sitting pushing civilian goodies into his face and drinking coffee, the next he was standing in front of me practically growling. His left hand was resting lightly on my chest to get the distance and his right was ready to do almost anything except pat me on the head. His young face – once frank and friendly – was now frank and very unfriendly.

'You're gonna tell me real quick how you know about that.'

Delicately, I lifted his hand off my chest. I'm not at my best as a target. 'Yes, I am,' I said. 'But first you are going to unbuckle that fist and calm down.'

At that moment the door opened and Dempsie stuck his big happy face round. The happiness soon left it.

'What's the trouble, boys?'

'Would you go and leave us, Sir?' Murphy's voice was high but firm. 'This is private.'

Dempsie looked at me, worried. I gave him one of those reassuring looks and nodded. 'I'll be in the foyer,' he said. 'Don't make it too long.'

Oscar tilted his head towards the door. 'He doesn't have to

know about this. You got that?'

'He won't. Nobody will. Tell me your end of the story.'

His end fitted exactly the version Palli had given me. Although their affair was supposed to be over officially, they still saw each other and they still planned to go back to the States. She'd gone through the stamp wedding with Palli to raise money. Once again he made me promise not to tell anyone.

And once again there was only one thing wrong with the story. Palli – like Jack Vale – had Oscar Murphy back in New York already. Yet here he was.

'I wouldn't have thought Palli was your type,' I said, wondering if I could turn anything up by chatting around the fringes.

'That's what a few people said. He's an old meatball. He used to laugh at me because I'd made corporal on my first tour – and I'll make sergeant on this one. I felt sorry for him at first. He's had a bad time. So we used to take him back to the Marine House and feed him a few Buds or Polars because you can't get any real beer here. He even played on our darts team once. Hey, you're a Brit – did you know we've got the only darts board in town in the Marine House? Sorry – I got to like him. He's mixed up but once you get past all that macho shit, he's okay. Hell, he got married for me, didn't he?'

He laughed, and so did I. It was authentic, every word of it. Yet it still didn't make any sense. I wished I'd got Jack Vale out of bed again before I'd come, to see if he'd dared to risk his social reputation by being seen in Jamaica.

Dempsie was waiting in the crowded foyer. All his geniality flooded back as soon as he saw Oscar and myself walk over to him chatting and smiling. We were doing those awkward triangular-handshake operations when a thin young waiter came through paging someone. It wasn't until he called it out the second time that I realised what he was saying.

'Mr Oscar Murphy. Mr Oscar Murphy.'

His mouth open, Murphy swung to Dempsie to see what to do. Dempsie did it. Three strides took him past a group of German businessmen and he grabbed the waiter by the shoulder and almost carried him off to the corner by the lift.

They talked for a while. I saw him stuff a note into the waiter's hand before he returned.

'He doesn't know who put the call out,' he told Murphy. 'It was a phone call.'

'Won't reception . . .'

Dempsie shook his head. 'They never remember phone calls. Let's get out of here.' Then he remembered I was there. A ghost of the old affable Dempsie flickered through this new swift-moving, hard-talking version. 'Sorry, Sam. Got to move. Small problem. Catch you later.'

They went out through the swing door so quickly they almost fired Christopher and Ivan across the lobby as they came in.

'Your friends seemed in an awful rush,' Ivan said.

'That was your old pal, Oscar Murphy.'

'Really?' He pushed back his flopping wings of hair. He still looked ill and tired. 'I wanted to meet him. You're not doing one of those awful scoop things, are you?'

'Not if I can help it. Excuse me a minute.'

I went to the big window but I was too late. All I could hear was the drumming of the Triumph Trophy's engine as it moved up through the gears.

Someone had put the finger on Oscar Murphy. I had a nasty feeling it was me. There was only one way to be sure.

32

'Collect?'

In Jack Vale's mouth the word sounded like an extreme form of perversion. Come to think of it, to him it was.

'Did I hear that woman correctly? You're calling me collect?'

I began to explain that I didn't have much choice when I was using a pay-phone at the hotel, to save time rushing back to Hulda's, but by this time he was practically keening.

'Is this some new sort of interrogation technique you are employing? First of all, persistent deprivation of sleep, and then you hit me where it most pains every man of breeding and culture – in the wallet. Are teams of men waiting outside my apartment door even now, ready to rush in and douse me with buckets of ice-cold water?'

Somewhere in among this catalogue of self-pity I managed to ask him if he'd been able to get down to Jamaica. He had. He then began to explain, yard by yard, what a tremendous distance this was from Greenwich Village, by way of preparation for his expenses, no doubt.

'And of course there's the matter of all these collect phone-calls . . .'

'Oh, can't you go and sell a sporran or something. Was he there? Did you see him?'

He needed a minute then to get comfortable, find his notebook and light a cigarette.

'Now, your first question. No, he isn't there, hence I didn't see him. I told you he lives with this girl, Vicky. On his instructions, she'd given his brother this story about having influenza and naturally enough the brother had believed her. Which is why I believed him.'

'So where is he?'

'Right where you are, Sam. He's in Iceland.'

I was about to say that I'd just had breakfast with him when it struck me I needed to hear every single thing he could tell me. This was the heart of the confusion.

'From the top, Jack.'

'As best I can, Sam, as best I can.'

It came out in bits and pieces, some from his notebook, some scraps he remembered as we went along, and some in response to questions from me. And in one form or another I'd heard most of it before.

Murphy was an exemplary marine. He had made corporal on his first tour. He had got his wings flying helicopters out of Cherry Point. For his second tour he did come to Iceland and he was on embassy duty. Then there was the girl trouble. He was sent back to the States. He began drinking heavily. He bopped a sergeant one night. And the marines didn't want him any more. It was true that he was now working for his brother and living with a woman called Vicky.

When Jack Vale arrived on the doorstep with his Hibernian charm she'd abandoned the story of his having 'flu. The truth was that she was none too pleased about him going off to Iceland like that.

'He's not a big success out of uniform?'

'He's struggling. This Vicky, she's pretty enough, or she has been. You'd give her seven out of ten for looks and one for brains. But she's sitting there eating food out of a can and killing roaches with her other hand. You know what it's like: no money, no clothes, no pretty hair-do . . .'

'Your story, Jack. Why did he decide to come back here?'

'This Vicky, she says about three weeks ago he got a letter from Iceland. She accused him of writing to his old girlfriend – is it Solrun or something? – and he showed her the letter and then gave her a smack in the mouth. We're talking about pretty basic communication here.'

'They'd do well in newspapers. Wasn't it from Solrun then?'

'Apparently it was anonymous. That's all she knows about it, or so she says. Oh yes, and there was a photograph too but again she says he wouldn't let her see it. Anyway the effect of it was quite dramatic. Old Oscar went right off his chump. He said he had to go back to Iceland, and that led to a free and frank exchange of views. He gave her a few more smacks in the mouth, flogged his old Toyota and headed north. Does that make any sense your end?'

'Almost. He's been here how long?'

'About a week, I think. She's not too clear on dates. She's been mooning about weeping most of the time, hoping he'll come back.'

There was a pause then, and I knew that was ominous. Jack didn't go in for costly pauses, not when he was paying.

'There's one thing you're not going to like too much. He took some of his old marine gear, sleeping bags and so on, as though he intended living rough. He also took a gun.'

'A Colt .45 automatic?'

'That's the one. They call that model The Mule because it kicks so much, but it's the old jar-heads' handgun, so it makes sense, I suppose.'

'What sort of state was he in?'

'I wouldn't think too good. He'd been hitting the booze and popping pills, she said, and God knows what else she wouldn't admit to. Apparently he didn't want to come back from Iceland anyway, and he'd been under a lot of pressure since then. I think he's going to be a mite fractious.'

'I'll remember.'

'As they said to Mrs Lincoln, apart from that, how are you enjoying yourself up there? Are the girls as dazzling as ever?'

'Do you know Iceland, Jack?'

'I did, certainly. When you were a mere twinkle, my boy. I was there with the real military, the RN, just after the war. You couldn't get any booze, there was almost sort of prohibition then, as I recall, but the women. Och-la-la, as we Scots say.'

'Land of the Midnight Fun?'

'And then some. But I'll tell you something, your man Murphy wouldn't have got past first base in those days.'

'How do you mean?'

'They actually had an official deal with the US Government. They weren't too keen on those of a darkish hue.'

'Those of what? I do wish you'd speak English, Jack.'

'Blacks, my boy. They wouldn't let any blacks near the place.'

'You mean Oscar Murphy is a *black*?'

'Yes.' He sounded quite blank. 'Of course he is . . .'

I stood holding the receiver and not listening. Pennies, dimes and krónur began to drop. There'd always been one man too many, right from the start. The one in the kitchen at Solrun's, who'd knocked me cold with the pan. The one who'd set up camp in the spare bedroom at Palli's. The one who'd almost certainly have damaged hands from beating up Kirillina. He was the little Mr Nobody who did everything but was never seen.

He was half-mad, stoked up with jealousy and anger, and he was out there running around with a Colt .45.

Then it struck me. The chances were that he wouldn't take too kindly to people taking his name in vain. The man I'd just met – the white man who claimed to be Oscar Murphy – had

133

been publicly identified. That made him a target.

I put the phone down without saying goodbye. There wasn't time.

So far as I'm aware, no one has yet done comparative studies on the time it takes to bash a sodding great Vauxhall estate out of the way when you're in a rush. For those who care about these things, the answer is about three minutes if you're in a Daihatsu jeep.

But you have to be very bad-tempered.

Whoever had parked the Vauxhall two millimetres from my rear bumper would come back to find it three feet further north, and with its front several inches nearer the back.

It's always the same when you're rushing. As soon as I'd got out of that, I somehow took a couple of wrong turns and got myself stuck in the town centre. They were all there: housewives who hadn't been told about indicators, blind tradesmen in their vans, tourist coaches pausing to photograph every lamp-post.

Teeth gritted, hand on horn, I hopped from brake to accelerator as I fought my way through. Minutes clicked by. I had to get on the road out to the base. And all the time I was thinking how much quicker you'd do it on a Triumph Trophy.

When I did break free of the town, it was one of those days that demanded admiration. The sun sparkled on the apartment block windows in the suburbs and threw cheap glitter over the sea. You could almost reach out and touch the mountains. But it was all wasted on me. I had a nasty feeling that I was too late.

The tick-drum noise of the diesel engine didn't seem anything like enough, and I found myself rocking in the driving seat like a kid as I tried to will more speed out of it. If only I'd gone for a bonnet full of cylinders instead of four-wheel drive.

When the road narrowed to a straight two-car strip, I could see that I was the only man on the move. I was out in lava-country again. On either side the wastelands of stones stretched out. I was the only man on the moon, me and my moon buggy.

By the time I saw the car I was almost past it. It was about twenty yards off the road to the left, in a gulley nearly, but not quite, deep enough to hide it. It had plunged downwards and rammed its nose under a rust-coloured boulder the size of a small house.

I stopped, reversed, pulled in, and walked over.

I didn't run. The time for running was over.

I walked across to it, picking my way across the bomb-site left by nature's civil wars. All around the air was sweet and pure and silent, and the first thing I noticed about Dempsie was the way the sun lit up the brilliant jewels in his mop of black hair.

You might have thought he was running for Queen of the May if it wasn't for his face. It looked like an uncooked beefburger. As the Ford came bucketing over the rocks, he'd been flung through the windscreen and he'd ploughed up the screen with his face. That was how I found him. The smashed windscreen had provided him with the tiara.

But he was alive and, as far as I could see, the rest of him was undamaged.

I looked in the car, under the car, and around the car. Nowhere was there any sign of his passenger. There was no sign of a motor-bike either.

A minute later I waved down two US sailors and sent them on their way to raise help. As I waited with Dempsie, the blood bubbled on his lips as he tried to talk.

I leaned close to him. 'Who was it?' His lips moved without making a sound. I asked him again.

This time I bent right down to hear his reply. There was no doubt about what he said.

'Oscar Murphy,' he said. 'The bastard.'

I waited. The sentence that kept coming back to me was the one Dempsie himself had quoted from someone else – I couldn't even remember who: 'The greatest threat to the American presence in the North Atlantic is the interface between the American male and the Icelandic female.'

Dempsie screwed up his eyes and shook his battered head in some wild dream. 'Oscar Murphy,' he whispered again. 'The bastard.'

33

Kids are the urban vultures. Wherever they cluster, you'll find the action – even if it's only a comical drunk or a domestic punch-up. This time they were gathering for a kill.

At Breidholt, the uniformed cop in the entrance to Palli's block of flats whispered urgent threats and curses and even took a swipe at them, but it didn't make any difference. On bikes and on foot, they circled the doorway, yelping and giggling and firing their finger-guns at each other. Don't ask me how they knew. Don't ask me how everyone knew. Outside the square was too empty and the windows all around were too full of faces.

Petursson exchanged words with the cop, who then started talking to his crackling radio.

'Palli's in,' Petursson said to me. 'With one or two friends, according to neighbours.'

Neither of us mentioned the name. We were both thinking he had to be up there – Oscar Murphy. On Palli's floor, we waited a few minutes until two more uniformed policemen arrived. They whispered and one of them handed Petursson a gun. It looked like a .38 police special. He checked it like a man who knew his way around guns.

'One thing,' I said, also whispering. 'I didn't notice – was the bike outside?'

He spoke to the uniformed men, then turned back to me. 'No. It hasn't been there all day. Why do you ask?'

I shrugged. I wasn't absolutely sure myself. Even so, I would've been happier if it had been there.

'Very well, gentlemen,' he said, more loudly. He dropped the gun into his pocket. 'I do not suppose we shall be needing that, not for one moment. Shall we go?'

The uniformed men ran into prearranged positions. One beyond the flat door, one almost opposite, and one at

Petursson's shoulder just in front of me. Palli's door was open.

At a nod from the fulltrui, I called out: 'Hello Palli, are you there? It's Sam. Sam Craven.'

We listened to the restrained rasp of our own breathing.

'Can I come in, Palli?' I shouted this time. Then, at another nod from Petursson: 'I'm coming in now.'

But it was Petursson who slipped in front of me and began to move down the narrow dark corridor into the familiar warm scent of soiled bodies. When he was one step from the open room, Palli's voice bellowed: 'See ya, you sonofabitch!'

I dropped to the floor. Petursson tried to flatten his bulk against the wall and I saw the .38 in his hand and heard the oiled click of the safety. Maybe he wasn't going to need it but he wasn't taking too many chances.

Then I heard Palli's laugh, bright with glee and malice: 'Come on in, Sam, and bring your spooky pals with you. We're having a friendly game of cards, is all.'

So they were. On the floor around an upturned cardboard box sat Palli and two younger men. He held his hand of cards up as proof. 'I just said I'd see these guys and, you know what, they'd only got a lousy pair between them.'

Chuckling, he began to scoop up the few notes from the box.

I had to give it to Petursson. No officer of the law above the rank of ink monitor likes being mocked, and he'd just been made to look foolish by a bunch of street-corner comedians. But he wasn't your average cop: he kept cool and his big face stayed as expressionless as a paving stone.

He split the three of them up between the rooms in the flat, the corridor and a police Volvo outside. The other two were only a pair of trainee vandals. In no time at all their triumphant sneers had turned to shrill protests.

Wisely, he didn't try to pressure Palli at all. No cops had anything that would frighten him. He'd been places and seen things that put him a long way out of reach.

We stayed in the living-room. The baby clothes were back on the radiators again, so that a fine skin of moisture put a sheen on the furniture. Again, it was hothouse damp.

It was all very matter of fact. The girl-mother came out of the bedroom and dumped the baby in a plastic chair. It slumped forward asleep, and she slumped beside it in one of the mutilated chairs, watching us through half-closed eyes.

Looking pleased with himself, Palli sat cross-legged on the floor playing Chinese patience now that his poker school had broken up. He whistled between his teeth, breaking off to swear cheerfully when he pulled the wrong card, and swigging Polar beer from the neck. He offered me a drink from the same bottle, and winked when I declined. I knew why he did it: to show the friendship between us was still there.

After looking at the choice of resting places, Petursson put his hat on his knees and kept it there. And he sat upright to keep contact with the Olafsson home – if it was his – to a minimum.

'Your bike was stolen this morning, was it, Palli?'

'Now that's what I call a fine bit of detective work,' Palli replied to him. He whistled his admiration as he faked amazement. 'How about that, Sam? Only had the bike stolen this morning and here's Mr Petursson knows all about it. Don't suppose you happen to know where it is, do you?'

Without lifting her sleepy head, the girl said: 'He has been here all day. I will tell you. Those two men, they will also tell . . .'

Petursson silenced her with a movement of his hand. He'd been outside talking to the other two. He knew what they were all going to say. Nothing.

'They're telling the truth?' I asked.

'Yes. No doubt. Those others cannot lie for long. They are what Palli's countrymen call chicken-shit.'

'Beer?' Palli held the bottle up.

'No, thank you.'

'Now that's a shame. Makes me feel I ain't offering you real Icelandic hospitality. Hey, good news. Red nine on black ten, here comes the eight, dammit.'

'Where is Oscar Murphy?' Petursson kept his voice level and emotionless. He wasn't allowing himself to be drawn by Palli's minor dramatics.

Once again, he mimed wide-eyed surprise. 'My old buddy Oscar? He's back home in the States. You security people know all about that.'

'Why did he come back?' I took that one. It was less painful for me to look a fool than it was for Petursson.

'Has that old rascal come back here and not told me? Well, I'll be damned. You tell him, you hear, you tell him to come and see his old pal. There's the eight, knew it was hiding in there somewhere.' He glanced up grinning. 'Just like old Oscar.'

'When did he move his stuff?' I pointed over to the bedroom where I'd found his camp.

'What stuff?'

'Clothes, money, booze, cigarettes.'

He went on playing cards.

'Colt .45.'

He flicked through the next few cards. 'That's cheating, but I know you two won't tell,' he said. Then, looking down at the cards again: 'I don't recall Sam here going in that room on his previous visit – his only visit, do you, sugar?'

'No.' The girl's lips moved in a patient smile.

'So you're just guessing.'

He went on turning the cards.

I tried again. I don't know why. 'Who told you about the other Oscar Murphy? Someone from the Soviet Embassy?'

'Now we've got two Oscar Murphys. Are you sure you fellers aren't getting just a little confused here?'

We were getting nowhere. Petursson pulled himself to his feet and I could see where the weight of the gun creased his well-pressed jacket. He moved towards the door.

'That will be all for now, Palli.'

He looked up from beneath his colourless brows. 'Hope I've been some help to you guys.'

'We will, of course, find Murphy and when we have spoken to him we shall be back to see you. Then you will have to talk.'

'Why, I'd be glad to.' Palli was milking it for every ounce of pleasure he could get.

'The only thing that surprised me was the old lady,' Pete went on, in the same quiet tone.

'An old lady now, would you believe. Was she called Oscar Murphy, too?'

'I didn't think you would do that. Torture her by pulling out her hair, then letting her die. No, I didn't think . . .'

Palli went quite still and his eyes closed. 'Don't try and tie my name to that.'

'I was surprised, but I don't know why. It was the crime of a vicious animal, wasn't it? Are you coming, Sam?'

The girl had opened her eyes and was staring at Palli. 'An old lady?'

'Shut up, dummie.' He took another slug from the bottle of beer. 'You tell him that ain't true, Sam.'

'How do I know what's true?'

He got up and jabbed a finger at Petursson. 'You wanna know about that you go ask those bums on the Russian trawler down in the harbour, okay? Just don't tie my name on it.'

He followed us down the corridor. 'Another thing, Sam.' He was back to his chuckling triumph again. 'You got your nationality as mixed up as me. There I was thinking you were a true Brit and the guy down the corridor here reckons you're a German.'

His voice echoed after us down the corridor. 'Auf Wiedersehen, buddy. Auf Wiedersehen.'

34

Solo females celebrate their status. They gather in wine bars on Saturday lunch-times and swap notes on how to change plugs and what's new in rape alarms, and laugh scornfully about their enslaved sisters who have to wash shirts.

Solo males don't. It's widely assumed that they weep in dingy basements with only a budgie for company and pine for those little female touches, like a pile of smelly tights on the bathroom floor.

For some reason, it's an achievement for women, but a failure for men. Actually it isn't like that at all. The reason we keep so quiet about it is that we're having a lovely time: we're just nervous that pitying women will burst in and rip the shirts off our backs to wash them.

By use of a secret international code, Petursson and I had established that we were both solo males. It's not all that secret – you simply never use the word 'We'.

He lived in a cramped flat above a shop in Laugavegur, a long shopping street which runs right through the centre of the town. Some stretches look like a branch office of Bond Street, others more like an Arizona trading-post a century ago, and it's the only street I've so far come across where you can get an Icelandic-Vietnamese meal. The flat probably wasn't cramped before he moved in. But by the time he'd packed in huge chunks of dark gleaming furniture, presumably salvaged from some earlier existence in higher and wider premises, a library that lined almost every wall, a baby-grand that was more grand than baby, plus a high-security wardrobe to keep his hat in, and then slid his own considerable bulk through the door, it was cramped. Each of the three main rooms had a central clearing in which it was possible to sleep, eat, or sit.

Once you'd seen him at home you no longer wondered where he got such nimble footwork.

'Are you interested in food?' he asked. I'd found him in the kitchen, apparently unaware of the fact that he was wearing a full-length plastic apron cut and decorated in the shape of a half-naked hula-hula girl.

'I am, actually,' I said.

That was another tricky one. You had to be careful where you made that admission. Solo men who like food have the same problem as male hairdressers – people are apt to make snappy and inaccurate judgements.

'Then perhaps you can do these.' He handed me some peppercorns between two sheets of kitchen paper and a rolling pin. 'Ah, an expert,' he said, when I set about crushing them.

He was peeling broccoli stems which he then placed upright in a pan. 'So,' he said, obviously pleased to be able to show off a little. 'The steam cooks the heads while the water does the stems. It is quicker this way.' He took two quarter-pound steaks out of a dish of red wine where they'd been wallowing and dipped them in the crushed peppers.

'*A point?*' He slid them under the grill.

That was an expression you didn't hear a lot outside France which was where he'd picked it up. When he lived in London he did a lot of Channel-hopping.

He knew what he was about, too. When I sliced into mine I saw the thin line of raw meat in the middle. It was *à point* all right. And I wasn't sorry to see that he'd removed his pinafore before he sat down. Hula-hula dancers' breasts may well stimulate appetites but not when they're slung beneath an elderly copper's face.

We tried some burgundy, then some more burgundy on top of that burgundy and they got along fine. When the brandy went down to join them, it did no harm at all, so we sent off some more, with dashes of coffee in between. Two table-lamps spread light as thick and yellow as custard.

He told me he wanted me to visit Dempsie in hospital the next day. The American PR man hadn't got any serious injuries. They'd kept him in case of concussion and his face had been badly chewed up. When I asked why he wanted me to go, he repeated again his idea that I was there for a purpose. Had he some contact with Batty? Or even with Christopher Bell? I didn't know and he wasn't going to tell me.

'Do you really believe that Palli did that to Solrun's mother?' I was interested in his answer. If he did, he was a good deal dimmer than I'd taken him for. To my relief, he shook his head.

'I tried to use it as a lever. It worked a little. At least he told us what he thought.'

'The Russian trawler. I thought you'd inspected that and found nothing but fish.'

'Sometimes you can have too much innocence.' He'd assembled his cigars, lighter and ashtray on a table beside his heavy leather chair. I noticed that he aligned them exactly along the edge of the table. That was how he liked things: neat.

'What was that old Icelandic saying that Hulda wheeled out for Palli?'

'Oh, yes. Something about we cannot save those who are doomed and we cannot send to hell those who must live. It's a saying you hear mostly from the old people.'

He looked at me carefully through the smoke from his cigar.

He wanted to see if I was laughing at it. Luckily I wasn't.

'Which did she think he was? Doomed to die or to live?'

'What do you think? To die, of course. Here, have some more brandy.'

'Why do you think she said that?'

He pondered on that for a while. He'd put on some classical piano stuff – Chopin at a guess – and he cocked his head to concentrate on that for a moment. After that he replied.

'Palli. Ah, Palli. I was thinking more about what you said about him. I tried not to be the policeman, to see him your way. I think that is why I wasn't so hard on him at the flat. Isn't it clear why Hulda said that about him? He has the smell of death about him. Perhaps it is from where he has been or perhaps it is a part of him, I don't know. But it is there, without a doubt.'

He wrinkled up his nose as though he could smell it there in his own warm den of a home. We sat in a comfortable silence before he carried on.

'Loyalties. That is what we are talking about here. Loyalties. Where do you think Palli's loyalties lie? With Iceland? With America? Or is he a maverick, a mad dog to be shot down?'

'No, he isn't a mad dog. He doesn't have loyalties to any country because he's a man without a country. All he has are places where they don't want him. You can't grasp that because your roots go ten miles down under this lot.'

I tapped my foot on the thick rug.

'So where does this man place his loyalty?'

'If you haven't got a country, it goes to your friends. Who are his friends? One. Only one. Oscar Murphy. Everything he does is for love of a friend. That doesn't make him too bad, Pete. Not with me anyway.'

At that he sat forward. 'That reminds me. Why didn't you tell me about your meeting with Murphy? I had told you things. I trusted you. I hoped you would return the favour.'

'If I did, you would've swamped the place with police and there would've been no Oscar Murphy, real or phony. Has he been picked up yet?'

He shook his head. 'Who else knew about that?'

'Ivan,' Even in saying that, I felt as though I was betraying him. 'And that means the entire Soviet Embassy, which also means Kirillina. Very possibly Christopher Bell too, for what that's worth.'

He gave a mock hurt look. 'Everybody in Iceland except me.'

'Who was he? The man who vanished?'

'That,' he replied, tipping some more brandy into my goblet, 'is something I trust Mr Dempsie will tell us tomorrow.' He raised his glass. 'Seriously, I do owe you my thanks. You have told me about the real Oscar Murphy. Thank you.'

I thought of the way the police had appeared unsummoned on that first night. He'd known what that Air Crew badge was from the start. They'd been expecting him. They were looking for the ex-marine at Solrun's when they picked me up.

'I think you knew all about Oscar Murphy anyway.'

'Well, I will tell you this. I didn't know he was running around our countryside armed with a Colt .45. So I am grateful to you for your clever piece of burglary.'

He raised his glass again. 'And where do your loyalties rest?'

I lifted my glass to him and we held each other's eyes over the rim.

'With Dr Barnardo's, of course.'

He examined the ceiling in search of further evidence of my lunacy.

'I thought people who were raised in institutions needed the warmth of others around them?'

'Mostly they do.' It was true. That was why so many of our lads went into the Forces. It was also why they tended to make well-balanced citizens. 'But with one in a thousand it bounces the other way. You come out emotionally self-sufficient.'

He lowered his eyes to mine. 'So you won't be going out to Chelmsford, I take it?'

'No. Not a chance.'

'Like this country of mine, you are trying to be neutral in a world where it is not possible.'

'I wouldn't say that. Palli's neutral.'

'Palli is also crazy.'

'Why does it fascinate you so much?'

'Because neutrality is wrong. It is a form of cowardice. No, no, please don't take offence. I mean intellectual cowardice. Personally, it is merely tragic. Don't you feel this?'

Deep down in his half-buried eyes I thought I detected a sparkle of mischief. He was going to get me again. Like that afraid-of-the-past stuff. He led you on then, wham, he got you. A conversational mugger. But not me. Not again.

'I don't think it's tragic,' I said, slowing down while I looked for the traps. 'Not if you don't need to use other people as props.'

'There,' he said, flopping back as though I'd made some major admission. 'It is all a question of viewpoint.'

'How's that?'

'That's where we differ, you see. You say you don't need to use people as props. I was thinking how sad it was for people you might've propped up yourself.'

A large neon sign saying 'Mistake' lit up in my head, but I ignored it. 'Like who?'

He waved his hands to show it was of no importance. Then he answered. 'Like anyone. Like Solrun, maybe.'

He'd got me again.

I got him back, though. I watched him put the pinafore on again as we collected the dishes. 'You know, you're going to have to make your mind up which you're going for,' I said.

He gave me a puzzled look.

'Well,' I said, nodding towards his twin-barrelled chest, 'which is it? A face-lift – or a bra?'

As I walked back to Hulda's, taxis were dashing around siphoning people from the blocks of flats to fill up the discos. The old gods of war had been at it again in the sky – the clouds dripped blood all over the sea. In all its vivid horror, it brought back the memory of Solrun's mother with her freshly-plucked head. The thought stopped me in my tracks. I shuddered. The light night air went clammy on my skin.

It was all right sitting drinking brandy and swopping ideas about loyalty, but I was several fathoms out of my depth here. Unseen armies were locked in silent conflict of which I knew nothing.

With a swell of sudden fervour, I hoped that Christopher Bell was my lifeline. I prayed that the inoffensive Mr Batty, between sneezes, had made allowance for my amateur status in the world of spies. Why me anyway? Why had he sought me out to fling me into the middle of this dress rehearsal for World War III?

I felt small, ignorant, and incompetent. I looked up at the butchery of the sky and silently mouthed the wish that God, Mr Batty or whoever was admin. night-duty was keeping an eye on me.

Two would be even better.

35

Overnight they'd done a quick spray job on the sky. They'd taken the pattern from some minor public school tie – it was eggshell blue streaked with pale gold. The sea wasn't having any of that fancy stuff: it stayed surly grey, lightly topped with angry white.

The wind was back with us too. It tugged hard at the Daihatsu as I drove out to the base, and I saw that someone had moved the crashed car.

Ivan had caught me mid-shave that morning with a phone-call to say he'd filed a story, and I was glad of it by the time I got to the base hospital. It gave me something to trade with.

Petursson wanted me along. He insisted that I was central to his inquiries and he also pointed out that it wasn't wise to have stray newsmen wandering around unrestrained at a time like this. Dempsie wasn't sure, but he let it go when I told them about Ivan's call. I didn't feel bad about telling them. Ivan and I had agreed to let each other know before we filed. In any case, the Western embassies would pick up his story the next day.

He'd phoned from the Russian Embassy. I could tell that by his businesslike manner – no mention of leg-breaks, his favourite waiters, or even the heavy glooms. What he'd written was basically an Outraged of Omsk piece about the beating up of Kirillina. Professionally, that didn't bother me too much. I didn't think the civil rights of Soviet citizens abroad were at the forefront of Grimm's mind. If it was big enough to have a forefront, that is.

What interested the other two was the interpretation that Ivan had added on the end.

'Once more, please,' Petursson said, bending his ear towards my notebook as though he could actually hear my shorthand.

It was all about flagrant acts of provocation . . . an indication of the increasing fear of the US imperialists that the peace-loving people of Iceland would no longer tolerate their nuclear bases . . . fears that the Americans planned further barbaric acts and that Iceland's friends would not stand idly by . . .

'What next?' Pete said, looking at the American.

'That's definitely cue-for-song,' Dempsie said. He was sitting up in his hospital bed wearing raffish black pyjamas with red piping, and flicking through a clipboard thick with notes.

Vaulting through windscreens and a rub-down with volcanic rock was obviously his idea of a work-out. Despite the extra belly and chin, he was a real toughie. Cleaned up, his face was puffy and swollen and red with dozens of tiny grazes and scars, and his glowing charm had modified to a brisk bonhomie.

'Switch that trash off, will you?' He waved at the television in a far corner of the room. 'No wonder the Soviets laugh at us – we invent the most complete form of communication the world has ever known and all we put on it is cats chasing mice.'

'What happened?' Petursson asked.

'What happened? I tell you, I don't come out of this too well.' There was an apology in his laugh, but the Icelander merely acknowledged it with a sombre nod.

Dempsie began to protest, then abandoned it and turned to a straightforward account of what had happened. He and his colleague – he didn't name him – were driving an open jeep back from town when he saw the motor-bike in the rear-view mirror. From the stance of the rider, he thought it was the desert-bike, but he couldn't be certain. The next few seconds were confusing. There were shots. The windscreen went and one of the rear tyres. In the mirror he fancied he saw the rider holding a big handgun. Then there was the crash. From tyre tracks nearby, he reckoned that the rider, the bike and his colleague had all been spirited away in a van.

'Neither of you fired back?' Petursson sounded stern.

'Come on, Pete. You know we wouldn't dare carry guns out there. Not on your patch.'

'I have to be sure.'

'I know that. And you know I wouldn't do anything like that. There's too much at stake. I wouldn't louse up things with your boys.'

With a solemn nod of his head, Petursson came to the question he'd been edging around. 'All I need to know then is the identity of your colleague who is now missing.'

'Not Oscar Murphy?' I thought a little light banter might help things along, but Dempsie gave me a warning look.

'You know I can't tell you that, Pete.'

'But he is one of your . . . department?'

'I can't even go that far. Hell, you know I can't. You're running up against our own security here. See it from my angle. Come on. We understand each other, don't we?'

He'd turned the full force of his warm sincerity on the Icelander. All Petursson did was to frown and get up and walk to the window. Dempsie shook his head with worry at the unfairness of it all.

'He was a great little actor, I'll say that for him,' I said. 'I thought he was going to take a poke at me when I asked him about Solrun marrying Palli.'

'We figured you'd try that one,' Dempsie said.

From the window, facing outwards, Petursson said: 'He would have learned everything that they had on Murphy. He would have had answers for questions you never thought of. That man would have been so well-briefed that he could pass any test except one. A friend of Oscar Murphy, or Oscar Murphy himself. Or both.'

There was only one question that was bothering me. And, since neither of them had asked it, they must both know the answer.

'Why did Oscar Murphy come back?'

Dempsie shifted his gaze to Petursson who had turned from the window to face me. He's with you, he was telling the fulltrui. Then he looked at me again and the American's blotched and battered face changed.

'Doesn't he know?' he asked.

Petursson had kept his eyes steadily on me all the time. Softly, he replied: 'I am not sure.'

'I'm damned sure . . .'

'Coffee, boys,' Dempsie roared. A white-frocked nurse wheeled in a trolley. 'And BLTs. Jesus, am I hungry?'

That was the only answer I was going to get.

As the American ate and appointed me on coffee duty with an impatient movement of the hand, Petursson half-sat on the window-sill. He wasn't picnicking. He was on official business. Patiently, he waited until the food had gone.

'I must make an official request for your full co-operation. I am inquiring into a serious crime. I can appreciate that your security is involved but so also is the security of the state of Iceland.'

Dempsie waved his arms to show how powerless he was. 'Think how they're going to be laughing over this in Gardastraeti. You're giving it to them on a plate, Pete. You're letting them get between us.'

Petursson's face was slowly hardening. 'Don't tell me my job. You had no business to instruct your men to try to conduct some sort of operation off this base . . .'

'Operation? What operation?'

'Creating false identities and fabricating evidence to confuse people . . .'

'Only a goddam newsman.' He was too good a PR man to leave that. Out of the side of his mouth he snapped at me: 'No offence, Sam.' Back to Petursson again, he said: 'Have you brought in Palli?'

'No.'

'Why the hell not?'

'Because he has not done anything. And please do not tell me how to conduct an investigation. I want that name.'

'Sorry, sorry, sorry.' The American hauled himself up in the bed. 'Let's remember what this is all about, right? Fundamentally we are talking about a PR exercise. That goddam thing,' he flung his hand towards the television, 'rules the world. That and you news guys. I am telling you, if we're not careful, and I mean very very careful, we're gonna come out of this looking so bad we'll make Herod look like Mary Poppins. My man will have to take his chance. What you've got to do is to get to Murphy and get to him fast. If he reaches the girl . . . You know what that means as well as I do. If he gets the girl, a year from now you'll have Soviet Typhoon subs calling in here to pick up ice to put in their vodka.'

He studied his clipboard. Without looking up again, he let one arm flop on the bed and released a small sigh. It was a signal of defeat. 'Okay, give me two hours and I'll get you all you need on the missing American. But I'll have to clear it first. From Washington.'

'Thank you.' Petursson was at his most formal. 'You also see my position. If my political bosses ask for an explanation, I cannot possibly say that I permitted anonymous and unauthorised agents to run amok.'

'Fine.' Frost had entered Dempsie's voice now. He wasn't backing off any more. 'And you take mine on board. It isn't easy sitting on our butts while a crazy man rampages around with a fistful of .45. Great ambassador for his country he's gonna be. And don't forget, if the shit does hit the fan, we told you the minute we knew he was heading this way. Don't forget that. You had your chance to get the girl out. That's down to you.'

'He was already in the country when you told us.' Petursson wasn't being bulldozed either. 'We didn't know how near he was. We had to telephone her to warn her. How were we to know she'd go into hiding? As it was, he attacked Craven only a few hours later at her flat. That's how close it was.'

So that was it. Solrun ran because she'd been tipped off. In my blissful sleep, I hadn't heard the phone. Too much pleasure, not enough duty – story of my life. That explained the 'Bless' and the goodbye kiss. Then I'd walked in on Murphy when he was searching the flat, with Kirillina sitting innocently downstairs waiting for her return.

'As soon as we knew, we passed it on.' Dempsie smoothed out

the sheet before him like a symbol of the solution. 'Pull him in, that's all. Then we want him. He's ours.'

'That,' Petursson said, 'depends entirely on what he has done. Leave it to us. This time.'

Slumping down in the bed, Dempsie humped up on to one hip so he could read his clipboard more easily. The audience was coming to an end.

As we moved towards the door, he played his last card.

'While you're looking, it might help you to know that the Soviet destroyer *Udaloy* has anchored half-an-inch outside territorial waters south of Iceland. They're probably bringing food parcels to those bastards sitting in that trawler down in the harbour.'

He didn't look at us. He looked like a big black rock among all that snowy linen.

Petursson's face went even grimmer. 'Leave it to us,' he said, and marched out.

'Yeah,' we heard Dempsie's final word, 'yeah.'

Outside in the cool bright sunshine, we stood while the wind beat at our faces. Petursson put his hand up but his hair-cream was holding out all right. He was making regretful clicking noises with his tongue.

'What's a Soviet warship doing on your doorstep?'

He shrugged and sighed. 'He was right. They will be laughing in Gardastraeti. They put a wedge between us and we are stupid enough to let them do it.'

We began to walk over to the cars. I'd seen these two men, each strong in his way, collide mightily and each draw back, a little hurt, wounded, but still full of fight and pride. I wasn't absolutely sure why. So, quietly, I asked him if he had to force the issue on the missing American's identity.

As we walked, he held his head down so his words didn't get lost in the wind. 'Dempsie was right about that too. This is public relations. Not what is the truth but what seems to be the truth. Already an old lady has been brutally killed and a diplomat attacked. If it becomes known we have allowed American agents to treat our country as a playground, how do you think people would like that? How would they like that in Britain? I will tell you what would happen here. Even the most conservative of politicians would find it difficult to defend. Everyone would be shouting, "Go home, Yanks." I'm not sure I would not be among them.'

36

In London we don't have weather. Instead we have days when you can get taxis and days when you can't get taxis, days when you have to hurry to the pub and days when you can stroll. Occasionally you get glimpses of weather in those spaces between the buildings if you look overhead. But for the most part weather is something that happens to you on holiday.

In Iceland they've got weather and to spare. When I got back from the base, I decided to let the day and myself just drift around. I spent four hours wandering round the city, and the weather got me wherever I went. On street corners the wind mugged me, tugging at my hair and pulling my tie. Plump white clouds, like the ones produced by smiling steam engines in kids' books, would without warning be replaced by scowling, sooty-coloured clouds so low they almost touched the roofs. Then the wind and the rain ganged up to scare me and, by the time I'd found a doorway to hide in, the wind scrubbed the sky clean and my face burned to a sun that was unfiltered by city muck and dust. If it had snowed too, it would've been a typical Icelandic day.

I sent Sally a card with a picture of a guillemot reassuring her that conservationists need not worry about its future so long as it retains its flavour. Then I bought her something white and woolly to put in the drawer along with all the other untouched presents from Daddy.

I even went right over to Vesturbrun. Outside Solrun's block of flats, two men sat in a car smoking and waiting for their shifts to end.

I passed the sports hall where, on my first trip to the country, I watched a Russian and an American locked in symbolic battle over a chess-board. They made a great pair. One – handsome, fancy dresser, pleasure-loving, never far from a pretty girl or a gin and tonic, dashing on to the tennis court. That was the Russian. So naturally the American spent all his time bolted up behind doomed moods of wild black genius. Somewhere the casting had gone wrong.

The battle was still being fought but with different champions now.

Later, I sat in the shadows of Hulda's sitting-room and listened to her soft voice, as the wind and the light prowled round outside looking for chinks in the defences.

Quite out of the blue she said that she'd hoped me and Solrun would make some sort of couple. I hardly knew what to say. Weakly, I muttered something about only spending a few days together.

She soon brushed that aside. 'Many people spend half their lives finding that they do not like each other,' she said. 'So why shouldn't you find love in a week?'

It's one thing playing the cynical old seen-it-all sod with young reporters, but it's quite another with someone who's twice your age and seen five times as much, so I shuffled my feet and settled for looking foolish.

I was thinking about an early night when the phone went. 'For you,' she said. 'An American.'

It was Palli. He was in a coin box. He spoke in a hushed, excited voice.

'You wanna meet Oscar Murphy?'

'Again?'

'Don't be stupid, Sam. The real Oscar Murphy. My buddy.'

If I didn't, I was the only one. 'Yes, I'd like to talk to him. But why would he want to talk to me?' Finger-tips to the head was all it took to remind me of the pan incident.

'He reckons you can maybe fix him a deal with that Icelandic cop you're friendly with.'

I remembered Petursson's words. 'That depends what he's done. Anyway, what's wrong with the Americans?'

'He thinks he'll get a better deal off the Icelanders and the

Americans won't dare to change it.'

He could be right. It wouldn't have mattered anyway – I had to go.

I grabbed a jacket and a few thousand pounds in case he wanted a Coke. As I was flying out Hulda stood by the door.

'You are going to see her?'

'Who?'

'Solrun?'

'I wish I was, I can tell you. No, I'm going to see a couple of blokes for a drink and a chat.'

'She is up there in the mountains. That is where she is.' The old lady smiled towards the distant hills.

The lime-green Ford was in the square outside the Hotel Borg and Palli was at the wheel.

'Where do we meet him?' I said, as I pulled the door shut.

He didn't answer. He didn't need to. My answer was a forearm like warm steel that slid across my throat and then thumbs searching for the carotid arteries.

If I'd wanted to show off my classical education, I could've told them they get their name from the Greek word for sleep because the Ancients supposed that it sent you to sleep if someone blocked them.

My last vision was a stocking-masked head in the mirror. I did a few karate chops and judo throws all by myself in the front seat. They caused about as much pain as a fly's final spasm does to sticky-paper.

I sank into darkness. Those Ancients knew a thing or two.

37

When I woke up, I was sealed inside my own body. Blind. Deaf. Dumb. And paralysed. Yet I was thinking so I must be alive – buried alive inside myself.

It was a nightmare so instantly terrifying that I made a convulsive effort to throw it off, and then the nightmare doubled. This was no mad dream. This was real.

Panic rocked my mind and shook my soul. I was being buried alive in a black coffin which was pitching from side to side as it swung down into the earth. Fear ran like flames through veins shaking sanity out of my finger-ends and putting reason to flight. It was true. I was locked up in my own body and my soundless screams rang only in my own head. I was the last man on earth. Me and Johnny Cash.

Johnny Cash.

Somewhere, far far away, Johnny Cash was singing.

Now I know that the end of the world isn't going to be a lot of laughs for the likes of me, but even a vengeful God wouldn't hit me with Johnny Cash in my last moments.

Intently, I listened again. It was one of those prison dirges . . .

I could hear. Not much. Indistinctly. But I could hear.

At that moment the pitching to and fro stopped and the floor beneath me rose up, smashed me in the back and on the back of my head, so that I bounced upwards, and then fell back again. On cold metal. It hurt but it was worth it. I wasn't cut off from the rest of the world after all. For that relief, they could bounce me all day.

Consciously, I set about finding out what bits of me were still working and what they could find out about my surroundings. The cold metal was against my fingers. My arms were tied behind me, my fingers free. And I really could hear. All around me was a dull roar, partly vibration and partly sound. I could smell. Oil, petrol. Then I knew. I was trussed up in the boot of a car.

Right then we hit what must've been a pothole and I was thrown around again.

At least I could do something about that now. Hope surged through me, washing away the panic. I was lying on my side. All I had to do was to wriggle until my shoulders were against the wall of the boot, then stretch out my legs to the other side so that I was firmly wedged. Better, much better. No more bouncing.

And my legs were free. Free and working, what's more. Fingers, legs, at least ten per cent of my hearing – I could always be a disc jockey.

I started to work on that. It wasn't my hearing that was on the blink. My head was bound too. I stretched the muscles of my face to feel it. Eyes, ears and mouth were all tightly covered by some stretchy, sticky binding – probably that bandage they use to hold pulled muscles. My nose was flattened but I could still breathe.

Then I remembered meeting Palli and the stocking mask in the rear-view mirror. They'd trussed me up and hi-jacked me, and were now ferrying me over rough Icelandic roads, with accompaniment by Johnny Cash on the radio. Which meant it was the base radio because the Icelandic government would not risk corrupting their citizens with that rubbish, and for once I was right with them.

Where? Where were they taking me? And why? Was this how they'd hi-jacked the fake Oscar? Perhaps they wanted me for a fourth for bridge. Ouch. We hit a pothole four-foot deep and my head rang bells on the back of the boot.

That focused my attention on where I was. It doesn't matter where you live, one of our old Barnardo's aunties used to say, so long as it's home. For now, this was home. I braced myself again to get more comfortable. I tried again to work my hands and my jaw against the bindings, but always they slackened, then resumed their tight grip. Arm fastenings. Same there. I was tied so tightly at the wrists that I couldn't even work my fingers back to feel what they'd used. I tried to push my hands down to get my legs through. I couldn't get anywhere near, and every time I tried I got another bouncing round the boot. One thing was for sure – I'd never make a television cop.

Television. On television, bound victims back up against a saw-edged strip of metal and free themselves that way. All the time. Grunting and sweating, I manoeuvred myself around my metal tomb, feeling with my fingers for anything like a saw edge. I couldn't find any edge at all, saw or otherwise. I banged my head a few more times and that made me conscious of the pain in my arms and shoulders with being trussed so tightly.

I sagged back. Lie back and think of Iceland.

I ran through the who and why questions again. It had to be Solrun. They must still think that I knew where she was. 'They' being one enraged Oscar Murphy with a Colt .45. And my pal Palli had set me up for it beautifully.

Braced on my side again, my fingers were doubled up in the dirt in the bottom of the boot. Dirt and paper. Slowly I realised that my half-numb fingers were resting on a small sheet of paper – as far as I could tell, about the size of a pound note. A garage bill perhaps. A petrol receipt. A love letter. Who cared so long as it bore a name or an address. It took me about five minutes to force my arms up my back so that I could push it down the back of my trousers. But I did it. That made me feel useful. It wasn't an emotion I'd experienced for some time.

I must have faded away then. The next thing I knew was silence. After the bouncing and the drumming, it was quite eerie. Before I could begin to evaluate that, I felt a big hand lock around my upper arm and heave me to my knees. Another grabbed the front of my cord suit and I was hauled clear of the car boot. When they stood me on the ground, I was shaking so much I had to lean back against the car.

'He can't hear you.'

'Sure he can hear me. You can hear me okay, can't you?'

'There. I told you he couldn't.'

Powerful fingers tugged at the bandages round my head. He prised an opening over one ear and another so that part of my mouth was free.

'This is the guy, Palli. See where I got him on the head with the pan?'

All the time he was pulling at the bandages, I was trying to assess my new surroundings. The first thing I realised was that almost immediately I was covered in a fine drizzle, and the drumming of the car was now replaced by a great whooshing roar of sound that seemed to fill the background. Together they meant something but, with my head still echoing from the journey, I couldn't quite piece it together.

'Evening, Oscar,' I said, as I managed to free my top lip from another layer of bandage. 'Nice to meet you after all this time.'

'Manners. All these Brits got such cute manners, Palli.'

'He's cute all right. I told you he was.'

'Is that why Solrun wanted him? I mean, Jesus, he don't look much.'

'It's because I'm nervous,' I said. 'It always upsets my complexion.'

Suddenly I could smell his gut breath as he came close to me, and feel the warmth of it on my lips.

'You gonna be nervous, don't you worry about that. You are gonna be very fucking nervous. Nervous and cute, eh? I never knew she went for nervous cute guys like you. To me you're just a man who played around with my wife and that means you don't have no future.'

'She wasn't your wife.' I said that because I wanted to give the conversation a push from my end. I had to try to work out what sort of man he was and what his reactions were likely to be and I only had my hearing to go on. Reaction was what I wanted – reaction was what I got. I felt myself jolted forward as he grabbed my clothes again and I could sense his face an inch or two from my own.

'She was my wife,' he screamed. 'Palli was standing in for me. I asked him to. That was me she was marrying, not him. Tell him, Palli.'

'Like he says.'

He was still shaking me. 'She was going to get the money and come over and join me in the States. Then, Mister Goddam Smart-Ass, we were going to get properly married. With choirs and things like that. It was all fixed up. You understand that now, you cute little bastard?'

I did understand it. I understood a few more things, too.

'Then she upped and ran off with her Russian fancy-man, did she, Oscar?'

I was halfway into a flinch, waiting for the blow that would bring. Or at least another gale of stomach-stench and rage. I got neither. He even let go of my clothes. When he did speak, his voice was easy and pleasantly conversational.

'Maybe she did. Or maybe that's what she's planning to do. I asked her little Russian boyfriend about it and he wasn't too helpful. I coulda made him more helpful but Palli here said we didn't want to start no Third World War or nothing. Me, I don't mind.'

As he spoke, chuckling gently from time to time, he spun me round, holding my collar with one hand and sawing through the binding around my wrists with the other. Then he spun me back again, one-handed. In the jumble of new sounds and voices, I'd at last managed to work out where I was. The spray and the whooshing sound – we must be close, very close, to one of the tumultuous waterfalls that you find in Iceland where the rivers, swollen with the melting snows, crash over the rocks. I rocked around for a minute, partly at the novelty of having my arms free and feeling the blood rush in them, and partly at the proximity of tons of cascading water.

'So now I'm gonna ask you. I'm gonna ask you where Solrun's hiding and you're gonna tell me and we'll all be friends. Palli here says you're a good guy and I believe him, so naturally I don't wanna hurt someone who's a friend of Palli's. It's reasonable, you gotta admit. She's my wife. I'm looking for my fucking wife. Nothing funny about that, is there? It's not crazy or anything, is it? So you tell us. Okay?'

That did worry me. The careful control in his voice, the way he had to rationalise what he was doing, the insistence that Solrun was his wife, the way he tried to hold a line of logic . . . he'd gone. He was mad.

'By the way, Palli,' I whispered, when I reckoned Oscar was out of earshot, 'just in case I don't get out of this alive, I'd like you to know I do appreciate your efforts on my behalf.'

'I had to get you out of the house,' he hissed back at me. 'He was going to come in and carve up the old lady, too.'

By this time we were actually doing that shouting-whispering up against each other's ears to be heard over the crash of the water. When I'd thought I was next to the water before, I was wrong. Oscar had walked me about thirty yards – I counted the steps – over rough rocks to what I now knew must be the edge of the waterfall. Here the spray streamed down my face and my clothes were drenched. He'd gone back to the car for something, which gave me my only chance to try to lay claim on the friendship I'd built with Palli.

'Anyway, you said you were going back to the States.'

'I was. I am. I just gotta get Oscar out of this hole.'

'He's in a hole? Oh that's great . . .'

'He's gone nuts, Sam, can't you see? They were working on him back home, phone calls and letters, drip, drip, drip, until his nerve went.' He held my arms hard to drive home the urgency of what he was saying. 'Do what he says . . .'

'Do I have a lot of options?'

'Listen. Do what he says, play along, I'll try to get you out from under . . . you'd better tell him, that's all. Hey Oscar, what's the rope for – we're not having a lynching are we?'

His laugh was too sharp and too quick to be anything other than apprehensive. I didn't like the sound of that. Palli wasn't a man who apprehended easily.

'Your friend here's gonna tell me and we'll go straight up and see my wife. No problem. It's make-your-mind-up time, cutie. Where is she?'

'I don't know. I really don't.'

He was chuckling. Anywhere else you'd have taken it for good humour.

'Look, I didn't come up here for the air, you know. Solrun's got a summer-house up here. Hell, I've been there, man. But they all look the same to me, all this fucking country looks the same to me. I was gonna ask her ma but someone got to her first and did some asking. But you know. You've gotta know. Which one, cutie? Tell me which one.'

So that's why we were out here. He was right. She did have a cabin, somewhere near Thrastarskogur, which was near a lake on the road out to Gullfoss – if I remembered correctly. It wouldn't have mattered anyway. There were dozens and dozens of the bright little cabins. I'd no idea which was hers.

I thought perhaps Oscar wasn't paying rewards for information like that.

'Why did you come back?' I asked, by way of an alternative.

'I told you.' He sounded stubborn and peevish, for some reason. 'I come back for my wife.'

'That didn't bother you when you left her.'

'I didn't know the truth then. They told me she was a tramp, even said she was some sort of spy and that she'd been twisting secrets out of me and making me into a traitor. That's a thing I'd never be, a traitor. Palli'll tell you that.'

'That's right,' Palli said.

'Sent me back and got me kicked out of the marines. Yessir, that's what they did to me.'

At least I'd got him talking, and while he was talking he wasn't doing any of the alternatives. 'So why did you come back then?'

'I got friends, see. Good friends. They told me what was really going on. Soon as I found out, I came out here right away.'

I was so soaked that my clothes were sticking to me and the shivers were almost making my limbs kick out. What I wanted most of all was to see what was going on, instead of this imprisoned feeling from the blindfold. But the minute my hands went up to the binding, Oscar's snapped warning was enough.

'Why worry?' I heard Palli say to him, quietly. 'Shit, he knows who we are.'

'Because he stays blind, that's why.'

If that was Palli's preparation for a getaway, it hadn't got very far. That made me think of Christopher. If he was Batty's man, I thought, where the hell was he now? And the thought that someone else out there might have some idea of my plight gave me a chance – remote, but a chance. I felt I had something left to play for.

'I don't get it.' Even to me, my voice sounded bold. 'You know about me and you know about Kirillina . . .'

'Who?' He sounded sharp.

'The Russian.'

'Oh.' He relapsed. For a moment he thought there was yet another man and he was all set to fire up again.

'You knew she wasn't a faithful little wifey waiting for you to come back. It doesn't make sense. Why come back?'

'Because of things.' He sounded like a petulant child.

'What things?'

'I told you. Things I was told by friends. Anyway, that's none of your business . . .'

'Why're you tying that to the car, Oscar?'

I was trying like mad to piece the scene together. Oscar's voice had strangled a little as though he was bending over. And

Palli did sound alarmed this time.

'Don't worry, Palli. He'll tell me, then we'll be pals. Anyway, look at him, he's wet already.'

I knew then what he meant to do and I still didn't believe it. He was right in front of me again. His breath smelt like a stable at dawn. I held a cold nylon rope in my hand.

'Hang on to that, cutie, you're gonna need it.'

'Christ, Oscar!' Palli was up close too, now. 'You can't do that. No more killings. You promised no more killings.'

'He ain't dead.' He said it in the steady, reasonable tone of a man who is raving mad.

Then he gave me a push in the chest with his finger-tips. Any other time it wouldn't even have dented my shirt-front. Here, on the edge of an unseen cliff, soaked and frozen, with all my black terror trapped behind a blindfold, I rocked wildly. And all the time I was winding the stiff rope around my hands and wrists.

'Course you can always take a shower . . .'

'You don't have to do that to him. Let me push him around a bit. I know a few things . . .'

'One quick dip under there and he'll talk. If he comes up again.'

The two of them were talking in raised voices above the noise of the water and all I could do was listen. I bent towards their invisible figures and raged: 'I don't know. I tell you, I don't know.'

It silenced both of them. In a quiet tone, Oscar merely replied: 'Tell me that again in a couple of minutes.'

Then he pushed me backwards.

For a moment, I dreamed it was one of those kid's party games where you trick a blindfolded victim into thinking he's standing on a chair, and get him to jump. He's really on the floor, of course, so when he expects to fall two or three feet, he only falls an inch.

It's that old trick, I thought, as my foot went out backwards feeling for the ground. Only there wasn't any ground. I was falling.

38

In my time, I've done my share of falling. I've fallen out of bed, I've fallen out of love, and I've fallen out of a few pubs with a little help from the landlord.

But this wasn't the sort of fall where you come off a ladder. I'd come off the whole damned earth. It was spinning away from me, leaving me behind, and I was left like a traveller in space who's missed the intergalactic bus.

I couldn't see. In a way, it didn't matter now. I could feel the echoing emptiness of the universe all around me. I was back to being a babe-in-arms with that first and most primitive of fears – the fear of falling. There was a timeless moment when I hung out in space as though nothing had really happened, then the rush of air as I dropped. The thick spray of water that I'd ceased to notice suddenly turned into a torrent as I swung under the edge of the waterfall. The force of it caught the right-hand side of my body, then my head and chest, as it turned me more inwards, pummelling me down, down, down.

Like a leaf in a hurricane, I was tossed and tugged as the force of the water threatened to yank my arms from their sockets. I'd run out of rope. For the moment, I was at the end of my fall. Then the force of the falling water doubled and doubled again as I failed to move with it.

Somehow I'd set my arms ready for the brake of the rope, and my feet – acting on no instructions from me – had managed to find a protruding rock and instinctively kicked me out of the heaviest flow of the river. Even so, I was left hanging there, face up, feet against the rock, while the vast solid weight of the water avalanched down upon me. The rope burned across my hands. Every whisper of breath was battered from my body by the hammering waters, and there was no air, nothing to breathe. Only the water, crashing ceaselessly on to me.

Seconds. I only had seconds. Then I would be choked and

swept away in the torrents.

I bent my knees so that I sank further into the sheets of water, then sprung myself outwards. I felt the water spew from my lungs and sucked in streams of clean sweet air. And, blind as I was, I could've sworn I heard larks sing in the bright blue skies as I felt the relief, away from that pounding crushing power. Then, as quickly, I was back beneath the hammer of water again.

Knees bend, press, spew, breathe. Again. I don't know how many times I did it. To my surprise, I suddenly felt myself rising up through the edge of the cataract. I couldn't think why. I'd forgotten there was a world above me, and people on it. I hung on to the rope and rose through the water like a gaffed salmon.

Face down on the rock, I pumped up quite a few waterfalls of my own. Someone sat astride me, working my back. I didn't know who. It wasn't important.

'I think he'll be okay . . .'

'Sure he'll be okay, I told you . . .'

'Jesus, I thought he'd been blown off . . .'

'He's a cutie, you said so yourself . . .'

There was plenty more. I didn't listen. I couldn't take it in. But, between the eruptions of my own body, one tiny frail thought was beginning to take shape. I had to cling hard to it.

A hand turned my head sideways. 'Where the fuck is she?'

'For Christ's sake, he doesn't know, he said . . .'

'He knows. I can tell. So where is she?'

'He's damn near dead, Oscar. The guy can't even talk if he wants to. He's only just breathing.'

'He's in great shape. Anyway, I think I'll give him another shower. Shake him up a bit more.'

'Don't be dumb, Oscar. You said no more killing. He can't take any more. Look at him.'

'He looks fine. One last time, feller, then it's bath-time again. Come on, tell me all about it.'

'He can't even hear you. He doesn't know we're here. Let's drop him off at the nearest house we can find – if we can find one at all in this goddam wilderness – and if they get a doctor right away maybe he won't die.'

Hands went under my arms and began lifting me. I was sitting up. Apparently.

'Let me try then, Osc. Let me talk to him.'

'Okay, but if he don't talk, he's over the edge.'

A hand slapped my face, both sides. 'Sam? It's Palli. Can you hear me? Shit, Oscar, I think he's dead already. Can you understand me? Try to open your eyes, Sam. Come on, open up. Where's Solrun? He's dying, Oscar, I know it. He's dying.'

In a last spasm I threw a gutful of water all over Palli.

As I sank back, the words came in a hollow rumble all the way up from my belly. It sounded like a belch, no more.

'What's he say? Bush something?'

'What was it? Once more. Tell me again. Where is she?'

I belched and groaned and spewed another bubble of water.

'The *Pushkin*? The trawler in the harbour?'

I groaned again.

I could hear them talking. Boat? What boat? Russian. Spy-boat. What'd I tell you. Said he knew. Knew he knew. Take him somewhere. Doctor. The hell. Live. Die. Out here, who cares? Let's go. Doc. No doc. Finished. Waste of time. If he gets back. Laughter. Nowhere. Going nowhere. He's going nowhere.

Peace covered me. Pleasure like I have never known filled me. If only they'd said what they wanted. Good old Palli. He knew all along. I lay there, going nowhere, finished, and the only sound was the hiss and crash of the falling water.

39

Nature woke me just in time to be principal witness at my own death-bed scene. Or so it seemed to me.

It was the cold that snapped me into consciousness. The stiff mountain wind had almost dried my trousers, shirt and jacket, and driven the aching cold of the waterfall deep into my bones. I could feel my whole body shaking. My teeth weren't chattering – they were taking burger-sized bites out of the air.

Yet my mind was diamond-sharp. I felt as though I could solve the mystery of the world's creation and still go on to do the *Daily Mirror* crossword. I was that good. I was so amazingly alert that I even knew the alertness itself wasn't real.

But I still couldn't see. Easy. Rip off bandages. I said it again: rip off bandages. No one did anything. Right. Hand, I said, with more severity this time, rip off sodding bandages. Slowly, lazily, hand plucked at them. Fortunately, the soaking and the drying had weakened them and eventually they fell in a thin rolled collar around my neck.

My eyes flinched from the light. I clapped my hands over them, massaging them slowly as they became accustomed to it. I'd no idea how long they'd been bound. My watch had gone, ripped away under the waterfall.

As my eyesight cleared, I looked around. The sky was a uniform pale grey and the light was the pearly dream light of the northern night. It was still night then.

They'd dropped me fifty yards or so from the waterfall. I'd heard it for so long now that its thunder was a perpetual background. The river came down from my left in a wide smooth sweep which broke up when it hit a series of stepped falls, each ten or twenty foot deep. There the water whitened among the first rocks, fell into a deep pool where it slowed and circled, recovering its dazzling blue, then gradually inched up to the cliff-edge where it crashed in one unbroken cascade. From where I was, it stretched out in a pretty lace curtain that had nothing to do with the boiling spitting mass which had pounded me. Around it rose the spray, in glittering clouds. After the falls, the river ran off unseen in a chasm across the wide flat lava field, whose perimeter was ringed in the far distance by saw-edged, white-tipped mountains.

Around me were bare rocks, every shade from black to bright rust red. Beyond that, a few yards away, was a long sloping incline of springy moorland grass, with deep tyre marks showing where the car had gone. The nylon rope was on the ground beside me. It must've been fastened to the bumper of the car – which explained why I'd risen so swiftly.

That was the way they'd gone. That was the way I'd have to go, too. Somewhere down that track there must be a road, and a road meant tourists and traffic.

So. All I had to do was to get up and go.

Up we go, wobble for balance, step forward, one two three four, crash, down. Damned legs withdrawn labour. Sit up. Try again. Stand. Slowly this time. Better. Straighten, right foot, left foot. Knees like broken hinges, legs go again. Christ. Down again. In the mud.

Stay here. Lie here. Till they come. Aha. Trick. No one coming. No one knows. No one cares. Unwanted orphan. Always alone. Dying, on cold rock on top of world.

Legs, I said, move. Up again. Right foot, left foot, right foot. Again and again. Brow of hill. At last. View across lava field. Oh, my God! Miles and miles of it. Thin brown track runs in long straight line to base of mountain range. Road at foot of range. How far? Three miles. More. Hours of walking. Can't make it. Never. Never.

Next time, it was the heat that awakened me. Before my eyes opened I felt the hot stable breath around my ear and neck and thought that Oscar had come back to give me another shower.

I turned my head and half-rolled over. A pony, its black rubber mouth and nose nuzzling my neck, swung its head round and trotted off. Then I saw I was surrounded by them. There must've been nearly twenty of the rough-coated ponies that run in herds there and come down to the road for salt.

As I sat up, swords of pain cut into me and my diamond-sharp mind felt about as brilliant as a bucket of mud. I knew where I was all right. And I could see the line of the road under the mountains in the distance. It must be another two to three miles away still. Two or three yards I could manage. Miles, never.

Some of the clouds had shifted now and pale sunlight was painting the lava field in moss-green patches. The night was over. I squinted again at the distant road and saw a cloud of dust moving jerkily along its course. A car, probably taking tourists up to the waterfalls at Gullfoss.

I looked at the ponies again. What's good enough for an Icelandic shepherd is good enough for a Fleet Street hack, that's what I always say. You never know: they might be on a good mileage rate.

But first I had to see what shape I was in. Christ! I lurched up, feeling terrible. The journey in the boot of the car and the hammering I'd taken under the water had beaten every ounce of strength out of me. I felt like a cut-out-paper man – I had the general shape, but none of the substance. Still, I was – for the moment at any rate – upright.

The ponies had moved off when I got to my feet. Now I had to address myself to horse psychology. It was around thirty years since I'd done that with a little fat grey kept by an even fatter girl near Sevenoaks. She let me ride the pony if I kissed her in the stable. I was crazy about horses, so I did. It was my first conscious act of compromise and the first bitter realisation that nothing comes without a price. It would probably have been more acceptable the other way round.

One thing about her pony, she didn't like being caught. So I had to learn all sorts of subterfuges.

One thing horses don't like are creatures taller than themselves. Which is why they moved off when I stood up. But something low on the ground, like a smaller animal, often makes them curious. That's why they were giving me the once-over when I woke up.

Knees creaking, I bent slowly, agonisingly, to my haunches. And I inspected the opposition.

The one that had come to have a look was the boss, a big grey, fourteen hands or more. He'd trotted off with neck arched and his tail in a proud curve. Any other day I'd have loved to ride him. Today, with no bridle and no saddle and no strength – no thank you.

What I wanted was something small, dull, placid and safe. Then I saw her, Doris. I thought of the name immediately. She was a little piebald, black and white, and by the look of her she'd dedicated all her waking hours to eating. The basic design was card-table, flat-backed with a leg at each corner. She was just what I was looking for. And when I moved and the others twitched their ears and shuffled off, she stayed, nose down, hunting one last blade of grass. Doris. She had to be a Doris.

The problem was, how could I interest her? The second problem was how could I hold her? And the third was how could I mount her?

First things first. I looked around to see what natural resources nature had given me. Answer: rocks. I could knock her out with a rock and sit on her until she woke up. Ha, ha. I checked my pockets. If only I hadn't stopped smoking... shake a matchbox and horses are always curious. Ah, the car keys. They'd survived the buffeting.

Doris was already having a good look at me while she ate. When she heard the keys, her ears went on red alert and she lifted her head. Then she turned her head on one side. Did she like it? Was it worth coming over for a look? Or was she far too sophisticated for all that catchpenny stuff?

Not Doris. She came swinging over, not too quickly, but definitely interested.

As she came I pulled my tie undone. It wasn't much more than a damp piece of string now, but a piece of string was exactly what I wanted. I looped it round into a thumb-knot and held it in my left hand.

Then I jangled the keys again. I made those clicking and cooing sounds that I used all those years ago. I don't know about ponies but the Sevenoaks girl always liked them. On came Doris. Good as gold. Then, a yard away, she stopped. She stood there. Come on, old girl, come on, darling, come here.

A whinny vibrated in the air and Doris looked up. The herd was at the top of the bank now and just about to disappear over the top. The grey, acting as courier on this package, was giving her the last call. As soon as I saw he was going to whinny again, I began coughing. Not too loudly, not enough to frighten her, but enough to cover his last call and to distract her from the herd.

Then, without any encouragement, she swung down her beautiful head and pushed her nose into the hand which held the keys.

'Oh, you lovely big softie,' I said, and the soiled, stained, ragged neckwear officially authorised by the Groombridge

Cricket Club slipped over her head and tightened just behind her ears. I'd got me a hoss. Question was, could I ride it now I'd got it?

With pain springing in every move, I weaved unsteadily to my feet. Doris didn't panic.

This is the point in all good cowboy films where the hero grabs the horse's mane, leaps astride and gallops off. With most horses, if you tried that you'd be left with a handful of hair and the dying clatter of hooves as it vanished over the horizon.

But Doris wasn't an inch over twelve hands. Tired as I was, there had to be some way I could get on board her. I leaned against her, resting and thinking. She dropped her head and started casting about for breakfast and, when something caught her eye, she moved off a couple of steps – and down six inches.

She'd stepped into a gulley. Still hanging on, I edged my way up a bump of rock so that I was now almost looking down on the broad, black and white back of our Doris.

I could mount her easily from there. Except for one thing. I couldn't.

It hadn't struck me until that moment. I was far too weakened to ride her. I couldn't even begin to sit upright on a moving horse. I'd caught her, got her in position, and now there wasn't a thing I could do about it. I could've cried.

In despair, I flopped against her. She stood there, willingly enough. Then a thought occurred to me. Whatever the Pony Club might think, there's no law that says you have to have a leg on either side.

I put my arms over her back. Then, with a small hop, I draped myself stomach-down across it. At first I felt dizzy and couldn't get my breath because of the weight on my stomach. But gradually I got used to it. I reached out my hand and took hold of the tie and gave it three sharp tugs. At the same time I tapped on either side of her ribs with my knee and hand, to impersonate the rider's leg action.

'Walk on,' I said. 'Walk on, old girl.'

Now I don't suppose Icelandic horses speak English, but the tones you use to animals are universal. Doris, not in the least unsettled by this flopped-out wreck on her back, lifted her head and began to amble down the track.

My face was full of her coarse scratchy hair and the sweaty stink of her and I could feel her strong warmth rising up through my own body. She reminded me of a girl I once knew in Aberdare. 'I know I got a big bum,' Hazel used to say, 'but it's only so I can roll nice for you, see.'

Doris rolled on.

I counted every time her front right hoof rose and fell. When it got to a hundred, I began again. Time after time after time. I watched the rough lava and the green moss rise and fall beneath my eyes. I rocked and rolled with Doris, love of my life, and I'd have been going still if she hadn't pressed the ejector button.

One minute I was hanging there, like a western baddie being taken back to town. The next, I was flat on my back on the floor looking up at the sky.

It wasn't malice that had done it. It was hunger. Doris just chanced to see a tempting clump of grass, put her head down to grab it, and I was fired down the chute.

Well, I'd done it before, I could do it again. I pushed myself into a sitting position and I was reaching out for the cricket club tie, when Doris threw up her head, pricked her ears and with a swerve and kick of her fat haunches tore off back up the track.

I looked towards the road. It wasn't more than four hundred yards away. From where I was, I could see two coaches and one car curving their way slowly up the hill. Even I could make that, somehow.

If it hadn't been for the Triumph Trophy that came kicking and skidding towards me. Oscar Murphy had come back to tidy up after all.

And everywhere you looked, on either side of the track, there were gulleys, ravines, sinks, potholes and craters – a hundred places where you could discreetly tuck away the remains of a discarded diurnalist.

40

With a plummeting heart, I watched the bike come nearer and nearer. He slowed and used his feet to get around the potholes and the craggy chunks of outcrop. There was no hurry. I wasn't going anywhere. Five yards from me he stopped, bracing the bike on either side with his legs. He pushed up the stocking mask. The wide smile on his black face was the smile of a happy man.

'You know, you really are cute,' he said, in tones of some admiration. If I'd had doubts before, that cleared them up: he was bats. 'How'n hell you get so far?'

'I got a lift.'

'A lift?'

As his confidence wavered he began to look around, so I told him: 'From a pony. Called Doris.'

'A pony called Doris. I don't get that. English jokes, huh? One of those wild ponies?'

I nodded. I was lying back on my elbows. The day I thought I'd never see had come to life all around me. Above me the sky was a lively blue, the sea wind was as clean as a razor on my face, and I could see humanity hauling its cameras up the road to see the wonders of nature. I'd fought my way back to within sight and sound of the world, but they weren't going to let me get on board. The sooner he shot me the better.

Then my eyes half-focused on a shape somewhere behind him and I knew I had to keep talking. Whatever happened I had to keep him talking, listening, anything except shooting.

I pushed myself up on one elbow and tried to look like a good listener.

'You know, Oscar, I don't think Solrun was ever serious about that Russian.'

'You don't?' Even he gave me an odd look – it wasn't a situation for cocktail-party gossip.

'No, not really. Like she wasn't serious about me. She was having a last fling before she got married to you. That's the way I'd see it.'

I'd always thought that Marje Proops stuff was rubbish. But it certainly didn't come easy off the top of my head in a one-to-one situation with a man who was about to make it a one-to-none.

At least I'd got his interest. He was standing over me and, where his camo-jacket fell open, I could see the big Colt stuck in his belt.

'Once you get her back to the States...' As I talked I narrowed my eyes so he wouldn't be able to see where I was looking. My sight was wavering from all I'd been through and at first I thought it might be a mirage. This was no mirage. Bright blue anorak. Vast white floppy hat. Baggy shorts. Striding towards us like some ungainly long-legged knobbly-kneed old bird...

Outside an ostrich farm, there was only one other pair of knees like that. Bottger, the Esperanto-speaking German, from the flight out.

'That don't bother me,' Oscar was saying. 'I don't give a fuck about her no more. All I want is the kid.'

Then, even as salvation came nearer, he had my attention. 'Kid? What kid?'

The kid in the photo?

'Mine, who else's? They kept it from me when they ran me out of the country. These friends of mine let me know. That's why I came back.'

'You mean she's had your child?'

'That's what I said. She ain't fit to have no kid of mine. Tell you something, it's strange to find you're a father. Makes you feel part of things.'

He'd dropped down on his haunches now and there was a glow of enthusiasm in his eyes as he spoke. Over his shoulder I could see the tall German lumbering over some rocks.

'It changes everything. The whole idea of it. I mean, you wake up every day thinking there's a little bit of you out there. Makes you think about your own parents, and their parents, and instead of feeling like just one person standing in one place during the whole history of the world, you feel more like a part

173

of a stream, a moving stream.'

I felt sorry for this man who was going to kill me. 'Take the kid and go, Oscar.'

His knowing grin came back. 'I'll do that, don't worry. But I ain't leaving witnesses around to talk about it when I'm gone.' In a kind voice, he added: 'Don't be scared, cutie, you won't feel a thing.'

He pulled the big Colt out and snapped back the slide, and it slipped contentedly into his pink palm.

'Not just yet,' I said. 'I don't think the injection's working.'

'Injection?'

'A thing we used to say at the dentist.' I pushed myself up on to my elbows. He shuffled quickly back on his toes in case I was going to try to jump him. Jump him – I couldn't even have leaned him.

'Excuse me a moment, will you? Over here,' I called out, in a feeble shout. 'Over here quickly, please.'

He glanced over his left shoulder and so didn't see Bottger advancing behind his right. 'Don't fool yourself. They can't hear you down there. They won't hear a thing.'

'Ah, my friend from the plane. Why are you shouting?'

When he heard Bottger's voice, Oscar was on his feet in a second, his face wide open with astonishment. Bottger was then about thirty yards away, waving one arm as he called out and using the other to help him slither down a bank. He was so intent on that he didn't notice the gun. By the time he looked up again, it had gone.

'You have had an accident?' He looked from one to the other.

If he's pushed, I thought, Oscar will shoot down both of us. He had the camo-jacket closed over the gun in his belt and his face was lined with concentration as he tried to work out what was happening. I had to give him a way out.

'Broke my leg. This young American here was going to try to get me on his bike, but I was just explaining, I couldn't manage that.'

That was the door. The question was, would he go through it. I saw him look quickly towards the traffic on the road.

He was wondering how many more Bottgers there were and what it would take to bring them all up here.

Bottger, thank God, didn't seem to find anything odd in this lugubrious young black man standing there not speaking. Happily he went on: 'That is out of the question, young man. We must get proper transport. You were lucky this man spoke English.'

'Why?' I didn't care what he said. I only wanted to keep the air filled with normal, unexciting sounds.

'Why? It is obvious, is it not? If you spoke Esperanto you could have shouted for help. Helpu! That is the word if you need it again. Helpu!'

Without speaking, Oscar backed towards his bike, mounted it and kicked it into life.

'Young man.' Oh no. Bottger was actually calling him back. 'Young man, would you ask someone with a Land Rover or similar to come and help us. Thank you.'

We watched him roar and slither away down the track.

'He will not remember,' Bottger said. 'Young people today. No manners. It is the same everywhere.'

'You don't know a Mr Batty by any chance, do you?'

'Please?'

'Forget it. But if a sneezing man offers you a part-time job with history, tell him where he can nudge it.'

41

'I don't know how you stayed on,' Petursson said.

'That's what Hazel always used to say.'

'Hazel?'

'Sorry. Private joke. God save us!' I spluttered on a mug of soup that Hulda had brought me. She'd been having a lovely time with an invalid in the house. 'What's this – condensed polar-bear droppings?'

Even after ten hours' sleep I still felt groggy. As soon as

Oscar had got out of sight, whatever it was that had kept me going had snapped, and I'd collapsed. I'd stayed that way while Bottger organised transport and had me shipped back to Reykjavik. The doctor and Hulda had battled over who got to play with my remains. Inevitably, Hulda won.

I'd come round for long enough to tell Petursson what had happened. In another lucid interval, I'd found Ivan and Christopher sitting beside my bed. Eyes brimming with tears, Ivan had gone all soppy: clasping my hand and saying whatever would he have told Sally . . . he embarrassed half the island. Christopher, his gypsy face bright with relief, could only say how lucky I was to have chanced upon – or been chanced upon by – the ambassador for Esperanto.

The next time I slept a hot, troubled sleep shot through with dreams that were hardened with reality. I kept seeing Oscar's face, a hopeless mixture of sentiment and madness, as he talked about his baby. I could see the stream he'd talked about, with all the faces I knew – his and Palli's, Solrun's, the baby's, her mother's, even Petursson and the American, Dempsie – all floating in the water, mingling and drifting together, then parting again. And I couldn't get into the stream. I don't know how, but I was trying to dive in but one of those mysterious dream-powers held me back and I was crying as I watched it flow past. Next, I wasn't crying at all. I was being my usual arrogant self. 'As a matter of fact,' I was saying, to Ivan of all people, 'I never join streams. I'm not a stream sort of person.'

When I woke again, more rested this time, Petursson was back at my bedside.

'I could go for one of your pepper steaks.'

'Invite me to London and I'll make you one.'

'You're on.'

It was neatly done. For some reason, bachelor gents have problems with social preliminaries. I was absurdly glad to think we'd salvaged something from this meeting. I've always found friendship even trickier to manage than love because you don't have sex to fill in the blank bits.

'You must be quite a tough chap,' Petursson went on. 'That waterfall business wasn't just a whim, you know.'

'No, I don't. How'd you mean?'

'Sensory deprivation, dislocation of time and place, water, sudden physical shock . . . these are all established torture techniques.'

'That's okay, then. I wouldn't want him trying any unestablished ones on me.'

'You held up very well.'

The truth was, I couldn't remember most of it.

'I wonder where they are,' I said. All that high wild country, a population the size of Southampton scattered in a country as big as England . . . they could be anywhere.

'We are looking. He has always been one step ahead of us. At Palli's. And wherever he is now. Of course he is trained in survival techniques, he's got that bike, he's got a car and a van somewhere too. He got back to you so quickly we think he must've been keeping the bike at one of the summer-houses.'

Suddenly I remembered. 'That's where he thought Solrun was.'

Petursson shrugged. 'We're looking, but there are so many. Who's this?'

Dempsie, swearing several oaths not to tire, distress or upset me in any way whatsoever, was reluctantly ushered in by Hulda.

'Great security you've got here,' he said.

After saying all the usual things you say to people who've been pushed off waterfalls, the big American turned to Petursson. He only had to raise his eyebrows. Pete only had to shake his head. There was only one question anyone cared about now.

'You're still watching the trawler?' he said to Petursson, and was answered with a curt nod.

He sat examining his shoes for a while. He was strangely festive in all the bright pastel shades of the golf course that seemed to be his style. Pete, stiff in his spotless tweeds, looked formal beside him. Then I suddenly realised. The Icelander hadn't got his hat.

'What's happened – your hat?'

'Don't worry,' he said, thinking I was pulling his leg. 'Hulda is keeping an eye on it for me.' Then I understood: it must be something of an office joke for him to catch on so quickly.

'You know that destroyer they've got sitting on the twelve-mile limit?' Dempsie's voice wasn't much more than a growl. 'They've got two Helix choppers on board.'

'That is not so surprising.' Petursson looked uncomfortable.

'That means they can be on the island inside fifteen minutes and maybe that will be surprising,' Dempsie snapped. Then he sat back and slapped his belly twice. 'Look, Pete, for Christ's sake. I'm not sitting on your tail on this.'

'I hope not.'

'But these guys are going to pull a big stroke. It's all building up for one. There was the business of Kirillina and the girl, there's the trawler down in the harbour with those two ghouls on board, and now we've got a Soviet destroyer parked outside the front door with a couple of helicopters warmed up and ready to go. And all we know for sure is that Oscar Murphy's out there on the rampage and we don't know where.'

'He is an American,' Petursson reminded him, quietly.

They were into all that again, each furiously flying his own flag. I was glad that I'd never got around to developing team spirit.

That reminded me of my dream about the stream, and I was puzzling over that when I saw that Hulda had put all the contents of my pockets on the bedside-table while she tried to rescue the remains of my precious cord suit. And in amongst the pile – the keys I'd used to catch Doris and the rest – was a piece of paper with writing that didn't look like mine.

I picked it up. It was an Icelandic bar bill. The writing on the front, in ink, had gone into a blue smear where it had been soaked and dried. The writing on the back, in pencil, was almost legible. Then I remembered. I'd pushed it into my pocket when I was in the boot of the car.

It looked like two columns of figures, each one crossed out, and it was familiar in a way I couldn't place.

'Did you know about this kid?' Dempsie was asking Petursson.

'No. It was a very well-kept secret. Hulda tells me – now of course – that many people did know but they kept it from people like me, naturally.'

'For the same reason as the marriage?' I asked.

'Yes. They thought she wouldn't be allowed to become Miss World. Here, of course, there is no shame about that. It has been a custom for many years for girls to have babies before they marry. Her mother used to look after it. That's why she was tortured – by people looking for the child.'

Even the thought of that made me feel sick. 'By Murphy?' I asked. It had to be him, I supposed, but I still couldn't see it. In his heart he was still a soldier, and that wasn't soldier's work.

I saw Petursson's eyes slide across to Dempsie, then back to me.

'No. Not Oscar. You've forgotten, haven't you?'

'What the neighbour said. The old lady with the brush. She said two men in dark clothes like uniforms, and a third man.'

This time it did sink in. The two men in dark clothes had to be the military blokes off the Russian trawler. So who was the other man? The two of them sat looking at me as I repeated the question to them.

'We kinda hoped you might tell us,' Dempsie said, gently.

Both their faces were turned to me, waiting. I knew what they meant. I'd known all along. Only it was something I chose not to think about. People pick their own loyalties.

There were so many other things jumbled in my mind after the chaos of the last few hours. Trying to find them and haul them up into the daylight was like fishing in mud. And I was tired, tired. Even the sky's light flooding in through the unguarded window couldn't keep sleep away.

42

As they say in the Bible, she came to me in a dream.

The first I knew was the ice-hard touch of her cheek against my burning flesh, the cold marble of her hands against mine. I dragged my eyes half open.

She was beside me, sitting on the bed. She was wearing – I think – a padded white jacket and a loose white scarf. I hardly noticed because I was fascinated by the way the lifeless light of the night had drawn all the colour and vigour from her, so that she was blanched to a bloodless beauty. She was the Ice Maiden.

Yet at the same time I knew that it was only the gruelling ordeal I had been through, together with the doctor's drugs, that freed my imagination to see her in this form. I was back in the car boot, locked inside my own skull. I was pounded under the waterfall. I was rocking to the rhythms of Doris, the horse. Whether she was real or not was of no importance. She was here, at least in my mind she was here, and that was all that mattered.

'I had to come.'

'Thanks. I'm glad.'

'You know about my baby now.'

'Yes.'

'Asta. She is called Asta. My mother's name was Asta.'

'Have you been in hiding?'

In the half-light I saw her give a quick sharp nod. 'It was Oscar. I was afraid what he might do.'

'He thought you were going to join him in the States. You know, because of marrying Palli and the stamp money.'

'Maybe I was. Maybe I still am. Isn't that where everyone wants to go – America? In any case, I had to have the money for a new life.'

'So that was it. The two men. Oscar and Nikolai. America and Russia.'

I could feel her cold fingers tightening and slackening around my hand. I felt there was more meaning in that than in the words which were echoing like gongs in my head.

'Or London,' she said, in a whisper so low it hardly rippled the night's quiet surface.

'London?'

She moved so that she bent down a little towards me. 'Yes. That was why I had to make sure you knew about the child.'

Then I remembered. I remembered what she'd said that first night, when she'd asked me if I would take her away. But she knew how useless I was with my own kid, let alone other people's, so she was making it quite clear.

'If you want to get out of this mess, then come to London.' I was sorry I couldn't drive my enthusiasm into my words. But I was tired and, perhaps, a little afraid. Then, weakly, I added: 'While you work out what you want.'

'I want a home and a father for my daughter.'

I didn't know what to say to that. A silence like a wall stood between us. 'What does Nikolai say?'

I felt more than saw her shoulders slump a fraction and thought I could hear defeat in her voice. 'Kolai? He said he was going to defect to live in Europe with me. Now he says it is not possible. I must go to Moscow.'

'And Asta?'

'He is a kind man. He says he will be her father. I think he means it. But if I go with him I will have to do certain things.'

'What things?'

She rose and walked over to the window and I saw the light, pale on her hair and the planes of her face. She looked out of the window, speaking at the same time. 'Propaganda things. There will be a ceremony. A public ceremony. They want you to come. Will you?'

'Why me?'

'They want a neutral observer. A journalist to write about it. Will you?'

'Yes, of course.'

'You understand?' She turned towards me again. 'That is the price I have to pay to go there. I have to say certain things. You do understand?'

'Don't worry.'

'It is all arranged. They have been ready for days now.'

'Weren't you sure what you wanted?'

She came back down the room towards me and took my hand again. 'No. I knew what I wanted. Asta's father.'

I thought of the big crazy man running around the island on his desert-bike waving his Colt .45, and there didn't seem much I could say. Anyway, it was her decision. It had to be hers. So I said nothing.

'Will you come to me, if I send a message?'

'Yes, I'll come.'
'I may need a friend.'
'I'm your friend.'

I lay there like a dreaming corpse. She sat like a colourless ghost. After some more time had died, she burned me with her iced lips. I had drifted back to sleep again when I heard her last word . . .

'Bless.'

As the door closed, a thin shaft of light swung across the room. It caught one evil eye, mocking me from the table-top. Stuffed puffins never sleep.

43

Conscience, the best early-morning alarm in the business, was off the mark sharp the next day. At six o'clock I was wide awake. And sleep, who's got this name for delivering solutions to problems under plain cover, for once lived up to his reputation.

I knew what the columns of figures on the back of the bar-bill were.

Petursson wasn't all that delighted to be woken up at that time – but he was when I began to tell him. He promised to pick me up in an hour.

Hulda emerged from the kitchen with coffee. Or one of the several Huldas who appeared on round-the-clock duty in this house, and it seemed as good a time as any to check up on my dream.

I had no problem in remembering it. In many ways it was like an enhanced form of reality. But I'd suffered so much mental confusion from the moment I'd awakened in the boot of the car that I didn't know if I could trust my own perceptions any more.

'Do you lock up at night, Hulda?' I asked.

'Most nights, yes. The young people today . . .'

Her purple-veined hand rose and fell in despair at the decline of youth.

'Did you last night, Hulda?'

'No.' That was all. No. She sat, her hands now linked in her lap, shoulders back, chin up. I'd reached the Please-Proceed-With-Caution sign.

'The door was open all night?' She gave one firm nod to that.

'Why?'

'Sometimes,' she said, rising to fetch more coffee, 'I lock the door, and sometimes I do not. Last night I did not. That is all.'

That was it. She could be a bit other-worldish sometimes, could Hulda, and this was obviously one of them. The Icelanders like a bit of the old mystic and cryptic. Solrun had been doing it in my dream – if it was a dream: in recollection, the conversation sounded like a *Times* crossword on a bad day.

As Hulda was halfway through the door, I thought of a question she might answer. Now.

'You know Solrun's baby?'

'Yes.'

'Do you know what they call it?'

'Yes. It is called Asta. After her mother.' With a flick of her long black skirt she slipped down the dark passage to the remoter regions of the kitchen. Anyone with any more trick questions could follow her down there – if he dared.

As I was waiting for Petursson, the phone went. It was Christopher.

'Did you say it was that Esperanto chap Bottger who found you?' he asked, after apologising for ringing so early.

'That's right.'

'You wouldn't happen to know where he's staying – I'm rather anxious to get in touch with him.'

'I don't think he'll need an interpreter.'

'What? Oh no, quite. No, I thought his Esperanto contacts might help me get the old musical loo thing off the ground. It's really not taking at all you know.'

I told him I didn't know for sure but I'd got the impression that he was camping somewhere up country. Before I had time to gauge his reaction, I heard Petursson's horn tooting outside.

At the entrance to Thingholtsstraeti, two uniformed cops waved our car straight through. We were expected.

The Marine House – three white-washed storeys of bed-sits, lounge, bar, television and games that's home for the marines on embassy duty – was buzzing with action. The door with the peephole in it was wide open. With an air of brisk urgency, several young men were bringing out loaded boxes and taking in photographic gear. They were all under thirty, they all had cropped hair, and they all had problems fastening their sports jackets over their chest development.

'I think you are right,' Petursson said, examining the limp piece of paper. 'Once or twice in London I played darts, and I remember this strange upside-down way of scoring.'

Why I hadn't recognised it immediately, I'll never know. The two columns began at three hundred and one and the numbers gradually whittled away until they came to the final dart. I can't think of any other game where they score from the top like that. And the only dartboard in town was the one in the Marine House basement bar.

In the bar, three young marines – two in pyjamas, one huddled in a striped-cotton robe – were lined up in front of Dempsie. He had one heavy haunch propped on the edge of the pool table. He was still in golf gear – powder-blue slacks, dark-blue sports shirt – but there was nothing playful in his manner.

'Later,' he snapped at a sharp-suited man who had to be something from the embassy and who'd apparently been rolling out the threats to the three young men. 'Right now I want to hear them talk.'

The one who'd got stuck with the spokesman's job had ginger hair and freckles – and a face blood-red with guilt. But he was trying hard to be a good marine and take it on the chin.

'Like we said, Sir, we felt sorry for him. I knew him from his last tour and he was a real squared-away guy then, so when he said he'd nowhere to sleep . . .'

At that the sharp-suit hissed: 'What about embassy security?'

Dempsie silenced him with one flap of his hand. 'Security's

my game and I play anywhere I want. Go on, kid.' He took a cigarette from the pack with his lips.

'He came in with us, then later he said he had to see a friend and the way he said it I took it he meant this girl. I heard some bumping around later on but I didn't think anything of it...'

'You didn't see him bring anyone else into the building?'

'No, Sir. I told him to take Gary's room because he was away fishing and naturally Oscar knew which room was which and didn't need showing around or anything like that.'

'He'd gone the next morning?'

'Yes, Sir. Just that note saying thanks fellers or something, and we didn't have any reason to go into the room until you came this morning. Look, Sir, if...'

The dartboard was on the wall behind him. I went round and picked up the darts. One, two, three, just like that. They all missed the board. Darts is like riding a bicycle. Once you can't do it, you never forget.

'And you've no idea where he's gone?'

'None, Sir.' The red-head gulped and his Adam's apple bobbed. 'We didn't like to think of the guy sleeping rough, was all, Sir.'

'All grunts together, hey?' As the man in the suit started to interrupt, Dempsie cut him down. 'Hell, we teach 'em to be a team, don't we?'

'How was he?' I asked.

'You mean health-wise?' the embassy man said, incredulously.

'No. His mood.'

The marine was grateful for a distraction. 'Well, Sir, we all thought he was kinda spooky. He kept laughing but it was that uptight sort of laughing.'

'You'd better see this.' Dempsie led us up two flights of stairs. On the way he called out to us over his shoulder. 'Question: Where'd you hide a big black in a country like this? Answer: The one place where he wouldn't stand out. Here. He must've found it tricky getting in and out of Palli's, so he rolled up here. Then, if he moved at night and kept his face covered with that stocking mask and goggles – no problem.'

At the top of the flight, he stopped. I think we both knew

what to expect. It was a light airy room with white built-in cupboards, wardrobes, and dressing-table units. Hi-fi and video equipment was stacked waist-high next to a turntable and television set. Bar-bells and sets of weights were arranged neatly by the window. Over a chair by the bed hung a dark green sweat-shirt bearing the slogan, 'This is a herpes-free zone', above a down-pointing arrow.

On the bed, his head raised on a pillow, his arms folded across his stomach, was the man I'd interviewed as Oscar Murphy. You might've thought he was resting there if it hadn't been for the hole where his right eye should've been. That's the way the pro's do it. It would look quite neat if you didn't have to dislodge the eyeball.

The ID propped on his hands made him Roddy Hermon of the Naval Investigative Service.

'Not public relations?' I said to Dempsie.

'Same thing,' he growled. 'Same damn thing.'

When I got back to Hulda's, I stood looking at my bed in the hope of some sign that Solrun really had been my night visitor. I don't know why. As soon as Hulda had confirmed the baby's name was Asta, I knew I hadn't been dreaming.

Unless, of course, I was developing a talent for clairvoyant dreams, and after my experiments with meditation that didn't seem too likely.

So what was it she'd said about a ceremony? Try as I could, I couldn't make any sense out of that fragment. I was lying on the bed trying to dredge my memory when I saw the puffin watching me. With its cocked head and glinting eye, it looked to me like a puffin that knew too much. I pulled a sock over its head. And it wasn't a clean sock either.

A ceremony. A public ceremony. It was the price for something, she'd said, but I was damned if I could remember what.

I was quite glad when there was a tap at the door and Christopher Bell came in. He was wearing his usual cosy clutter of jumble-sale rubbish and his thick black hair was hanging down so that only one bright eye showed.

'You know, Christopher, either you're growing to look like

those bloody puffins or . . .'

'Quite possibly,' he said, not at all affronted. 'Get the old hooter painted and I'll be in business, I dare say. Although, come to think of it, I shouldn't think my beak's straight enough.'

'How'd you get it?' I'd been wondering that since we met.

He tapped it with a knuckle and grinned. 'Awful, isn't it? Trouble is, I've got this high threshold of pain. Bust it in the first ten minutes playing scrum-half for Cambridge, didn't realise, and went on and played the whole damned game. Terrible mess.'

'Well, I've got this high threshold of nerves and that bird of yours was giving me the evil eye. Hence the sock.'

'Poor little chap. No word from Solrun, I don't suppose?'

'Not a cheep.'

'Actually,' he said, drawing the word out to four times its normal length, 'actually, I believe old Ivan's scooped you. Isn't that what you chaps call it?'

'I call it a damned nuisance,' I said, wondering if it was anything that might bounce back on me. 'You wouldn't happen to know what it is?'

'Well, I was wondering about the ethics of that,' he said, his dark face gleeful at all this mystery.

'The ethics are that you tell me about Ivan's stories, but not the other way round. How does that sound?'

Nothing would've stopped him anyway, he was so pop-eyed with the fun of it all. He'd called at Ivan's room and found the door standing ajar. And he had somehow been unable to prevent himself hearing what Ivan was saying down the telephone.

A man had been found dead in the Tjornin.

'Name?'

'Heavens, Sam, I wasn't eavesdropping, you know.'

'I know, and while you weren't eavesdropping you didn't happen to hear any more, did you?'

A crafty grin curved under his crooked nose. 'All Brits together, eh? I did actually. He said something about it being linked to an attack on a Russian embassy official. Does that mean anything to you?'

'Something. I'm not quite sure what, that's all.'

'My nephew Matt keeps his in his study at Eastbourne College.'

I looked up wondering what on earth he was talking about. He was stroking the puffin's back. 'He finds it restful,' he said, with a gap-toothed smile.

'Anything else?'

'Yes, sort of. He seemed to be suggesting that this person had met a violent end.'

'Whoever he was, he was in step with the spirit of our times,' I said, sitting up and reaching for my jacket. 'I think I'll go and take a look.'

'Can I come?'

'Why not? By the way,' I said, as casually as I could manage, 'I didn't know you counted Russian in your apparently endless repertoire of languages.'

'Only a smidgin,' he said, apologetically. 'Only about the-pen-of-your-aunt level.'

The bird didn't say a word as we left. If it had, Christopher would probably have replied. In fluent puffin.

I'd always had my doubts about him. Now I was beginning to assemble an entirely new set . . .

44

All that was left at the lakeside was a wet patch on the pavement where they'd dragged the body out. But there were still some loitering spectators around, and still with that slightly festive air that sudden death often inspires in people.

I was just thinking we were too late when I spotted a lanky youth from the local morning paper. Luckily, he was familiar with the pass-it-on principle that governs most media work.

'Found by a workman early this morning,' he said, flipping

through the pages of a notebook the size of a gravestone. 'Police called. Ambulance. Body recovered and identified. Are you the journalist from London?'

'That's right. Identified, did you say?'

'Any chance of me getting a job there?'

'Not a chance.'

'Why not?'

'You look honest, intelligent and you can probably spell. Who was the drowned bloke?'

'Everyone knows him around town. He was a bit of a hoodlum, as the Americans say. In a small way. They recognised him as soon as they saw the tattoos on his arms.'

'Palli? It was Palli?'

'Yes, Palli Olafsson.' He was surprised I knew him. 'He was a friend?'

'In a way, I think he was.'

'And was he drowned?' It was Christopher who asked that question. Either it was a very silly question, when a body has just been heaved out of several thousand gallons of water, or an unusually clever one. By the look on this chap's face, it wasn't so foolish.

'I heard them talking,' he said. 'They are not so sure.' He pointed across town, past where the Hallgrimskirkja's new tower soared to the skies. 'They've taken him to the mortuary.'

I set off back to the jeep when he grabbed my arm. 'Don't say I told you,' he said out of the side of his mouth, like real reporters do, 'but his fingers – ugh, they were a horrible mess.'

Much against his wishes, I dropped Christopher at his hotel. I was beginning to think he couldn't be Batty's man, or he would surely have identified himself to me by now. And if he wasn't, then whose man was he?

I drove straight round to the state hospital which also doubles as the medical school and the mortuary. Standing in the doorway was Petursson. As he saw me, he shook hands with a white-coated elderly doctor and walked across.

'I would have let you know but it was something of a rush,' he said, bending his head down to see through the Daihatsu's side window. He was looking grave and thoughtful.

'Palli?'

'Yes. Your friend.'

Well, he didn't have a lot of friends and if they wanted to put my name in, they could. He never did get around to going back to America. Now he was in a cool steel drawer in there. At least that was as much American as it was Scandinavian: all stainless steel and controlled temperatures. It never seemed quite right to me in Britain. I always thought our morgues ought to have them dressed in cardigans and sitting up in rocking-chairs holding the *Radio Times*.

'A violent man, a violent end,' he added.

'Not drowning?'

'No, not drowning.' He paused and moved his head to look around. Mid-morning. The lawns were quiet and peaceful. The sun lit up the white buildings. He seemed to take in some of that tranquillity before he began to explain.

'His fingers were smashed. The finger-ends, I mean.' He rubbed his own together to show what he meant. 'The nails were broken, the flesh was torn and lacerated. They looked like . . . stubbed-out cigars.'

'Nasty. But you don't die of biting your finger-nails.'

'No, and he didn't drown. At first we thought he did. People who drown generally go a strange pink colour, but in Palli's case, the pinkness – a sort of dusky discoloration – was limited to the knees, the elbows and the hips. We cannot confirm this until a full post-mortem, but there doesn't seem to be any froth in the air passages and lungs either.'

'Which means?'

'Which means he didn't drown.' He stood up and leaned back so he could still see me. 'Palli was frozen to death . . .'

Then I did remember what Palli had said.

'Hop in,' I said. 'I think you're going to like this.'

45

Like new lovers, the sea and the boats played all afternoon. The sea surged in with sloppy kisses, the boats giggled and wriggled like schoolgirls.

'What are they cooking up? What the hell are they cooking up?'

Dempsie had been asking the same question, in assorted forms, all afternoon.

We were sitting in an unmarked car at the top of the slope that led down to the harbour. Below us, the *Pushkin* was tucked hard against the wall.

We'd been there for four hours, waiting for Petursson to arrive with the necessary authority to board the vessel. He was clearly having problems. He'd said himself that his government wouldn't like it. No one particularly wanted to go and kick the Soviet Union on the shin if they could avoid it.

It was when he'd said Palli had frozen to death that I remembered what he'd said to me. He pretended that I'd said Solrun was on the *Pushkin*. He'd done it to save my life, I knew that. Oscar was going to throw me under the waterfall again, and I wouldn't have stood another minute of sub-aqua rope-tricks by that time. He'd pretended they'd beaten the answer out of me. But there was more to it than that. He wasn't a stupid man. He wouldn't have suggested it unless he thought it could be true.

And the *Pushkin* was a freezer trawler.

Dempsie and I had spent four hours sitting in the car, me thinking about the stateless man in the cold steel drawer, and Dempsie trying to read the minds of the men below decks on the trawler. There was little enough life on board. Two fishermen – real sloppy unshaven fishermen, not the clean-cut military types – had come ashore and returned with some shopping. Three of them had been doing some repair work to the gantry over the aft-deck. Otherwise, it was quiet.

We waited. Dempsie smoked his menthol cigarettes and opened the windows so the smoke was swept away.

He squeezed his fleshy face between his fingers and pounded at his knee with his fist. 'Come on, what is it they're lining up for us? I know these bastards. Every time we work out one move, they've made three more. Where are they taking us? What are they leading us into? Christ, Sam, here he is.'

It was Petursson. If he could feel the pressure from Dempsie urging him on, he didn't let it show. Stone-faced, he unwound without haste from the back of the official Volvo and the two uniformed men accompanying him waited while the driver passed out his hat and his raincoat. Again, as though preparing for a stroll through the park, he put on the latter and held the former and marched up to the gangplank of the *Pushkin*.

'What're they saying, dammit?' Dempsie muttered as he leaned this way and that to try to make sense out of the babble of voices. A tall woman in a straight grey dress appeared to be Petursson's interpreter. She stood between him and a skinny wilting figure, wearing what looked like a soiled vest under a heavy overcoat. Beside him was the wide-bodied man-woman I'd greeted a few days earlier. By the way she pushed in she must be the commissar.

Then Petursson raised one arm and waved me down.

'Don't let him foul it up,' Dempsie said. He knew there wasn't a chance of smuggling an American intelligence agent like himself on board.

'It has been made clear to the captain here,' Petursson said, as I ran up to them, 'that this document here authorises us to board this vessel. Follow me.'

With delicate steps, he picked his way up the gangplank, with me, the interpreter and the two uniformed men in tow. The captain – in the grubby vest and overcoat – shouted, and the woman grunted at the captain and jabbed him in the back. But they parted.

'Hurry,' Petursson whispered to me, taking me by the arm. 'Once the Soviet Embassy gets here, things will become very difficult.'

I followed him down into the belly of the ship. Steep

companionways let out into dark narrow corridors. On the mess deck a dozen or so men were watching a film. It was either porn or the history of a pink blancmange factory. They hardly gave us a glance as we clattered by. A minute later we heard them cheer: presumably the pink blancmanges had clashed.

We went past the gutting benches and the vertical plate freezers, down through the factory floor until we came to a steel cover in the deck. Petursson had to put on his hat so he could use both hands to move it. I took hold of the iron-ring beneath and heaved out the foot-deep plug which blocked the hatch.

The gasp of cold air that swirled out behind it was like a draught from the grave. We both peered down into the half-lit space around the ladder.

'So,' Petursson said. 'No Oscar.'

That didn't bother me too much, but then I didn't have to justify raiding Soviet ships.

He handed me a pocket torch. 'You first.' I turned and went down the steel-runged ladder.

It was only about a seven-foot drop and when I got to the bottom I turned and swung the torch beam round. I've never seen so many damned eyes in all my life, and they were all looking at me.

I was in a space maybe a yard square. On all sides, stacked from deck to ceiling, were slabs of frozen fish. Wherever the torch beam went, it found glittering silver bodies, caught and crammed and crushed into hundredweight blocks. Tails, gaping mouths, scales and fins all solidified in motionless shoals, shimmering in the torchlight. But mostly it was eyes, bulging, white-framed, glassy, glossy eyes that caught the light.

When I breathed in, the air was like broken glass. It was thirty below. The cold bit like a rusty razor and was just as deadly. A weak yellow light in the deckhead hardly took the edge off the dark once I moved the torch away. And the only sound was the soft groan of the generator – to remind you that you were being frozen to death.

Forty-five minutes, the pathologist had said. That's how long a fit man could live in those conditions. I shivered. And it had nothing to do with the temperature.

What had it really been like for Palli down there? There was only one way to find out.

'Drop the bung back in.'

Petursson's face, unusually anxious, appeared above me. 'There is no need for that.'

'Seriously. Put it back in place.'

It dropped in with a heavy sigh. I switched off the torch. The deckhead lamp was no more than a clouded moon of light. In the dark, the generator's hum sounded like the voice of the cold itself, sawing roughly into your bones. Tiny flashes of light darted between the heaped shoals so that I glimpsed a lolling mouth, a fierce eye, a sudden sweep of the iron-coloured fish.

I climbed two rungs up the ladder and switched the torch on. Dark stains, black by torchlight, marked the steel rim. Where a ragged lip of metal stuck out, I found a sliver of ripped flesh. Then more, where he'd rammed his fingers into a crack to try to tear his way out.

I banged the underside of the bung. I was ready to come out. The silence that followed was too long. I flashed the torch around at the banks of gaping fish and the shiver which ran through my body owed nothing to the freezing air: that one was hatched in the imagination. Briefly I knew the fear that Palli must have faced. Then the bung rose and with relief I saw Petursson's friendly face.

'That's where he got his manicure.' I heard him curse at the grisly sight.

'And that,' he said, pointing to ripped wires on the deck, 'is where they disconnected the emergency alarm.'

'Probably spoiling their film-show.'

The bottom of the plug, which was made out of some sort of cork-type insulating material, was rough cast and it had taken tiny chunks of flesh off his fingers where he'd been scraping and pushing at it. And all the time he'd be getting weaker and slower, the warmth of his body draining away until he folded up and died. In the dark, with only his terror for company.

Even for Palli, it was a hell of a way to die.

46

'There's only two ways you can hold a fork,' Dempsie was saying. 'There's the logical way and there's upside down. How do the Brits hold it? Upside down. Perverse? They are the most perverse nation on God's earth.'

He gave one of his deep-belly chuckles.

I was finishing off a light meal that Hulda had knocked up for me when the two of them, Dempsie and Petursson, came round. The first thing I noticed was that the American had eased back into his mood of effortless charm as though it was an old sofa. Petursson didn't attempt to hide his concern.

Ostensibly they'd called to tell me about the *Pushkin*. Between the lines of the Russian protest and their own inquiries, it looked as though Palli and Oscar had raided the fishing-boat looking for Solrun the previous night. There'd been a hell of a set-to, by all accounts, and Oscar had escaped. They'd stuck Palli in the deep-freeze and transferred him to the lake later in the hope it would look like a drowning.

By way of trade, I told them about Solrun's visit the night before. That brought them upright and shoulders-back in their chairs. There was a pause while they restrained themselves from laying me on the floor and jumping up and down on me for letting her go.

They listened quietly while I told them, as well as I could recall it, what she'd said.

'I don't get it,' Dempsie said. 'She said she was scared of Oscar but he was her first choice?'

'That's how I understood it.' In daylight, before witnesses, it did sound ambiguous to say the least.

'Her next choice is the Russian. Don't forget.' Petursson frowned at the American.

I thought of offering some cheerful comment on the fascinating unpredictability of women, but decided against it.

'What advice did you offer?' Dempsie asked. He was leaning forward, his arms resting on his knees, and the hard intelligence shone in his eyes.

'None.'

'None.' He repeated it. What he left unsaid was more interesting: it was a long explosive rant about how I do nothing to restrain the one woman the whole island is looking for, and then decline the chance to advise her.

But he didn't say it, and he didn't say it for the same reason he'd put his charm on full-beam. He needed me.

'Sam,' he said. He stopped there, leaning forward with his hands dangling between his knees and his face turned up towards me for maximum sincerity. 'You know they're going to come for you again?'

'I think so,' said Petursson, anxious to put in his two-penn'orth.

'Why?'

'Let's talk it through,' the American said, although it was obvious he and Pete had done plenty of talking through and that's why they were here. 'The Soviets see you as neutral. No disrespect, you're entitled to your views, but they see you as an uncommitted sort of guy. Is that it?'

'I don't see why that should interest them.'

He looked up at Petursson who was leaning with his elbow on the mantlepiece. I didn't know how he'd found room between the photographs.

'You can influence her, right? She listens to you. That's why she came here last night, which – though don't take this as a knock – you should've reported to us. That's by the way.'

'I think he's right,' Petursson put in. 'They are planning some sort of major coup. They think it's possible she will turn to you for guidance.'

They were probably right. That was why Batty wanted me near her – to use my influence. And I was still left with the question I'd put to Batty.

'What makes them think I'll give her the advice they want?'

Petursson gave an embarrassed shrug. 'You say yourself that you're not on anyone's team . . .'

'I'm not. I never have been. If Solrun wants to advertise

package holidays in the Lubianka, let her.'

Petursson stood there shaking his head. 'The bell only tolls for someone else, isn't that it?'

I was a bit peeved at being quoted back at myself but I wasn't going to back out of it. 'That's about it, yes.'

From behind the ramparts of his face, his eyes were on me. 'And you meant it when you said you don't go to that address in Chelmsford?' Then added: 'To see your grandmother?' – as if I needed any explanation about an address I'd carried round in my memory since I was a child.

'I don't see the connection, but yes, actually, I did mean it.'

'I don't think I'm too interested in your grandmother . . .' Dempsie began to say, but he fell silent again as Petursson continued.

'No loyalties, then, Sam?'

'Except the ones I choose. Personal ones.'

'Like?'

I tried to lighten it. 'I could be personal to anyone who could arrange to look like Solrun. Or even someone who could make a good pepper steak.'

'What we want to know,' Dempsie cut in, 'is what advice you give her if she's asked to defect?'

That's a heavy word – 'defect'. When she'd talked about going with Kirillina, somehow I hadn't seen it like that.

'It's not as though she's exactly a nuclear physicist . . .' I began.

'Nuclear physicists rate one paragraph in *The Times*,' Dempsie said.

Of course, he was right. In terms of newsprint and television time, outside of Hollywood a top model was the best you could hope for. If anyone should've seen that, it was me – up to my ears in Sexy Eskie stories. But I'd been too close to see Solrun as anything other than a woman.

I sauntered over to the window. In the street, the man in overalls was still under his jacked-up car. It was Hulda who'd noticed him earlier and said that it was just like an American to carry overalls in case he broke down. Didn't he live there? I asked. Oh no, she knew everyone who lived in the street. She'd never seen him before. And you could always tell Americans they had happy faces.

'No one's going to approach me if you have your sneakies crawling all over the place.'

Dempsie began to deny it but my smile and Petursson's frown were too much for him.

'There's a lot at stake,' he said, flinging his arms wide to show how honest he was.

'Your men have no business on our streets,' the Icelander said. 'We will do whatever is necessary.'

'Look, both of you,' I said, turning round and resting on the back of Hulda's head-teacher's chair. 'Stop playing games. If you're right and they do want me, you'll have to let them come. You're going to have to trust me whether you like it or not.'

I saw Petursson confirm it with a nod, and I watched the American shake his head in doubt as he rose to his feet.

'What's he going to tell her?' he said out loud, as he made for the door. 'We still don't know what he's going to tell her.'

'Neither does he,' Petursson said quietly to me. 'Does he?'

Half an hour after they'd gone I went for a stroll around town. It was late afternoon, warm and pleasant now. I got a bag of dried fish from a stall and sat and nibbled at it.

One of the Vietnamese kids came round, the clanging northern words sounding hard and wrong coming from a face you instantly linked with sunshine and suffering. He paused in front of me and held out a newspaper. I shook my head.

'Hallgrimskirkja,' he said. 'Midnight.'

I remembered. It was Palli who said they used to send them with grenades. Nothing changed.

When I got back, the roadside mechanic had gone.

47

As soon as I drove into the square I saw them. A Range Rover – so we were equipped for rough country – with three heads showing.

I drove right round the square and pulled up behind them. When I got out I took a quick look around. The square was deserted, but from open yellow windows in the houses I could hear people being young and carefree. It was a thousand years since I'd felt like that.

For the first time in my experience there were no men working on the new church. Its tall elegant grey columns, which look as though they've been dripped down from heaven rather than built up from this end, were black against the light sky.

'In the back,' I heard Ivan call out. I got in.

We'd got one murderer each, which seemed fair enough. They were the two non-fishermen that Petursson had pointed out to me that day on the harbour. The two men who, with a third, had called on Solrun's mother. One was driving, with Ivan beside him, and the other was beside me in the back. When he turned I saw that his right eye was almost closed and he had a fat lip and a missing tooth.

'Ah,' I said, always keen to communicate, 'Oscar or Palli?'

He gave me a look that almost melted my fillings.

'You're keeping classy company these days, Ivan.'

He'd turned so that his arm hung over the seat. He looked dishevelled and distraught and repeatedly kept sweeping back his lank hair in a troubled way. I wasn't quite sure how sorry I felt for him any more.

'Needs must,' he said.

'I'd like to think you didn't make up the trio when these gents called on the old lady.'

He did look genuinely appalled at that. 'Sam, my dear boy,

however could you even begin to imagine that?'

'Christopher Bell, then?'

He pulled a don't-ask-me face and gave a deep sigh at the same time. 'Whatever are we doing mixed up in all this?'

'I can only speak for myself, Ivan, and I'm not.'

He shook his head rapidly, drawing in his breath at the same time – a gesture of deep distaste. Then he opened his eyes wide.

'I mean, it's nothing to do with us really, is it?'

'Not to do with me, but then, I'm not a patriot.'

He bit his bottom lip and jerked his head to the front. I was almost sorry then. He was a delicate little flower, our Ivan, and I suppose he'd hoped that I'd let him play innocent-victims with me. And I thought we'd got well past that stage.

'One thing you can tell me – why me?'

He turned back, his head on one side, and appeared genuinely surprised.

'Why you, Sam? Well, because apparently a gentleman in Whitehall thought you would be a sound influence on the delicious Solrun. As a matter of interest, were you?'

'I didn't join in. Is she going to defect? Is that it?'

He raised his eyebrows. 'Dash for freedom you always call it when they come from East to West.'

'It is rather a one-way traffic.' Outside, the houses had slipped away and we were heading out into the country. The driver spoke to the other man in the back and he studied the road behind, then answered him. Whatever he said, it meant there's no one behind.

'That's why our chaps wanted you there,' Ivan went on. He was choosing his words with care. This was Ivan being official. 'Whenever we give a press conference in Moscow of someone who's run Eastwards, our fellow diurnalists tend to mock and say it's staged. So we thought, since you were here already, that you might like to act as an independent witness.'

I remembered what the others had said about my neutrality. At this moment, I wasn't sure I liked it any more.

'I'm hardly likely to write it your way, am I?'

He made a beautiful gesture of indifference with hands, shoulders and every facial muscle. 'You'll write it in your inimitable style, as always, dear boy, but I think you'll be obliged to admit it isn't fixed. That's all. But, as you'll see, we're doing it anyway.'

So that was why he'd fed me titbits of information. Oscar's name. The young Russian. Whenever I came to a halt, good old Ivan was always there to point me in the right direction. And I'd followed the trail they'd left me like a faithful old hound, right up to this point. At least it wasn't a kill. So far.

As Dempsie said, they'd become the world's best PR men. They even wanted me to endorse their product now.

'How do you know for certain that Solrun will turn up?'

Ivan turned again. 'I do wish you wouldn't talk to me as though I'm responsible for the whole thing.'

'You're not?'

His face sagged and, side-glancing at the driver, he mouthed: 'You know how I hate all this.'

I still wanted an answer. 'I was under the impression she'd gone missing.'

'Apparently, she had. She was in one of those summer-house things. Everyone was looking for her, including your tattooed friend and his exotic visitor. We were all ready for this press conference when I flew in, then she did a runner which led to any number of frayed nerves all round, as I dare say you noticed. However, she turned up.'

'Last night?'

'Yes, last night. Apparently she was hoping that an old chum would throw her a lifeline but he declined.'

I was trying to work out who that could be when I saw the watchful look on his face, and suddenly I knew. He meant me. I wanted to ask him how he knew she'd been to see me, and what he meant by it, but he cut off my thoughts.

'Don't worry, we know all about her late-night call. You rather muffed your chance there, I think. So she returned to Kolai, our handsome prince. No doubt someone will give him a biscuit.'

'Wasn't he . . .' I didn't trust myself to ask him about my part. 'Wasn't there a time when he was supposed to be coming West?'

It was a silly question and it showed all over his face.

'Really? I should be most surprised if Kolai's superior

officers encouraged too much of that line of thinking.' He even managed a small laugh.

Piece by piece, it all began to slot together. Poor old Oscar gets pulled out by the Americans to avoid diplomatic embarrassment. Heartbreaker Nikolai is put in by the Russians to fill the gap. He offers to defect to demonstrate his sincerity, then asks her to do the same instead.

Then, in case she's in any doubt, the Russians provoke Oscar into returning on a half-mad mission to find his daughter. Oscar was the ferret they'd put in to frighten her into the net.

No wonder the Russians had the best ballet. The choreography was perfect.

The only remaining puzzle was why Ivan thought Solrun had appealed to me for help. The rest of his information was uncannily good – that was a puzzle in itself – so how could he get that so wrong? Muffed my chance. That was what he'd said. I didn't understand. Why did he think that I might stop playing Switzerland, abandon my neutral status and try to drag her back? Surely he knew me better than that. Unless he knew something I didn't.

'There's something else I have to tell you.' This time he didn't turn round. I found myself studying the back of his scrawny neck.

'What's that?'

'It's not . . .' I could see him plucking at his fingers. 'It's not something that makes me terribly proud actually. I'd like you to know that.'

The driver was whistling through his teeth with some country music on the car radio. The one beside me was fingering his swollen lip. All I could see was Ivan's neck. My heart was bouncing against my ribs.

'Tell me, then.'

'Well, have a care before you speak out of place, Sam. As a friend, I suggest you simply watch the proceedings. No more.'

'Why?' One blank word.

'For Sally's sake.'

'Sally?'

'They've arranged . . . someone's holding her in London. If you do anything to make yourself unpopular . . .'

He was fast, I'll give him that. The gorilla next to me had my hands before they had Ivan's neck, but not by much. He slammed me back in the seat, smacked me once on the side of the jaw, then held me there. I didn't mind.

Ivan was cowering forward to get out of my reach. He needn't have worried. The urge to kill him went as swiftly as it came. All I wanted now was to hear the explanation.

'Don't worry, Sam. It'll be perfectly all right. It's all under control. They're holding her, that's all. And when this has gone off successfully, as it will, the word will go back and she'll be released. Not a hair of her head . . .'

My mind was spinning but I was beginning to grasp it. 'Just to make sure I don't foul things up for them tonight?'

'Yes, that's all.' He was almost pleading. 'I mean you can imagine how I feel about this, can't you, old dear? You know how I love the wondrous Sally.'

I thought of all the drinks and dinners we'd had and how I'd laughed at his limp jokes about cricket. Friends. Yes, we'd been good friends. No doubt about that. I heard the catch in his voice and saw his sad wet eyes.

'You disgusting bastard, Ivan, you must've told them. That's the only way they could know what a good arm-twister that would be.'

'I swear I didn't, Sam. On my life. Insurance, they said. It's only insurance. Do please remember that nothing at all will happen to her. She is perfectly safe.'

I stared out of the window. I couldn't bear to see his face. The gorilla eased his grip on me. He knew it was over.

'As a matter of interest, what made you give them that tasty morsel, Ivan? What did they say to tease that out of you? It must've been good.'

'Oh, Sam,' his voice whined with self-pity. 'Moscow. Imagine it. Me in Moscow. I'd die, dear boy, I'd simply die.'

There were a lot of things I could've said to that, and none he'd have wanted to hear. But I didn't. Ahead, I'd just seen a foaming spout of water shoot up into the air. It was Strokkur. We were there.

48

Immediately, I knew why. If you wanted to shoot a film that was unmistakeably Iceland, that's where you'd do it.

There's no other stretch of countryside quite like it. At the foot of a red-stained hump of a hill, water and steam sizzle and bubble in the holes in the earth's crust. The Great Geysir – the one that gave its name to the whole lot of them – sulks underground now, but the rest of the springs boil steadily away. Strokkur, the one I'd seen from the road, blasts up a thirty- or forty-foot column every few minutes. All around, over an area the size of a football field, steam hisses and spits through fissures in the rocks; mudholes like vast paint-pots, every colour from pale blue to burnt brown, bubble; in others, waters of pellucid clarity swirl, rising and sinking. Put in your finger and it'll skin it. And even the stiff wind that night couldn't shift the stink of sulphur.

That's what they were all set to do: shoot a film.

Three men – one with a shoulder camera, one with a hand mike, one with a clipboard – were testing angles around where Strokkur had erupted. Watching them, and chipping in occasionally with his own comments, was Christopher Bell. Ivan was standing deferentially a yard or so behind him.

Down by the road, our Range Rover was parked near a Helix helicopter, one of those fat-bellied models that looks like a flying cow, which Ivan told me had ferried the camera crew in from the destroyer, *Udaloy*. Our driver and his mate had taken up their positions by the car, as relaxed as chauffeurs in the car park at Ascot.

When it dawned upon me that no one cared where I went or what I did, I walked up the hillside where I could watch the film crew prepare for action. Even so, I kept my distance, perhaps thirty yards or so away from them. In some ways I'd have been happier as a prisoner. Being unrestrained made me feel as though I was in collusion with them. It was an odd feeling. Quickly I saw why they weren't worrying about me. What could I do? Run to Reykjavik? And at this time – the middle of the night – no one would be coming here. They were perfectly safe for hours yet.

But when people watched the film on their front-room tellies, they'd see the jewelled light, the eggshell sky, the miniature mountains in the distance – all as innocent as a country wedding.

'Ah, there you are.'

Christopher turned away from the group by the water and came towards me. He was so little concerned about security that he hadn't bothered to see where I'd gone.

He was wearing a cheap imitation sheepskin and he had to hold his hair down in the wind. At first I couldn't think what it was that was wrong about him, then I knew. Nothing was wrong. He still had the same merry look in his black eyes, and the same boyish quality of mischievous innocence. Despite what I'd learned, he was the same man.

'Did you know this was what we were after?' Again, inexplicably, I expected him to have acquired a foreign accent. But he still spoke the same prep-school English, and with the same gushing enthusiasm.

When I didn't answer, he looked into my staring eyes and nodded in understanding. 'Of course, Sally. Sorry, I should've realised.'

'Where is she?'

'Perfectly safe so long as this goes off okay. That's all you need to remember. She's my guarantee of your good behaviour, if you like.'

'And if I don't behave?'

He frowned and pushed his lips out as he looked around. 'All we need now is the bride and bridegroom. There they are, I do believe.' He pointed to a puff of dust making its way up the road.

'And if I don't?'

He shot me one of his clever sideways looks. 'Fair enough. Perhaps you should know. If not, then she's run over by a hit-and-run driver. Killed. Tragically.'

He could see the anger inside me but he didn't back away or show any apprehension at all.

'So you see,' he said, with a quick smile. 'No nonsense, eh?'

He jerked round again at the sound of men's voices. Strokkur had fired again. A tall column of boiling water stood in the air, then crashed down. On the windward side of the pool, not a drop had fallen. But two of the Russians had strayed towards the other side, and the shouting came as they scrambled back to safety.

Christopher called over to them in Russian. To me, he explained: 'I told them to watch that equipment. I had a terrible job getting it issued.'

I felt as though I didn't know what to say to him. All the stuff about cricket and stuffed puffins didn't apply now. Yet we were the same people. Absurdly, and to my own confusion, my reaction to him was still the same: to like him.

He must have sensed this because he reached up and slung his hand over my shoulder. 'Don't worry about the little girl, she'll be fine.' He gave me a reassuring smile. 'It isn't personal, you know. It's a game. We played rather better than you this time, that's all.'

I could hardly bring myself to ask the question. 'What about Solrun's mother? She was clean bowled, was she?'

He gave one of those small impatient signs that you save for favourite children on their bad days. 'Really, Sam. What about the pensioners who die of hypothermia? What about the miners who die of pneumoconiosis? What about the Light Brigade? What about the Holocaust? People die of politics every day, I'm afraid. There's no halting that. All we can decently do is to make sure they don't die in vain. To make sure their deaths bring us a little closer to a better world. Hers will, you know.'

I remembered her scalped skull. 'How?'

He marked off a square in the air like film producers are supposed to. 'That's the scene. Solrun, symbol of Iceland's proud patriotism, stands there and tells what it is like to have your land occupied by a foreign power. She even holds a child she was given by a foreign soldier. What's worse, a black soldier. In that picture, Icelanders – certainly the older ones – will see their daughters being despoiled and their race which has until now been little more than a large family being tainted by unwanted outsiders. I'm not saying they're right. I'm saying that's what they will see on their screens. And Solrun has a story to tell. She will tell how desperately she regrets this, and how, once she decided to speak out against the crimes of the colonialist power who occupies her country, she was hounded. The man who made her pregnant, a homicidal American, was unleashed to hunt her down and kill her. Even her own mother was tortured and killed by the Americans. And what you must admit, Sam, as a man who knows something about publicity, is that it is very close to the truth.'

The look on my face was all he needed to continue.

'Oscar Murphy is homicidal – yes?'

'By now he is, the poor devil.'

'You and I know that we had to prime him a little to get him in that state but the fact remains that it's true.'

'Are you seriously saying the Americans killed her mother? It was you. You and those two thugs down there.'

He held out his hands in a gesture of open honesty. 'But it would never have happened if the Americans weren't here. You must admit it, Sam. And what the viewers will see is a happy ending. That's what they love, isn't it? I'm sure it'll make a great story for Grimm. The heroine swept off to safety by the handsome hero. To Russia. Mark my words. Ten years from now there won't be an American left on this island. And here, unless I'm much mistaken, are the happy couple.'

I felt lost without confetti to throw.

The black car pulled up on the road. Very correctly, the driver came round and opened the door. Solrun, baby in her arms, got out. Kirillina, immaculate in his naval officer's uniform, came round and took her arm and posed beside her.

Despite the strip of plaster across the corner of his left eye, and the other scrapes and bumps on his face, he was debonair, attentive, polished. You could almost hear how all the mums would catch their breath when they saw him on their screens.

This time, I thought, it's Solrun who's in a dream. She looked beautiful, but she couldn't really look otherwise. She certainly hadn't dressed up for the event as Kirillina obviously had. She was wearing one of her crinkly cotton things, turquoise trousers and jacket, which instantly became glamorous when she put them on.

But she seemed isolated from all this weird scene. If she knew Kirillina was there, she gave no sign of it. She lifted her chin up another notch and, with short graceful steps, began to mount the gentle slope towards the hissing, smoking pools.

At that point, ludicrously, the camera crew gave a small ragged cheer. That was another layer of irony. If they were technicians, of course, they probably did believe she was a gallant freedom-fighter who was escaping to Mother Russia.

Christopher hurried down the hill to meet them by Strokkur. I didn't move. I watched. I saw him talking to them, and setting them with their backs against the geyser, and then shouting instructions to the camera crew. Solrun continued to stare ahead, even when Kirillina whispered in her ear.

This was what it was all about. All the lies, all the blood. I walked down to listen to what she would say.

'English version first,' Christopher was saying. 'This is the one for the whole world. I need hardly say that this is the one that matters. When you're ready, Solrun . . .'

She didn't speak. Instead she tilted her head even higher. But still the tears ran down her smooth tight cheeks.

'That's okay.' Christopher sounded pleased. 'Quite natural. Crying at having to leave her beloved country. We'll have some of that, I think. Ah, Sam, just the man. Give her some encouragement, will you?'

'Encouragement?' He was so informally cheerful that I had to make a conscious effort to remember what he'd done – and, even now, what he was doing.

He nodded towards her. 'Last-minute doubts. Not uncommon, I dare say. Tell her she's doing the right thing.'

I've no idea what expression he saw on my face. Horror? Disgust? Whatever it was, he leaned over and said the one word: 'Sally.'

When I turned towards her, Solrun saw me for the first time. Awkwardly, her arms tight around the child, she shook off Kirillina's grasp and ran forward to me. I put my arms out to hold her and the child. That was the least I could do.

When I looked down and saw the baby's face, it made me

start with a shock I couldn't quite define. It was white. Somehow that was wrong. But there was no time to work out what it meant then.

'I can't, I can't,' she was sobbing.

'Of course you can, dear,' Christopher said. 'That's it, Sam old boy, cheer her up. You're among friends, Solrun. Look, I think it might be easier without the baby. At least to start with. Let's give it a try. I'm sure you'll remember your words if you don't have to think about the baby.'

Without any force, he seemed to slip the bundle out of her arms. 'Sweet little thing, isn't she?'

With a quick move of his head, he sent one of the two trawler thugs over to her. He wrapped his thick fingers around her arm and marched her back to the position in front of the camera. The goodwill was beginning to thin out.

'Now,' Christopher said, his voice hardening a fraction, 'let's hear your piece, shall we? Now.'

The small bald man with the clipboard, obviously the reporter, stepped up beside her. I saw him moisten his lips before asking her, in goodish English, why she wanted to leave Iceland.

She began to say something about the United States, then broke down in heaving, racking sobs. Those stopped too, as her whole body seemed to stiffen and her hand crept out and pointed.

The baby, a two-foot pink bundle, was on the move. From where Christopher had set it on the ground beside him, it had dropped forward on to hands and knees and was plodding with slow determination with the gradient of the hill. Towards the geyser.

Christopher broke the silence as we all saw with horror what was happening. He snapped something in Russian. Kirillina immediately grabbed Solrun, his right arm round her, his left holding her right. The trawler thug also moved within arm's reach.

'Just the incentive we need,' Christopher said, with a smile that swept all around our group. 'Can we get it over with now, dear?'

He took two unhurried steps after the baby and stooped to

take hold of the bottom of its coat. It tried to move forward, this time without making any progress.

'Now?' he suggested, looking up at Solrun.

She tried again, and again collapsed in tears. A third time she couldn't get beyond half-a-dozen words. By now she was blubbering and shaking her head from side to side in distress. Suddenly she jerked her face round to me. 'What shall I do, Sam? Tell me. Tell me for God's sake. What shall I do?' Kirillina was watching her closely, with something in his face I couldn't quite place. Christopher was down on his haunches, still restraining the baby. Without glancing up, he said: 'Remember Sally.' Then he sat back and let the baby go.

The centre of the geyser is a four-foot hole which shows black and deep when the water is sucked back down. Then it slowly builds up for another blast, and this is what it was doing now. The water, diamond-clear, was swirling busily and then angrily around, until it flooded over the hard lip of the hole. From there it spilled out over a dish of rock burned bare by the boiling water, and spread to the craggy surround.

Horrified, fascinated, we all watched as the baby, like a large pink tortoise, crossed on to the rock: hand, foot, hand, foot. Her hand went in a tiny pool, not half a cupful of water, left from the last burst. It must have been very hot. She snatched her hand back and sat up looking at her fingers, a high wail breaking from her lips. Then, in fear and pain, she dropped again on to all fours and set off again.

Down the slope. Across the rock. Towards the swirling waters.

Solrun's cry tore the heavens apart and it was a few seconds before I understood what she was saying.

'She's yours, Sam. She's your daughter. She's your baby.'

Christopher pointed one finger at me. 'Sally,' he shouted.

But I ran, I ran like hell, I snatched the kid up under my arm and as I dived off the rock I heard the terrifying rush of hundreds of gallons of water boiled up in the guts of the world come bursting out.

As I looked up, I saw Oscar Murphy coming down the hill. He was riding his Triumph. And he was holding his big Colt .45 in his left hand.

49

The baby was dangling over my left arm, kicking and shouting. I never did know how to hold the damned things. Behind me I could hear the rush and gush of the steaming geyser. Suddenly I knew they were all looking at me. They hadn't seen Oscar. Stocking mask high up on his head, brandishing his gun like a cowboy, he came bucking and rearing down the hillside at a rare old rate – but they couldn't hear the bike for the noise from the waterhole.

My first thought was that he'd really flipped this time. You can't ride a bike over rough country like that one-handed, and you certainly can't hope to aim a big hand-gun like that. Even so, it might just give us a chance.

'The car,' I shouted to Solrun. 'Run for the car.'

'Stay where you are.' Christopher sounded crisp and commanding. 'Remember Sally.'

Fleetingly, I did. Sally in her straw-hat, with all her silly chatter about her giggling friends. And Asta: this pink bundle in my arms. Two daughters. One to live, one to die. And I had to make the choice.

Solrun was struggling to break free from the trawler thug who'd been our driver. He'd got her by the arm and collar and was shaking her to subdue her.

Then it was his turn. He glanced up, past where the camera crew and Ivan were backing towards the helicopter, and saw Oscar charging down on us. Instantly the driver flung Solrun from him so that she sprawled on the ground. Crab-like, he scuttled past Christopher and I could see the grin on his face. He knew the chances of being hit by a pistol, one-handed, from a bouncing bike. So he was smiling as he pulled a revolver from inside his jacket, and that was as far as he got. The first shot spun him to one side and the second kicked him six-feet down the hill. Those big Colts do that. He died grinning. All the odds were on his side, but he was dead, just the same.

The other thug, the one with the bruised face, had rushed up from the cars and dropped to one knee. With both hands, he fired. Once, twice.

The crazy glee on Oscar's face switched to hurt surprise as the bullets caught him. He rose in the saddle like a stunt-man. The bike roared and slid away from beneath him, skidding on its side and finally coming to rest with the rear wheel in a brown mud pool.

Bellowing oaths, Oscar staggered to his feet and came rocking towards us, firing the gun. Some shots went into the ground, some into the sky. His limbs were all over the place.

He crashed to his knees with a jolt, still with his torso upright, and I saw his eyes fix on the pink bundle in my arms.

'Baby,' he shouted, in a voice that echoed all the way to the mountains. He stretched out one long arm, pointing. Then he crashed forward on to his face. The squared-away marine.

The engine of the bike phutted weakly to a halt. The baby was silent. Only the water still gurgled.

Before I even had time to think of it, Christopher was beside Oscar's body, and he came up with the Colt in his hand. He shouted in Russian to Ivan and the crew who were by now down by the helicopter. They wanted none of this rough stuff. But slowly, muttering, they began to come back up the slope.

Kirillina turned over the Russian who'd been shot and whatever it was he said meant only one thing: dead.

'Now.' Christopher sucked in a deep breath and flicked back his hair. He'd got everything under control again, but he was still using the pistol to underline his authority. 'Now we'll have this film made, shall we?'

Solrun came over to me and took the child. 'You really didn't realise? You didn't know she was yours?'

I shook my head. 'No. I didn't realise you wanted to come to me.'

'I said the father. I said I wanted Asta's father. Did you think I meant Oscar?' She saw the answer to that on my face and she reached out and squeezed my arm. 'I brought the birth certificate to show you. It will make you laugh.'

'Solrun.' Christopher's snappy command broke in. 'Over

there with Kolai now, please.'

She didn't even turn to face him. 'What shall I do?' she asked me.

'Oscar was mad,' I said. 'They drove him mad.' She glanced at Oscar's body. Tight-lipped, she moved her eyes to show she understood me.

'They killed your mother too. The Americans had nothing to do with it.'

The baby began to cry. She patted its back. 'Why?'

'For this,' I indicated the waiting camera crew, 'and the gaunt Ivan. 'And me. It's a great story. Beauty flees with love child to escape wrath of Yankee spies. And can you imagine what the Icelanders will think of it?'

'Cut that out,' Christopher said. He raised the pistol and gripped it with both hands. It made a thin bitter sound in the open air. I felt my left arm jump like a twitched string. But oddly, no pain.

'You're a bloody nuisance,' he said.

A bloody nuisance. I looked around. Oscar's crumpled body face down. One Russian thug on the floor with half his head missing and the other with his revolver looking in the general direction of myself. A bloody nuisance. It didn't seem adequate, somehow.

'Kolai, get that crew up here,' Christopher went on. He was trying again to impose order on the scene. 'We are going to do this interview whether they want to or not. Ivan, get up here, man. You're supposed to be a professional.'

'I can't,' Solrun said. She was holding the child tight to her and facing out across the open countryside, across the bubbling pools and the plumes of steam, to the high mountains. 'I won't.'

'She can't,' I said to Christopher. I had to make him see it was impossible. 'Don't you see, she's not being stubborn, she can't. Before she half-believed it, but not now. She's not going anywhere with him,' and I pointed to Kirillina. 'It's all different now. It won't work any more.'

I could see in his eyes that I'd won. He stared at me, then flicked a glance over the rest of them. It had gone. It had been a great scheme, but now it was in broken bits all over this wild landscape.

'Get in the helicopter,' I added, in a friendly reasonable tone. 'Just go.'

'He's right,' Ivan called over. I could hear him try to force some strength into his trembling voice, and I was glad. The rest of them were listening and watching. They knew a deal was being made.

Without warning, Christopher suddenly gave one of his pleasing smiles. 'Fair enough.'

Then we all froze and looked at each other.

A high penetrating voice called out: 'Drop those guns please. Drop your guns, all of you.'

After a moment's silence, the voice came again: 'I said, drop those guns, and I meant it.'

A rifle cracked. The windscreen of the Range Rover shattered and crashed inwards.

The remaining Russian thug threw his revolver down noisily on the rock and locked his fingers on top of his head. Professionals don't take on rifles with handguns. But Christopher kept a grip on his, and like all of us he combed the landscape to see who was doing the shooting now.

All except Kirillina. His eyes were on Solrun. In them I saw passion and pleading and tragedy, and I understood then, with a jolt, that for him it hadn't been acting. He did love her.

'Mr Bell now, please,' the voice called again.

Whoever it was, he was on the side of the angels. But he didn't know I'd struck a deal with Christopher, and there was no way I could start to tell him. My hand felt hot. When I looked down I saw it was soaked in blood. I'd forgotten about my arm.

'No. I don't think so.' This was Christopher's reply. Once again he'd raised the Colt, and he'd also taken a step forward. He pointed it now at the baby's back, as it snuggled against its mother. My baby.

'Shoot me and you risk the child. You may get away with it, you may not. Well? Is it worth the risk?'

You had to give it to him. His voice was level and controlled.

In the silence, I saw a movement on the hillside. He must've been lying down in some sort of cover. When he did stand up, I recognised him immediately, even at two hundred yards. I'd know those knees anywhere. It was Bottger.

We'd all seen him, except Christopher. He wasn't moving his eyes or the gun away from Solrun and the baby. They were his last chance.

Only two yards stood between them. But it was two yards of electric tension. She had her left hand under the baby and her right behind its head. Her face above was burning with the will to live. Between the two of them, but a little to one side, stood Kirillina, his dark eyes running from one to the other.

In tones of ringing clarity, Christopher gave his instructions to Solrun and to the man on the hillside he still hadn't seen.

'The girl is coming down to the helicopter now. With me. You know what will happen if you shoot.' Still with a raised voice, so the man would understand, he added: 'Come along now, Solrun. Let's go.'

He stepped towards her. After a moment's hesitation she moved back a step. It was weird – like watching a patient dancing teacher with an awkward pupil.

On the hillside, Bottger had lowered the rifle. It wasn't his battle now. It was between these two.

At that moment, Strokkur blasted. With our own drama, we'd all forgotten about the waters grunting and grumbling underground, and when the sparkling silver column climbed up above our heads, we all gazed at it. Even Christopher lifted his eyes.

At that moment Kirillina sprang. He didn't go for the gun. He grabbed him around the shoulders and the top of his arms, and with his weight – he was much taller than the Englishman – and impetus, he ran Christopher backwards. He was shouting in Russian: let go, get off, something like that.

Maybe he'd expected Christopher to give more resistance or perhaps he'd just caught him off-balance. Whatever the reason they stumbled down the hill until they were on the bare rock which surrounded the geyser. Just then, it broke. One second it was a shining pillar, the next it was gallons of boiling water crashing back to earth. I went staggering back as some of the hot spray, caught on the wind, touched my face, but even then I knew that Christopher had fired the Colt. I couldn't hear the noise for the bellowing rush of the water, but I felt the disturbance in the air as the bullet rushed past.

Then I saw that Kirillina had flung himself sideways and was rolling away from the water. Christopher had gone.

In its rush to get back into the hot earth, the water raced in furious circles over the rocks. As the last streams were sucked into the plughole, I saw its black mouth gaping. That was where he'd gone.

'The girl.' It was Bottger who shouted as he ran towards us. We were all watching the waters close over Christopher's grave. Vanishing like that was somehow more complete than death.

When I spun and saw Solrun I knew instantly what had happened. She was still clasping the baby with both hands, but now she was on her knees. Her eyes and mouth were wide open in an expression of wonder, like a child's on Christmas morning.

As I reached her, she sank down on to her haunches, and if I hadn't put my arms around her she would have crashed over. I'd seen the neat hole the bullet had left in the baby's pink back. My fingers told me it had blown a hell of a chunk out of Solrun's back on the other side.

They were still locked together, mother and daughter. So, as gently as I could I lowered them to the ground just as they were. Solrun was still breathing in fluttery little gasps. Then her mouth closed, her top teeth bit briefly into her bottom lip, and she died. I sat there, holding the two of them. For a while, a sense of time must have left me. No thoughts passed through my mind. I wasn't thinking. But I was awake and aware. I could smell the sulphurous air. I could hear the waters hissing and bubbling around me. In the distance, I could see the saw-edged mountains. Strokkur fired again, three, or maybe four, times. The wind must have dropped for I no longer felt the hot spray.

I don't think I would have noticed the Helix going, if it hadn't churned the air so that Solrun's cropped curls lifted and moved. Gradually its clatter died away as it headed out over the sea. I didn't even notice the cars arriving. The next thing I knew was Petursson's hand on my shoulder. Then I remembered.

'Sally. They're going to kill Sally.'

In the police car on the way back, I wouldn't take Petursson's word for it. He radioed Reykjavik. They telephoned England. But it wasn't until they'd done it again, and the police operator in town had assured me personally that the nuns had been up to the dormitory themselves, that I believed them. Sally was asleep in bed.

50

'It was a bluff then?' Bottger said.

I still called him Bottger. It didn't seem worth breaking in a new name at this point. What I couldn't get used to was him having no accent. He spoke fee-paying English, like Christopher.

'Yes, apparently,' I replied.

'Of course, if you don't know any better, a bluff is every bit as effective as the real thing.' The stewardess was hovering. 'A drink? We don't want that disgusting brennivin stuff that Bell inflicted on us, do we? Let's be civilised and have a Scotch.'

I tipped all mine into the glass and I didn't wait for the water. I'd had quite a few of those in the twenty-four hours it had taken to tidy up the loose ends for Petursson before leaving.

Most of them had been necessary when I was writing my piece for Grimm. I owed him that. However you looked at it, I was representing his paper and it was a hell of a big story. But it was far from painless to do, with her death so vivid in my mind. My fingers were still sore where I'd had to scrub them to get her blood from behind my finger-nails. And having my arm in a sling didn't help much, come to that.

Anyway, one way or another I'd managed to get it written. Grimm was so overjoyed he even offered me a staff job, at which point I became too overwhelmed to give him any answer.

Distressed as I was, I could see why he was so pleased. He'd got an exclusive on a major international story. He jibbed a little at my approach to it – I'd done it straight down the middle, emphasising the political significance and playing down Solrun's part personally – but in the end said not to worry, he'd get one of his word-mechanics to sharpen it up.

Our flight rose into the clouds almost immediately. I was glad I wasn't able to look down on that wild country. I'd never go back again.

'I'd like to think you were keeping an eye on me all the time,' I said to Bottger.

He shook his head. 'Hardly at all. It wasn't possible most of the time. And I must say you seemed to be coping admirably. Admirably.'

'It didn't feel like that.'

'I was telling Batty that this morning and he rather thought he might have some more work to put your way. Interested?'

'What – nudging history again?'

He laughed. 'Did he say that to you? Nudging history? It's one of his favourite expressions. What shall I tell him?'

'Tell him I'll leave it.'

'Just as you like.' He crossed his long legs, an awkward operation with restricted knee-room. 'I can't say I came out of it with a great deal of glory.'

'You weren't to know we'd done a deal.'

'Still,' he pulled a face at the thought of it and brushed a crumb off his trousers. It was the first time I'd seen him with his legs covered. In some odd way, it made him seem younger. 'I'm sorry about the puffin, by the way.'

I had it on my knee in a carrier bag. Bottger had insisted on beheading it. Sure enough, he'd found a bug inside. That was how they knew Solrun had been to my room that night. I'd fastened the head back on with sticky tape, but it didn't look the same. I wasn't at all sure why I'd brought it with me. I wasn't planning to give it to Sally – not now.

That reminded me. For about the tenth time I took the slip of paper out of my pocket. Petursson had given it to me at the airport. It was the birth certificate they'd found on Solrun.

There it was. 'Asta Samsdottir.' She'd promised it would

make me laugh. It didn't, not then, but perhaps one day it would make me smile. Dear God. Daughters. Fathers. Families. What a mess!

'And your chum Ivan has gone back to Moscow?'

'So they say.'

'That hardly seems fair, does it? Getting away scot-free like that.'

'Maybe not.' I couldn't begin to explain how much Ivan would hate it. I'd die, he'd said. Dry up and die. When I thought about it, I still felt sorry for him. Emotions don't always change as quickly as experience instructs them.

Once we'd cleared customs, Bottger and I stood together, uncertain how to end it.

He checked his watch. 'I hope Ursula's cut the lawn. That's the one job I loathe. Well, Hammersmith, did you say? It's more or less on my way. A lift any use?'

'No, thanks. I'm not going straight home.'

'Not to the office, I hope. You've had a rough time, you must take it easy. How's the arm?'

I wagged the sling and immediately regretted it. 'Only a flesh thing. Not too serious, but rather painful.'

'Be careful. Any bullet wound is serious, I can assure you. It isn't like those cowboy films where they all get up and walk away afterwards, you know. The real thing is a good deal more disagreeable.'

It was disagreeable all right. People missed. They shot the wrong people. Like a knife in the heart, I had a quick vision of her face when her eyes closed. Her damp lashes lay like a brush on her cheeks. So long, so absurd, so lovely.

'Take my advice, Craven. Have a couple of large ones and get yourself to bed. Don't dwell on it. It doesn't do. And don't sit around by yourself, if you can avoid it. Are you going to see friends?'

'Family actually. In Chelmsford.'

I left him and took a cab. The driver's paper was stuck up behind his sun visor. It was Grimm's. The headline was so big I could've read it from Reykjavik.

SEXY ESKIE – THE SPY WHO DIED FOR LOVE

Ah well. As Grimm always said, that was what the punters wanted.